She could have him in her bed for a night.

But Sally didn't want one night with Cotter.

Being with him and his son and her daughter had raised the specter of dreams a girl from the wrong side of the creek should never have. Dreams of a husband and children, of a cared-for home on a tree-lined street. Of going to sleep every night knowing you had dignity and respect. That you were safe. That you were loved.

She thought those dreams had died with her innocence.

Besides, she already had the child and the house. And if she wasn't considered a lady by some in town, well, she had self-respect. She didn't need the husband. Didn't need any man.

She certainly didn't need Cotter Graham to make her ache and want and dream of what could never be.

But was she strong enough to stay away from him?

Dear Reader,

Well, it's that loving time of year again! Yes, it's February—and St. Valentine's Day is just around the corner. But every day is for lovers at Silhouette **Special Edition,** and we hope you enjoy this month's six novels dedicated to romance.

The February selection of our THAT SPECIAL WOMAN! promotion is *Sally Jane Got Married* by Celeste Hamilton. You met Sally Jane in Celeste's last Silhouette Special Edition novel, *Child of Dreams.* Well, Sally Jane is back, and a wedding is on her mind! Don't miss this warm, tender tale.

This month also brings more of your favorite authors: Lisa Jackson presents us with *He's My Soldier Boy,* the fourth tale in her MAVERICKS series, Tracy Sinclair has a sparkling tale of love in *Marry Me Kate,* and February also offers *When Stars Collide* by Patricia Coughlin, *Denver's Lady* by Jennifer Mikels and *With Baby in Mind* by Arlene James. A February bevy of beautiful stories!

At Silhouette **Special Edition,** we're dedicated to publishing the types of romances that you dream about—stories that delight as well as bring a tear to the eye. That's what Silhouette **Special Edition** is all about—special books by special authors for special readers.

I hope you enjoy this book, and all of the stories to come.

Sincerely,

Tara Gavin
Senior Editor

Please address questions and book requests to:
Reader Service
U.S.: P.O. Box 1325, Buffalo, NY 14269
Canadian: P.O. Box 1050, Niagara Falls, Ont. L2E 7G7

CELESTE HAMILTON

SALLY JANE GOT MARRIED

Silhouette®

SPECIAL EDITION®

Published by Silhouette Books
America's Publisher of Contemporary Romance

For Terri Andes Rice
& Susan Bladen Reed

Carrick Hall couldn't have housed
three more different girls.
Our reunion made me proud
of the women we've all become.

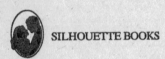 SILHOUETTE BOOKS

ISBN 0-373-09865-0

SALLY JANE GOT MARRIED

Books by Celeste Hamilton

Silhouette Special Edition

Torn Asunder #418
Silent Partner #447
A Fine Spring Rain #503
Face Value #532
No Place To Hide #620
Don't Look Back #690
Baby, It's You #708
Single Father #738
Father Figure #779
Child of Dreams #827
Sally Jane Got Married #865

Silhouette Desire

*The Diamond's Sparkle #537
*Ruby Fire #549
*The Hidden Pearl #561

*Aunt Eugenia's Treasures trilogy

CELESTE HAMILTON

has been writing since she was ten years old, with the encouragement of parents who told her she could do anything she set out to do and teachers who helped her refine her talents.

The broadcast media captured her interest in high school, and she graduated from the University of Tennessee with a B.S. in communications. From there, she began writing and producing commercials at a Chattanooga, Tennessee, radio station.

Celeste began writing romances in 1985 and now works at her craft full-time. Married to a policeman, she likes nothing better than spending time at home with him and their two much-loved cats, although she and her husband also enjoy traveling when their busy schedules permit. Wherever they go, however, "It's always nice to come home to East Tennessee—one of the most beautiful corners of the world."

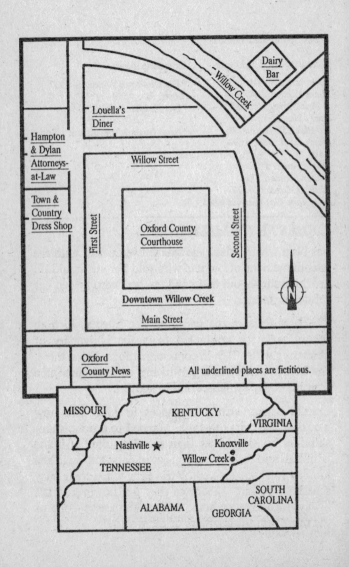

Dairy
Bar

Willow Creek

Louella's
Diner

Hampton
& Dylan
Attorneys-
at-Law

Willow Street

Town &
Country
Dress Shop

First Street

Oxford County
Courthouse

Second Street

Downtown Willow Creek

Main Street

Oxford
County News

All underlined places are fictitious.

MISSOURI   KENTUCKY

VIRGINIA

Nashville ★   Knoxville
                Willow Creek
TENNESSEE

SOUTH
CAROLINA

ALABAMA   GEORGIA

Chapter One

"Ever wonder where all this salt goes?"

Sally Jane Haskins looked up from a stack of receipts she was tabulating. "Salt?" she asked, eyeing her companion.

Lana Sanders, a petite, red-haired teenager, was seated across the restaurant booth, methodically filling a tray full of saltshakers. She appeared mesmerized by the stream of white crystals flowing from an industrial-sized box. "We just go through so much of it."

An intense contemplation of the mundane was typical for Lana. Another day Sally might have ignored her, but her bookkeeping was boring enough for Lana's musings to seem interesting. "This is a restaurant," Sally pointed out. "People eat food. Some put salt on their food."

"But this is the *Dairy* Bar. We serve ice cream more than anything else."

"I don't know about that. There are lots of burgers and fries woofed down around here, too, thank goodness. We couldn't survive on the strength of shakes and sundaes alone."

Sighing, Lana held up a filled shaker. The glass glinted in the bright September sunlight that streamed through the window. "I bet you could tell time by the level of salt in these."

"You know, you're right." Quickly Sally counted the unfilled shakers on the tray. "You've got half a dozen left to go, so it's *time* to get your butt in gear before the afternoon rush starts. That's why you get the last two periods off from school on Mondays, you know, to work."

Lana wrinkled her nose but stepped up her efforts. "You know what this salt consumption proves, don't you?"

"No, but I'm sure you'll tell me."

"It proves our predictability."

"Is this something you learned in calculus or physics?" Sally reached for her receipts again. "Because I've already told you that stuff just makes my eyes glaze over. My brain doesn't work like yours. I barely squeaked by in school."

The teenager rolled her eyes. "I'm sure the only reason you weren't an honor-roll student was because people encouraged you to get by on your good looks."

Sally shook her head. "No, darlin', I think it's more that nobody encouraged me at all."

"Well, I know something held you back," Lana said with staunch loyalty. "You're the smartest person I know."

"I appreciate that."

"But to get back to the saltshakers and our predictability—"

"Somehow I knew you would."

Lana's glare was admonishing. "What is it you and I do every Monday afternoon?" She answered her own question before Sally could venture a guess. "You do the books and I fill the shakers. During the week, the same amount of salt will be shaken out, the same amount of paperwork will pile up for you. And we'll be at this again next Monday. It's like the tides—"

"Or like salt through an hourglass," Sally interrupted, mockingly somber.

Lana sniffed. "There's no point trying to be philosophical with you."

"A point that we have agreed upon before." Sally laughed as Lana took the tray and flounced around the small restaurant, sliding saltshakers into place at booths and tables.

Lana was fond of flouncing, dramatic statements and intense conversations. Her clothes were usually kooky—like the loud red-and-white checked shorts, black T-shirt and green suspenders she wore today. In many respects, Lana reminded Sally of herself at the same age. Oh, there was little surface resemblance. The girl was a brilliant student, while Sally truly had coasted through high school, using as little of her brain as possible. But beneath Lana's bravura, beneath the zany personality she had adopted, Sally knew she often felt out of step with the world, especially out of step with the world as defined by the tight confines and strict guidelines of Willow Creek, Tennessee.

As Sally had, Lana was growing up on the "wrong side of the creek." Her mother was one of those women who drifted from one relationship to the next. She had four children by two different men. Lana had learned to be independent early. Sally knew the girl often felt alone in the world. Sally had known that feeling. Still knew it at times.

With an impatient shrug, she dismissed her sudden melancholy. The receipts in front of her and the restaurant around her proved she was solidly in step with the world. In step and winning the race. She had come a long way from her beginnings. She had worked hard to buy this place. In less than five years, she had taken a crumbling piece of real estate and a fading business, applied some elbow grease, some ingenuity and made it a success.

Sally looked with pride at the well-waxed green-and-black tiled floor, the starched curtains at the window and the two cash registers that sat at either end of the Formica counter where orders were placed. The current lack of customers was rare. On weekends it was usually so busy they had lines at both registers. Even with national fast-food chains going up on the other side of town near the interstate, her Dairy Bar was managing to turn a nice profit.

Smiling, Sally checked the totals for the weekend receipts once more. Business was good. She was building a future for herself and her daughter, Betsy. Sally Jane Haskins was making it just fine, a fact she knew was unexpected by the smug know-it-alls in Willow Creek.

She supposed it was just the small-town mentality that caused some folks to continue thinking of her as "that fast girl from the wrong side of the creek." She didn't care what they thought. At thirty-three years of age, she didn't apologize for her past or her present. She was who she was. Those who still criticized and judged her might be surprised to know she was content to measure her life by the amount of salt that flowed through her restaurant. Lana called it predictable. Sally called it secure.

Maybe not blissfully happy. But secure.

Sally frowned at the unwelcome thought. She was happy enough. What was bliss, anyway? From her experience, few people ever attained such a state.

Bells jingled as the front door opened. Sally glanced at her watch. It was still early for the after-school crowd. She looked up, prepared to quiz whoever entered about why they weren't in class. Instead of a group of teenagers, she encountered a man's smoldering, intense gaze. A very attractive stranger. Not strictly handsome. With strong, chiseled features and tawny hair, clipped short on the sides but longer and tousled on top. This was at least six foot of solid manhood encased in a well-cut gray pin-striped suit. He looked like a bank president, Sally thought. Then she mentally measured the breadth of his shoulders. Maybe he was a bank president who worked out. Whatever the case, the Dairy Bar rarely welcomed the likes of him.

"I'm looking for Ms. Haskins," he said, his voice as completely masculine as his looks.

Though there was a grim set to his mouth, Sally smiled. Smiling at men was just second nature to her. Which was probably one reason she got herself talked about around town. But what woman wouldn't enjoy smiling at this man?

He didn't smile back. And Sally wasn't used to that.

Nevertheless, in her most friendly and forthright manner, she stood and stuck out her hand. "You've found Sally Jane Haskins. What can I do for you?"

He ignored her hand and held up a crumpled sheet of paper instead. "You can tell me what this means."

"What is it?"

"Something my son wrote." The man's angry gaze raked Sally from head to toe and back again. "I think he wrote it about you."

Sally's friendly facade began to waver. She was used to admiration, even speculation, in men's eyes. But she didn't care for this man's hostility. She withdrew her proffered hand and thrust it into the pocket of her short denim skirt. "Who's your son?"

"James Graham. He's fifteen years old."

Lana, who was on the other side of the counter listening with unabashed interest, cut in. "He means *Jamie*. The new guy from Atlanta."

The new guy Lana had been displaying an inordinate amount of interest in, Sally thought, smiling as she turned back to Jamie's father.

But he was staring at Lana, a thunderous expression on his face. "Yes, that's my son. *Jamie.*"

Lana straightened from the counter, her fair skin flushing beneath her freckles.

The last vestige of Sally's smile slipped away. This father was evidently upset about something, but he wasn't going to take it out on anyone but her. "Lana, why don't you go check our hamburger patty supply. Make sure there's plenty to last until Wednesday's shipment. Then you can clean the grill, okay?"

Lana scampered away without argument. When Sally heard the back storeroom door close, she turned to the man in front of her. "Listen, Mr.—"

"The name's Cotter Graham."

"Well, it's so nice to meet you, Mr. Cotter Graham," Sally said with measured politeness. "I don't know what Jamie has written that has you in such a stew, but I can't imagine that it merits such—"

The man cut her off by shoving the crumpled piece of notebook paper toward her. "Read it."

Sally took the paper and smoothed out the folds. Her name was written in a boyish scrawl at the top. Down one margin was a drawing, quite a good one, depicting the sort of voluptuous woman Sally often glimpsed on the covers of the science-fiction fantasy novels the kids liked to read. Beside the drawing was a poem, at least it looked like a poem in between the scratched out words and scribbled phrases.

Haltingly, Sally began to read aloud. "She is the fantasy who visits me in my nights alone. She is a goddess, a warrior-queen, a mother-lover, full-breasted beau..." Sally bit her lip and stopped. The words that followed elaborated on Jamie's fantasy woman, a woman he had named after her.

Mr. Cotter Graham's voice was low and tight, filled with anger. "Now maybe you understand why I'm in such a *stew,* as you put it."

Sally silently finished the poem. The words were descriptive, but there was nothing pornographic about it. For that she was grateful. Mr. Cotter Graham would probably have the sheriff in tow if the poem had been any more colorful. As it was, Jamie had only praised and—or fantasized about what most fifteen-year-old males, or most males of any age in Sally's experience, found interesting—breasts and hips and legs and the mysteries of the female form.

Nice, polite Jamie, Sally thought with a fleeting grin. Outwardly, the boy bore little resemblance to the hard-featured man who stood staring at her now. She never would have put them together as father and son. But the poem showed there was more to Jamie than a baby face and a sweet smile. Of course, she had sensed his puppy love back in the summer when he first started showing up at the Dairy Bar. He was new in town and lonely. He had told her his mother was deceased, his father busy with a new job and—

"Why would Jamie write this?"

Graham's question made Sally look up. "What did Jamie tell you about it?"

"Jamie?"

"What did he say about it when you asked him?"

For the first time since he came through the door, the man looked uncertain. He pushed a hand through his hair, frowning. "I didn't ask Jamie about it," he admitted after a slight pause.

"Don't you think you should?"

Graham's face hardened again. "I don't think you're in any position to be telling me what I should do with my son."

"You're right," Sally retorted. "I'm in no position at all. *Your* son wrote the poem. And it obviously bothers *you.* So I would suggest that *you* take this—" she thrust the paper at him "—and deal with it the way *you* see fit."

"Are you saying that you don't know why he wrote this?"

"Oh, I know why. He's fifteen years old, and his hormones are in a major rage. Surely you understand that."

Graham looked ready to argue the point some more. Then the hard set of his jaw eased as his gaze again traveled over Sally from head to toe. But he didn't study her in anger. Not in an insulting manner, either. If she knew nothing else, Sally understood the difference between a disrespectful glance and complimentary regard. And this time, there was an open, if somewhat rueful, appreciation in Cotter Graham's hazel eyes. "Yes, I guess I can understand raging hormones."

Sally had read about people who took your breath away. She had never believed it before. She had been dealing with men since she was twelve years old when her body had blossomed prematurely into a woman's curves.

But she had never lost her breath over any man's interest. Not until now. Not until this man gave her an appreciative look on this sunny Monday afternoon in mid-September. Dimly, Sally could hear Lana cleaning the grill. She could smell onions and hot fudge. It was just a normal afternoon in the Dairy Bar in predictable, boring Willow Creek, Tennessee. Normal, except that Sally Jane Haskins, a woman who should know better, found it completely impossible to look at Cotter Graham and catch her breath at the same time.

Rather whimsically, she imagined all the saltshakers in the place turning over and beginning to pour at various speeds.

Graham didn't seem to notice anything was wrong. He just shoved his son's poem back in his suit pocket. He looked positively shamefaced. "I guess I've acted like a damned idiot."

"No." Sally managed to force the word out. Feeling unaccountably nervous, she fiddled with the deep neck ruffle of her peasant-style blouse. She was being foolish. This was just a man, she told herself. A man who exuded more raw masculinity than any she had ever met. But still just a man. And she knew how to deal with men.

"It's generous of you to let me off the hook, but I know I've made an idiot of myself here." Graham's quick smile was charm in its purest form.

Sally managed to hold on to her poise by glancing away. "You're not an idiot. I mean, you could have talked to Jamie about this first. But he's your son, and you saw the poem . . ." She paused, struck by a thought that made her look at him again. "How did you run across this, anyway?" Though she didn't know Jamie all that well, she doubted the poem was something he would freely share with his father.

Graham looked even more ashamed. "Jamie left a notebook in the car when I dropped him off at school this morning. It's a notebook he's been lugging around for a long time. In fact, he's rarely without it. I noticed it on the front floorboard at lunch. Curiosity got the best of me and I picked it up. I don't usually go through Jamie's things. I trust him . . . I guess."

Sally didn't mean to question this stranger's relationship with his son, but the words just slipped out. "You guess?"

"All right," Graham admitted. "I do trust him, but that doesn't mean I understand him."

"Sounds about normal for a parent."

"You think so?" For a moment, he looked absurdly relieved. Then he frowned again. "I don't understand Jamie. That's why I went through his notebook. I thought I might find out what's going on in his head. This poem was the first thing I saw. The name he used for a title made me think Sally Jane Haskins was a real person, a girl from school maybe, so I asked the lady at the diner downtown—"

Sally's groan cut him off. "Not Miss Louella who runs the diner?"

"That's right," Graham said. "I've been in her place a number of times since Jamie and I moved to town. She's very friendly, easy to talk to."

"That's Miss Louella." Sally sighed. If Graham had been talking to Miss Louella about her, then no wonder he had charged in here ready to accuse her of seducing a fifteen-year-old. "I guess she filled your ear full."

He seemed puzzled. "She just told me who you were and where to find you."

"Did you show her the poem?"

"Of course not."

"Thank God," Sally said. "Miss Louella is the biggest gossip in the three-county region. I'm sure your asking about me made her foam at the mouth." Eyes narrowed, Sally glanced toward the street, where a car passed at a slow rate of speed. "I wouldn't doubt that she's already dispatched someone to see if you came over here."

"But why?" Graham looked completely perplexed now. "I just asked a simple question about you. She seemed to know you quite well."

Sally laughed. "She knows everything about everybody in all of Willow Creek and Oxford County. She knows who's happily married. Who's not. Who everyone is sleeping with. Who's behind on their bills. Whose kids are in trouble at school. Miss Louella and her sister, Miss Clara, and their circle of buddies—or biddies, if you will—have their fingers on the pulse of this community."

"That's nonsense."

She regarded him with pity. "You're from Atlanta, aren't you?"

"That's right."

"Always lived there?"

"Yes, but—"

"Then you don't know what life in a small town is really like."

"I've been here since June, and I'm finding things pretty darn pleasant."

"Oh, it is pleasant," Sally agreed. "There's less traffic, less crime, less of a lot of things. And more of others. Like nosy busybodies."

"I hadn't noticed."

"You will." Sally smiled, pleased that looking at him no longer caused such a tight feeling in her chest. She was getting a grip on herself. "Just wait until Miss Louella starts presenting eligible females to you at every opportunity."

His dismay was obvious. "You don't really think she'll start that, do you?"

"Well, of course she will." Sally looked over to make sure Lana was still at the grill and out of hearing range. Then she lowered her voice. "Just make sure you don't get stuck on a date with Miss Louella and Miss Clara's niece, Thomasina Baldwin. Thomasina's a very attractive woman, but when she laughs..." Sally shook her head. "Well, let's just say that when Thomasina laughs, hounds from miles around answer."

Cotter couldn't stop his laughter. Not because this poor Thomasina sounded so funny. But because Sally Jane Haskins had the warmest smile and the easiest manner of any woman he had met in a long time. She might not like the comparison, but she had the same genuine quality that he had found in so many people in Willow Creek, including the infamous Miss Louella of Louella's Diner.

"You may think it's funny," Sally continued in her low, sexy drawl. "But Thomasina Baldwin has been through three husbands in eight years. And I hear it's that laugh that drove the men away."

"Now who's gossiping?" Cotter asked, still chuckling.

"This isn't gossip. It's God's own truth. I got it from Miss Louella herself."

"She talks about her own relatives?"

Sally's incredibly clear, incredibly gray eyes fairly danced with good humor. "Heavenly days, Mr. Cotter Graham, a good gossip doesn't discriminate when it comes to a tasty tidbit."

Cotter continued to grin. "I'll have to remember all of this and be on my guard the next time I visit the diner."

"You could come over here for a burger and fries instead. Your son seems to like what we serve."

"I think Jamie likes you," Cotter retorted. Once more he took in her heart-shaped face, her shoulder-length, midnight-dark hair and shapely figure. But quite apart from her stunning looks, this woman had a glow about her, an openness, that would make anyone respond to her. He certainly didn't blame his son for fantasizing about her.

A concerned look replaced her smile. "About that poem..."

Cotter made a dismissive gesture. "Oh, hey, look, I've got to apologize about that poem. I shouldn't have come bursting in here, thinking the worst. And Jamie would die if he knew I confronted you."

"I won't tell him."

"Neither will I. I'm sorry I came on like a crazed parent. I guess I've been watching too many smut journalism television shows or something. It's just that Jamie having those kinds of thoughts...writing them down that way..." He shook his head. "I still think of him as a ten-year-old in ripped jeans and a T-shirt."

"The jeans and T-shirts haven't changed all that much. But underneath he won't be a boy much longer."

Thinking of Jamie as a boy metamorphosing into a man brought Cotter a familiar bewilderment, followed by a profound sense of failure. He wasn't used to failing at anything. If only Brenda were here... He quickly shook off the thought. If Brenda were alive, he wouldn't be here. He wouldn't be dealing with Jamie at all. The facts were that his wife was gone, and their son was his responsibility.

Perhaps Sally Jane Haskins sensed his inner turmoil. For she reached out and touched his arm. A brief touch.

Impersonal, yet as warm and comfortable as her smile. The gesture made Cotter aware of how close they stood and how very attractive he found her.

She was talking about children. "Raising them is hard enough when you've got a partner. It's especially hard when you're alone."

He summoned a smile. "Sounds like the voice of experience."

"My daughter is ten going on thirty-five."

"Her father?"

Her chin lifted a bit. "He's never been in the picture."

"I'm sorry."

She gave him a straight-ahead, level look. "I'm not."

She turned away and began stacking papers on the table beside her before Cotter could come up with a reply or an apology. Which was just as well, he decided, since there were no words appropriate to the situation.

Before the moment could grow too strained or awkward, she said, "As I started to say about that poem, Mr. Graham. Don't worry about it. Back in the summer, when Jamie first started stopping by, he was lonely and anxious about a new school and new friends—"

"He told you that?" Cotter asked, thinking of the silences that usually stretched between him and his son. He had known Jamie wasn't thrilled about moving from a suburb of Atlanta to a small East Tennessee town, but the boy had seemed to adjust fast enough. Jamie wasn't a complainer. And he had said nothing to Cotter about being lonely or worried. But why should he? A discussion about what to have for dinner was as intense as it ever got between the two of them.

"Jamie and I have talked quite a bit," Sally confirmed, as if that weren't a small miracle. "I think he had a little crush on me for a while. Probably about the time he came up with that poem." Her voice dropped. "Lately I've noticed his attention shifting in a new direction." She nodded toward the counter, where Lana was once more in position beside the cash register.

"Really?" Cotter surveyed the young redhead in the bizarre outfit, wondering if his problems were over or had just begun. His worry eased a bit when she grinned shyly. Colorful attire or not, this girl was certainly a more suitable romantic interest for his son than Sally Jane Haskins.

Behind him, the bells over the front door jangled. He turned as four young teens filed in. They called greetings to Sally and lined up to place orders with the girl behind the counter. Cotter found himself regretting the intrusion. He had been enjoying this private talk with Sally.

She scooped the last of the paperwork from the booth she had vacated. "I should go give Lana a hand, but if you want to stay, Jamie often comes in after school—"

"He does?" Cotter asked, surprised. They had lived here for nearly three months, and his son had never mentioned this place that Cotter could remember. But it sounded as if he had spent plenty of time here. Cotter was under the impression that Jamie came straight home after school. He was always there when Cotter arrived at six or later. Together, they usually shared a meal prepared earlier by the housekeeper Cotter had hired to come in three days a week. More than ever Cotter realized how little he knew about Jamie.

"Are you going to wait for him?" Sally asked.

"Somehow I don't think Jamie would be too happy about me invading his territory."

"You might be surprised."

He shook his head, then stuck out his hand. "I want to thank you, Sally Jane Haskins."

She placed her fingers in his. They were slim and cool and fit perfectly against his own. Once again, Cotter decided his son had very good taste when it came to fantasy women. "Thanks for listening to me instead of booting me out."

"Don't be silly."

"And thanks for being a friend to my son."

Her eyes tilted up at the corners, her lashes thick and dark against her creamy complexion as she smiled. "That's no problem. He's a good kid."

"Is he?" The question slipped out before Cotter realized how much he was revealing about his relationship, or perhaps lack of a relationship, with Jamie. Quickly he dropped Sally's hand and backed toward the door. "I have to run. I'll come back sometime for that burger and fries you mentioned. We'll compare notes on single parenting."

Something he said must have amused her, for a teasing lilt slipped into her tone. "You come back. We'll compare notes, Mr. Cotter Graham."

"It's just Cotter, okay? Not even folks at the hospital call me Mr. Graham."

"Hospital?"

"The regional hospital just outside town. I'm the new administrator."

The news appeared to dismay her for a moment, but then her smile was firmly in place again. "Well, *Cotter*, come back and see us again."

At the door, he stopped and surveyed the restaurant. "You know, this is what I was looking for when I decided to move to a small town. A nice place like this for Jamie to hang out." With a flash of his brilliant smile, he was gone.

Hugging her paperwork to her chest, Sally watched until his black Bronco pulled out of the parking lot. She wondered what Mr. Cotter Graham, big-time hospital bigwig, would think about this place if he knew the two well-patched holes beside the front counter were made by bullets. Or about the mistakenly jealous wife who had slashed Sally's tires a few months back in the parking lot. Or about Betsy's father. About Sally Jane's entire misdirected family and the string of mistakes and misadventures that dotted her life. No doubt Miss Louella or some other well-intentioned biddy would soon fill him in on all of it. He would make sure Jamie stopped hanging out here. And he would never come back for that burger and fries or to compare those notes. And that was too bad.

For the second time today melancholy got the better of Sally. But again, she didn't indulge in the emotion. She put her paperwork in the cubbyhole she called an office, and she went to work assisting Lana in the after-school rush. She kept her mind on business as she gave evening instructions to Craig, the college student who lived in the apartment over the Dairy Bar and supervised the restaurant part-time. She went home to her daughter and the hundred-year-old house she had purchased last summer and was still remodeling. She made dinner and helped Betsy with a history homework project. She combed the tangles out of Betsy's long, dark curls and listened to all the reasons the child should have a new outfit just like her best friend, Laura. It was a normal, some might call it predictable, night.

It was only later, after Betsy was in bed, that Sally stood at the kitchen sink and allowed her thoughts to drift back to the man she had met today. His face came to mind clearly.

Sighing, she leaned against the edge of the counter. A warm September evening breeze stirred the white café curtains at the window and washed over her as she thought about Cotter Graham. But she didn't dwell on his gorgeous eyes or muscular physique. Not his tawny hair or the male magnetism that had taken her breath away. No, what she recalled was the look on his face when he talked about his son. He was so uncertain, so in need of someone to tell him if he was getting the parenting thing right. Sally sensed Cotter Graham was about as lonely as Jamie had been when he walked into the Dairy Bar early in the summer. Both of them were lost.

Lost souls.

Sally groaned at the thought. All her life she had been able to resist handsome faces and slick come-ons. But a man in need was a different matter. Lost souls were her greatest weakness.

It was no good telling herself that helping people in need, especially men in need, had led to most of the trouble in her life. It was no use admonishing herself to steer clear of this particular lost soul. By virtue of his occupation and the unwritten rules of Willow Creek, he was far beyond Sally Jane Haskins's reach. But Sally had often broken the rules.

So by the time she dried the last pot and put away the last pan, her mind was busy devising a plan by which she would come to Cotter Graham's rescue.

In the hall outside his son's bedroom, Cotter hesitated and glanced down at the notebook in his hands. Maybe he should just put it back in the car. Jamie would discover it in the morning, and nothing would need to be said. Cotter didn't have to let his son know he had read anything in it. He couldn't tell the boy about his confrontation with

Sally Haskins. Pretending he had seen nothing might be the safest route. But was it the best? Cotter wasn't sure.

If the poem about Sally was any indication of what was on Jamie's mind these days, there might be a few things Cotter should discuss with him. Throughout his professional life, he had dealt with problems and issues head-on. He had to operate in the manner that worked for him. He had put off talking to Jamie all evening, but it was nearly ten o'clock. So it was now or never.

Taking a deep breath, he tapped on the door. "Can I come in?"

He heard a scrambling sound from inside the room, a drawer opened and closed, then Jamie called out, "Door's not locked."

Inside, the teenager was hunched over a computer keyboard, his young profile outlined by the lamp on the desk beside him. A black Labrador lying across the foot of the bed raised his head as Cotter crossed the room.

Holding the notebook slightly behind him, Cotter paused to stroke the dog's head. "Hey, Jet, old boy, how're you doing? Did Jamie let you out after dinner?"

"I'll take him out when I'm through here," Jamie said, not looking up from the computer.

"Busy on something special?" Cotter asked his son.

"English essay. It's due tomorrow."

"Any problems?"

"Not with English."

"How about your other subjects?"

"Chemistry's a bitch."

"I could hel—"

"I got a tutor," Jamie cut in before Cotter could complete his offer of assistance. He turned to look at his father for the first time. "You told me to get a tutor if I needed one."

"So I did," Cotter conceded. God, how he hated this. It wasn't that Jamie was hostile or hateful. He just treated Cotter with a polite disinterest. And Cotter always felt off-balance with him. He hadn't intended this conversation to begin with a game of twenty questions, but that's the way it always seemed to work out. He wished he and his son could, for once, just talk.

Silently, Cotter studied Jamie, who went back to work at the computer. The boy looked like his mother, with dark hair and brown eyes, his features cut with a gentler hand than those that had shaped Cotter's own. He was like Brenda in other ways, too. Kindhearted and sensitive, an animal lover who would rather be reading a book than playing sports. Only in his height, already nearing six feet, did he resemble his father.

At Jamie's age, Cotter had been a football player working toward a scholarship. He had run a paper route from the time he was twelve. And because his father was gone and his mother worked two jobs to keep food on the table, he also had the lion's share of responsibility for his younger sister. At fifteen, Cotter had no time for daydreaming or writing poetry or reading books that weren't school assignments. Even if the time had been there, he knew he wouldn't have done things differently. Brenda once told him he had a worker bee's mentality. It was years before Cotter realized she hadn't meant it as a compliment.

But it didn't matter that Jamie wasn't like him, Cotter told himself. This was his son, and he had promised Brenda he would be the best father he could, a better father than he had been while she was alive. He had done little for Brenda when she was alive; this was one promise he would keep. Accordingly, he dropped the notebook onto the desk beside the computer keyboard. Jamie looked up in surprise.

"You left it in the car this morning," Cotter explained.

Jamie was silent for a moment, contemplating the notebook. "Did you read it?"

Cotter had never been any good at lies. From the back pocket of his slacks, he withdrew the poem and drawing he had taken to the Dairy Bar. He unfolded the paper and dropped it on top of the notebook. "It's a nice likeness of Miss Haskins."

Jamie gave him a quick, sharp glance. "How do you know her?"

Determined not to reveal exactly how he had met Sally, Cotter shrugged. "I've been in the Dairy Bar."

"The poem is just something I scribbled down," Jamie began.

Cotter held up a hand to silence him. "Nothing wrong with writing down what you feel. Nothing at all wrong with having thoughts like this about a woman. I'm not saying this was wrong. Not at all."

Clearly striving for nonchalance, Jamie made a dismissive gesture with his shoulders. "It was just a poem. I didn't mean any of it."

"Really?" Cotter picked up the paper. "So you didn't mean what you wrote about her breasts or the curve of her thigh—"

Red faced, Jamie stood and snatched the paper out of his hand. "Just stop making fun of it, okay? You don't understand."

"I'm not making fun of what you wrote," Cotter said as the boy turned away. Damn, but he was handling this all wrong, as usual. Directness might work at the hospital, but it wasn't right for relationships with a fifteen-year-old boy. He should have just given Jamie the notebook and walked away.

"I'm not making fun," he repeated. "I mean, Miss Haskins is definitely the kind of woman who would inspire thoughts like that in me."

Jamie made a sound of disgust. "You would say that."

"What does that mean?"

"It's not how she looks that matters."

"Of course it isn't. But it's her looks that you wrote about."

"But I didn't mean..." Jamie broke off, shaking his head as he sprawled beside Jet on the bed. "Never mind."

Watching his son stroke the dog's silky coat, Cotter thought about leaving. It would be easier to allow Jamie to dismiss him, to let this conversation end like so many others had over the years. But he couldn't. This tall boy with shaggy hair and earnest eyes was his responsibility. His alone. Brenda wasn't here to pull up his slack. He had never counted on this kind of responsibility. But it was a fact, and he had to start dealing with it. He had left his high-pressure job in Atlanta and moved them to Willow Creek in order to remove some of the barriers between them. Somehow he and Jamie had to stop behaving like strangers who happened to live in the same house. Cotter had lived that way with Brenda. He wanted it to be different with Jamie.

Sighing, he turned the desk chair so that it faced the bed and sat down. "Jamie, I didn't come up here to nag you about what you wrote. I'm sorry if it came off that way."

Jamie continued to stroke his dog, saying nothing.

Cotter leaned forward, bracing his hands on his thighs. "I just thought we should talk." He paused to clear his throat. "About women."

The boy pushed himself up on his elbows, his dark eyes wide. "Women?"

"About your feelings, about theirs, about respecting—"

Jamie's laughter cut him off.

"What is it?" Cotter demanded.

"Mom and I had this talk about four years ago." Jamie sat up. "Jeez, Dad, I'm almost sixteen."

Heat suffused Cotter's face. Almost sixteen. Almost a man. Of course Jamie didn't need his father delivering a lecture about sex. Most of the time it seemed Jamie didn't need much of anything from him. He might have at one time. But now it was too late. What was his life, anyway, except one big missed opportunity.

Cotter stood. "I'm sorry," he said stiffly. "I just thought..." As his words trailed away, he impatiently pushed a hand through his hair. "I'm sorry," he repeated and walked toward the door.

"Dad?"

At the soft entreaty, Cotter paused in the doorway and glanced over his shoulder. Jamie was sitting just as he had before, one hand on his dog, his eyes downcast.

"Son?" Cotter prompted.

Jamie looked up, surprising Cotter with a faint smile. "She is a babe, isn't she?"

"Pardon me?"

"Sally."

Frowning, Cotter turned around and leaned a shoulder against the doorjamb. "You mean Miss Haskins."

His son made an impatient gesture. "I'm not being disrespectful, Dad. Everyone calls her Sally. And she is a major babe."

Thinking of Sally Jane Haskins's voluptuous figure and pretty face, Cotter had to agree with his son. "Yeah," he admitted, returning his son's grin. "I would say Sally Jane Haskins is a major babe."

"But nice, too."

Cotter nodded. "From what I could tell, yeah, she is."

"She reminds me of Mom."

The statement caught Cotter off-guard. Brenda Graham had been a petite whirlwind of a woman. Cute and perky rather than pretty, she bore little resemblance to Sally Jane Haskins.

"It's not the way she looks," Jamie said, effectively following Cotter's train of thought. "She's just nice, she just..." He paused as if searching for the right word. "She's nice to everybody. Like Mom is...was."

Cotter was at a loss to know what to say. Jamie rarely mentioned his mother. Not to him, at least.

"The point is," Jamie continued. "That poem that I wrote and the picture I drew were...like a first impression. And Sally is, well, Mom always used to say that girls...people...aren't just how they look. And Sally isn't. She's just not like my poem. Some guys say crude stuff about her, but that's not how I think about her, you know?"

Cotter's chest literally expanded with pride. Jamie sounded thoughtful and mature, a far cry from most teenagers. Brenda, with little help from him, had done a good job imparting some values to this kid. She had taught him to look beneath the surface, to make judgments based on more than superficial qualities.

"I'm glad you like Miss Haskins...Sally," Cotter told Jamie. "She likes you, too."

The boy's eyes widened. "You and Sally talked about me?"

"Well...yeah," Cotter replied, remembering that he wasn't going to tell Jamie about the conversation. "There

were some kids at her place and I mentioned you and..."
He cast about, trying to save himself, when he remembered something Sally had told him. "There was this waitress there, a redhead. Is she what you would call a babe?"

Jamie got up from the bed so abruptly that Jet barked in protest. He headed for the computer, not looking at Cotter as he said, "Lana's a babe-in-waiting, I guess."

"She seemed..." Cotter searched for the correct word. Colorful? Dramatic? He settled on, "Nice."

"Yeah." Jamie turned his chair around and sat down. "I'm, uh, sort of...gonna catch a ride with her to the Friday night football game. Is that okay?" he added almost as an afterthought.

"Sure, but football?" Sports were usually Jamie's last choice.

"It's what everyone does here on Friday nights. Their mall is just too lame for hanging out."

"I thought Sally's place was the hangout."

"After the game, yeah." Jamie squinted as he peered at the glowing screen in front of him. "Listen, Dad, I gotta do this paper, so..."

"Okay." But Cotter hesitated, reluctant to end what had been their most substantial conversation in some time, perhaps ever.

"Dad?"

He looked up to meet Jamie's quizzical regard.

"You want something else?"

"No, nothing else. I'll be working downstairs in the den if you need me."

Jamie looked at him as if he had grown an extra head or two. "Sure, Dad," he murmured, shaking his head slightly as he turned back to his computer.

Cotter left before he could do something Jamie would find completely insane. Downstairs in his masculine, walnut-paneled den, he sat before his own laptop, trying to review a portion of the hospital budget while his mind kept straying to the boy upstairs. It had been silly of him to try to initiate a talk on something as intimate as sex. But in the end, it had worked out. Sally Haskins was a subject which certainly got Jamie talking.

Sally Jane Haskins.

He abandoned the budget, thinking instead of how well the common Southern double name seemed to suit her. Sally Jane. The name went with her silky drawl and her warm manner. It fit her about as well as that snug denim skirt had fit her rounded hips and thighs. Cotter smiled, remembering the smooth expanse of tanned leg revealed by that skirt. One by one, his mind clicked through a series of erotic scenarios involving one Sally Jane Haskins.

A major babe.

He was pleasantly aroused by the time Jamie and Jet came clattering down the stairs and slammed out the back door. The commotion snapped Cotter back to reality, sent him back to work on the budget, determined not to think about black-haired beauties with hourglass figures. He kept at it until he had to admit defeat. The problem was that he had gone without a woman for far too long.

After Brenda's death, it had been a while before he even noticed other women. His marriage might not have been ideal, but he had never been unfaithful. Before moving here, there had been a woman or two, mostly people with whom he could scratch a mutual physical itch. But outside of bed, the relationships had been unfulfilling. The women were looking for commitments; he wasn't, and there was no room for negotiation. His move had merely accelerated an inevitable ending to the liaison with the woman he had been seeing last.

Since June, he'd had his hands full settling into a new and highly visible position. Outside of work or work-related social events, he stayed home with Jamie. Not that they had done anything significant together, but Cotter had felt that in a new place, he should make himself available to his son. Now that Jamie was making friends, it might be time for Cotter to do the same. He wouldn't object to some female companionship, as long as the females in question knew there was no hope of a serious relationship. There were a couple of women at the hospital who had given him the come-on, but it wouldn't be very smart to get involved with a colleague or employee. No, if he was looking for sexual gratification, he was probably out of luck.

Or was he?

There was always Sally Jane Haskins.

"Damnation," Cotter muttered to himself. He was losing it. First of all, the woman probably had a significant other. A boyfriend, live-in, at least a lover. She was a striking, vital woman. He doubted she was alone. Second of all, she was his son's friend. Cotter certainly wasn't going to interfere with that. No matter how sweetly alluring she was, Sally Jane Haskins was off-limits.

He kept telling himself that over the next few days, when her face and figure popped into his mind at odd moments. He repeated it when he sent his Bronco cruising by the Dairy Bar on Saturday afternoon. He reminded himself of it when he went to the country club for a Saturday night dinner and dance and found every available female lacking. He had to face it. Sally Jane Haskins was the most attractive woman he had met in a long, long time.

By the time a week had passed, he had uncharacteristically built up quite a fantasy life involving Sally. That's why he thought he was dreaming when she called Tuesday morning to tell him they were going to have lunch.

She didn't invite him. No, in her honeyed, husky voice, she said, "I want you to meet me at the gazebo in the middle of the park."

"Park?" he repeated, thinking this was the most vivid delusion ever.

"City Park, a block over from the courthouse square. You can't miss it. It's the only park Willow Creek has."

She gave him no opportunity to refuse. So Cotter, telling himself he had no other lunch plans, met her. He fully intended to keep in mind all his reasons for not pursuing her. But he forgot that vow when he caught sight of her shapely legs beneath her short, pleated pink skirt. He damn near forgot his name when she smiled up at him, her heart-shaped face vivid and welcoming.

His only coherent thought was how he would explain to Jamie that it was Sally's "niceness" that made him as randy as any self-respecting teenager.

Chapter Two

As Cotter mounted the steps of the gazebo in the center of City Park, Sally leaned against the ornate white railing and admired the way he moved. He was a tall, solidly built man, but he had a catlike grace, a natural athlete's easy stroll. And there was a sense of purpose about him, too. He looked like a man who always knew where he was going, she decided. And as he approached her, one word kept running through her mind.

Breathless.

This man had once again robbed her of breath. Though she had half expected this giddy, weightless sensation, she told herself she had to get a grip.

Last Monday she had stood in her kitchen, plotting a way to rescue Cotter from what she was sure was a lonely, unhappy state. She thought he needed some flirting, some fun, some simple companionship. And maybe she needed the same. Maybe Lana was right in saying things had become too predictable around here. The most unexpected thing Sally had done in the past year was move out of the apartment over the restaurant and buy the old McAllister house on Willow Creek's oldest street. With the repairs needed there and the demands of the business, and Betsy, Sally hadn't had the time, nor the inclination, to become interested in a man in a long time. Despite what the gossips claimed, she didn't have dozens of men at her door. She didn't have even one.

Oh, she flirted. That was, after all, what people expected from her. But nothing had come of that flirting for quite a while. A romantic diversion might cure her of the melancholy that was wont to descend upon her at odd moments nowadays. And Cotter was new in town. The social divisions drawn by those who had appointed themselves guardians of such things might not be important to him. Last Monday night Sally made up her mind to get to know him much better.

But the next morning she hesitated. Needy males like him were dangerous. Her life was safe and secure and relatively peaceful just as it was. She told herself to thank her lucky stars for the relative lack of trouble.

Yet her mind wouldn't cooperate. As the week wore on, she found herself looking up every time the bells jangled on the Dairy Bar door, hoping Cotter had decided to pursue her. It was possible. She hadn't imagined the electricity between them. He had felt it, too. She knew interest when she saw it in a man's eyes. She *could* sit around, waiting for him to act. But Sally Jane Haskins had never been much of a "sit around" woman. Her take-action ways were, at least in the eyes of her critics, chief among her many faults. And since everyone in town would expect her to pursue any man she wanted, she finally just invited Cotter to lunch.

So the deed was done. Here he was, walking toward her. And now, somehow, some way, she had to do something about the debilitating effect he had on her lungs. Being attracted to a man was one thing, but a woman had to maintain some kind of control or she would get hurt. Sally had been hurt enough for three lifetimes.

Summoning her strength as well as her best smile, she held up a white paper bag as he approached. "You, Mr. Cotter Graham, are in for a treat. I've got cheeseburgers here, fresh off the Dairy Bar grill."

He came to a stop in front of her, grinning as he rolled up the sleeves of his crisp, white shirt. "You didn't ask if I liked cheeseburgers, you know."

"You'll like these."

He shook his head. "I've got to tell you. You're ruining my reputation."

"How?"

"At the hospital I used to run in Atlanta, they called me 'Cotter the Barbarian' when they thought I couldn't hear them."

"Sounds ferocious."

"Being ferocious gets the job done."

"You must be one mean slave driver of a boss."

"Exactly. I've been cultivating the barbarian image here, too. But if word gets out that you coerced me into lunch—"

"Coerced?" she repeated. "You barely protested."

His smile grew wide. "You didn't give me a chance."

"Sorry you came?"

"Not as long as you made those burgers all the way, nothing held back."

"Of course." She tilted her head to the side and watched him loosen his red-and-gray patterned tie. "I sort of pegged you as an 'all the way' kind of guy."

He arched one eyebrow. "Did you now?"

She laughed. Yes, she had control. Some innocent flirting with this man was just what she needed. "The burgers are getting cold and the ice is melting in the drinks I brought. Why don't we eat?"

They settled beneath the park's oldest tree, on a patchwork quilt Sally had brought from home. Cotter sprawled back, apparently unconcerned about picnicking in well-pressed gray linen trousers. Sally liked his easy manner. She kicked off her sandals, tucked her bare legs beneath her and set out the food, prepared to enjoy this rare midday break from the usual grind.

It was a gorgeous day. The September sun still had the heat of summer, but a light breeze stirred the air, rustling the leaves overhead and carrying the scents of earth and grass and the roses that grew in a well-tended bed nearby. Visible, but still at a distance, a group of children shouted and laughed as they romped on the park playground. Their happy voices provided a pleasant backdrop to the serene surroundings.

A big smile spread across Cotter's face after his first bite of cheeseburger. "This," he said after swallowing, "is one damn fine burger."

"The secret's in steaming the bun on the grill."

Cotter grinned again, his gaze warmly suggestive. "Something tells me that Sally Jane Haskins is pretty good at 'steaming' anything."

She pretended affront. "Is that a compliment or a criticism, Mr. Graham?"

"Just an honest observation."

The intensity of his gaze took Sally by surprise. Faced with this particular gleam in his eyes, flirting with him didn't seem quite so lighthearted. She glanced away and took a long sip of her cola before changing the subject. "Did you tell Jamie about our talk?"

Now intent on his burger, Cotter shook his head.

"I wondered. He asked me about you one day last week."

"What'd he say?"

"He just wanted to know how I knew you. I told him you'd been by for a burger." She gestured toward the bag that sat between them. "I figured you should sample the menu, just in case he asks."

A frown knit Cotter's brow as he polished off the first cheeseburger and reached for another. "I did try to talk to Jamie about that poem he wrote."

"*Tried* to talk?"

His expression was rueful. "He said it was nothing."

"Of course it was nothing. He was just being his age."

"But I wanted to be sure. I mean, I could understand his sentiments..." His gaze swept over Sally with the same appreciative gleam they had held moments before. "But I also think he should have respect for women . . . for everyone, for that matter."

"I don't think he meant any disrespect toward me."

"You're right. After I talked to Jamie, I felt pretty good about his attitude. But I wanted to make sure of what he was thinking. If his mother were here, she wouldn't want her son thinking of women as purely sexual objects."

"Maybe it's none of my business," Sally said hesitantly. "But aren't you worrying a little too much about something that has to do with normal teenage hormones? I believe you need to keep things in perspective here."

"I'm just trying to do the right thing." Cotter paused, squinting as he looked toward the crowded playground.

"Respect for others was something Jamie's mother tried hard to impress upon him. I don't want him to forget it."

After a moment's silence, Sally said, "You've done a good job with Jamie."

Cotter didn't turn from his contemplation of the distant children. "His mother did a good job."

"You weren't involved?"

"Most of the time I was too busy to care."

The blunt words shocked her. "Too busy for your son?"

"Yeah." He turned and looked at her then, his dark-lashed hazel eyes full of regret. "I was too busy for Jamie. That's a crummy admission for a father to make, isn't it?"

She had to agree. "Pretty crummy."

Setting aside his half-eaten second burger, Cotter reached for a napkin. "You didn't have to confirm my failings as a father quite so quickly, you know."

"What are you going to do about those failings?"

His grin reappeared. "Oh, I'm doing irrational things, like barreling around town ready to battle wicked, older women who inspire my son to write poetry with definite sexual overtones."

Seeing that he didn't want to get into a serious conversation about his relationship with Jamie, Sally laughed. "You want to know something? That poem has given my confidence a boost."

"Your confidence needed boosting?"

"Well, sure."

"Somehow that's hard to believe."

"Listen," she said with characteristic bluntness. "I'm thirty-three...and a half, as my daughter would say. That's not old, I grant you. But the bloom is gone. So it's not too painful to hear that someone thinks I've still got it."

Cotter turned toward her, shifting so that one arm rested on his right, up-drawn knee. Sally couldn't help but notice how his slacks molded to the outline of his muscular thigh. And she found herself distracted by other small details, as well. The smooth golden hair on his tanned forearm. The masculine breadth of his hands. The small indentation in his chin. The faint scar that split his left eyebrow. The lines carved on either side of...

"Sally?"

Hearing her name made her realize Cotter had been speaking while she had been caught up in an inventory of his very attractive attributes. Her cheeks grew warm as her gaze met his. "Did you say something?"

"I said I don't believe you need a teenager's poem to remind you that you've still got it."

"We'll just see how you react the next time some sweet young thing makes goo-goo eyes at you."

He reached out and touched her face, lightly, with just the tips of his fingers. "All right. Let's see."

Though she tried not to betray any reaction to his touch, her voice shook. "See what?"

"Make goo-goo eyes at me," he murmured. "We'll see how I react."

"But I'm no sweet young thing."

"Is that so?" His whisper was deep, teasingly sexy. "I could have sworn you were." The lines bracketing his generous mouth deepened as he smiled. "Uh-oh, Miss Sally Jane Haskins, I think these..." His finger trailed up the side of her face. "Yes, these are definitely goo-goo eyes."

Though she was breathless once again, Sally managed a grin of her own. "Maybe they are. How does that make you feel?"

"How do I look?"

Her flip reply stuck in her throat. She couldn't describe how he looked. For in spite of all of her supposedly infamous experience, she had never been regarded with the sort of blatantly sexual invitation now in Cotter's expression. Damn, but he could change so quickly. From teasing to an intensity that bordered on the dangerous. Raw desire shimmered in the air between them. It was real enough to touch. Solid enough to shatter.

And so it did. Cotter pulled abruptly away, and the thread that ran between them split into pieces and disappeared. Sally wasn't sure whether to be disappointed or relieved. All she knew for certain was that the breathlessness she had been battling since the moment she saw him was squeezing her chest in double-time rhythm.

Cotter gathered up the remnants of their lunch, intent on looking anywhere but at Sally. He was a fine hypocrite, he thought. He talked about how his son shouldn't objectify women, while all he had thought about for days was getting this woman in the sack. Uppermost in his mind for the past half hour had been visions of how her body might feel when pressed against his own.

Since the moment he had seen Sally today, he had been ogling her trim legs and sneaking glances at the cleavage revealed by her scoop-necked pink blouse. He had wolfed down two cheeseburgers in an effort to concentrate on something other than how she was affecting him. He had kept talking about that damn poem of Jamie's in an effort to keep his mind off the tantalizing curve of her bottom lip and the adorable curl of her pink-tipped toes. She had him so rattled, he couldn't remember half of what he said to her.

The desire to touch had grown so insistent, he had found just the right moment to stroke her cheek. He should have known her skin would be as smooth and delicate as the petals on the roses blooming nearby. And he should have known that touching her would stir him to full arousal. He only hoped he could get himself under control before he had to stand up.

He spared a look at Sally, only to find her regarding him with an unreadable expression in her clear, gray eyes. They sat, looking at each other, until someone called Sally's name and saved the moment from becoming hopelessly awkward.

Cotter turned to look as a strawberry blonde, wearing a light blue maternity dress and pushing a stroller, came toward them across the grass.

"Well, hello, you two," the woman, who was faintly familiar to Cotter, called as she neared them.

Thanking God for small reprieves, Cotter got to his feet and lent a hand to Sally. Once standing, she snatched her fingers quickly away from his.

She looked rather dismayed, but she managed a friendly, "Hello, Marianne," for the woman who pushed the stroller to a halt in front of them.

The other woman swept Sally into a brief hug before turning to Cotter and extending her hand. "It's Cotter Graham, isn't it?"

"That's right." He shook her hand, trying to think of a name to go with her face.

"Marianne Dylan," she supplied. "Publisher of the *Oxford County News.* We've met at a couple of civic affairs."

Recognition dawned quickly. Cotter had been told Marianne Dylan was the daughter of two of Willow Creek's oldest and most prominent families. The newspaper she operated had been in the family for several generations. Her uncle, Jeb Hampton, a retired attorney, sat on the hospital board. His wife, Delilah, was an active community volunteer. And Marianne's husband, Jack, also an attorney, was currently running for a seat in the state legislature. Cotter had seen Jack at several recent civic luncheons. He had been told Jack was fighting a tight race against a veteran but vulnerable incumbent.

"I remember you and your husband," Cotter said now, grasping Marianne's proffered hand. "I'm sorry it took me a minute to recognize you."

She brushed his apology aside with an airy wave of her hand. "It's no problem. I'm sure you've been meeting and greeting lots of people since you took over at the new hospital." Her pretty blue eyes rested for a moment on Sally. "I'm glad to see you've made friends with one of my favorite Willow Creek neighbors."

Sally laughed. "I guess we really are neighbors since I moved to the right side of the creek."

Wrinkling her freckled nose at Sally, Marianne stooped to hand a pacifier to her fussing dark-haired child. "We've always been neighbors, Sally. I wish you would stop this 'right side of the Creek' nonsense. In my opinion, this town has never been big enough for those ridiculous distinctions about this or that side of the creek."

"That's because you're such a flaming liberal," Sally retorted, hunkering down to murmur something to the little girl in the stroller. "You'd better watch that kind of revolutionary talk, Marianne. That handsome husband of yours might lose the election if word gets out that his wife doesn't recognize the unofficial boundaries of our fair town.''

Marianne's short curls bounced as she tossed her head. "Oh, fiddle. I guess I'll say what I want. I've already given up any kind of writing or editing at the paper for the duration of the campaign so no one will think Jack has an undo influence with the press. Not that I had any other reason to take it easy," she added, briefly touching her rather prominent stomach. She laughed up at Cotter. "What do you make of our small-town ways?"

It was impossible not to respond to Marianne Dylan's winning smile. "From what I can tell so far, Willow Creek's a terrific place."

"Anything you like in particular?" Marianne cut her eyes down toward Sally, who was now playing peekaboo with the baby.

"Well," Cotter replied, grinning. "I just found out I'm particularly fond of cheeseburgers in the park."

He glanced down to find Sally looking up at him. And once more there was a sizzle in the air between them, a nearly undetectable zing that made him wish he hadn't pulled away from her a few minutes ago. He should have kissed her. Although he was sure kissing Sally Jane Haskins's deliciously full mouth in a public park wouldn't begin to satisfy the ache she had engendered inside him, he should have done it, anyway. Now he was going to have to wait. And he wasn't sure this much anticipation was healthy for a thirty-nine-year-old male.

Marianne cleared her throat, and Sally broke the spell she had cast on Cotter by standing up. Only then realizing he was holding his breath, he exhaled and thrust his hands in his pockets. Damn, but this woman got to him on the most basic level.

"I should go," he said quickly. "Sally, lunch was...great."

"Yes," she murmured, tucking an errant strand of ebony hair behind an ear. Her gaze didn't quite meet his. "Now that you know our burgers are better than anything Louella's Diner serves up, you'll have to come into the Dairy Bar again."

"I'll do that." Cotter murmured some innocuous parting words to Marianne and then took off, resisting the urge to give Sally one last, lingering look.

Sally knew Marianne was chomping at the bit, but Cotter was barely out of earshot when her friend started fanning herself. "Lordy, lordy, woman, are the two of you in heat, or what?"

"Just hush," Sally hissed.

But there was a gleam in Marianne's eyes that Sally recognized all too well. Her friend, who had tried to fix Sally up with every available man in a ten-county sweep, smelled romance. And she wasn't going to miss out on one small detail.

"How and when did this happen?" Marianne demanded, shading her eyes to watch Cotter climb into the Bronco he had parked at the curb in front of the gazebo.

Sally glared at her. "You know, Marianne, in the two years since you moved back to Willow Creek, you've developed this very unattractive, very nosy side to your personality. Folks are saying that when Miss Louella kicks the bucket, you'll be next in line to pick up the gossip torch."

"Just because I caught you red-handed with that luscious man is no reason to get nasty, you know."

With a resigned sigh, Sally said, "Be at my house, tonight at six-thirty for dinner. I'll fill you in."

"I have to wait that long?"

Marianne's disgusted expression made Sally laugh. It would do her good to have to stew about this for a while. "Jessie here has a dirty diaper, and I have to get back to work. Bring Jack and the girls to dinner. I'll grill some chicken and you can grill me about Cotter Graham."

"You've got a deal."

By seven o'clock, Sally's kitchen was in chaos. Marianne's daughter, Laura, and Betsy had spread their homework across the drop-leaf maple table in the windowed nook and were refusing to move until they were finished. Marianne was trying to assist the girls, her swollen feet propped up on a cushioned chair. Her husband, Jack, was walking back and forth, jiggling baby Jessie in his arms in an attempt to cajole her out of a fussy mood. All he had accomplished thus far was to hamper Sally's dinner preparations.

When he bumped into her for the tenth time in about as many minutes, she demanded, "Shouldn't that child be asleep?"

"No way," Jack replied, shifting the baby to his other hip. "If she goes to sleep this early, she wakes up at three o'clock in the morning."

Sally sprinkled croutons into a glass bowl of tossed salad and shrugged. "So what?"

"So maybe I need my sleep," Jack said. "I have to stay sharp in order to win this election."

Marianne laughed. "Jack, I don't think you had better get used to sleeping. In a couple of months, we'll have another baby, who will no doubt wake us up every two hours."

"But *he* will take after me and sleep through the night," Jack proclaimed as he lifted his eleven-month-old daughter high over his head and nuzzled her in the stomach. Jessie squealed in delight.

Pausing while she checked the rice pilaf on the stove, Sally smiled at Jack and his daughter. "Even if the new baby has your temperament, he couldn't look any more like you than Jessie does." The little girl was her father in miniature, with the same dark hair and unusual sea-green eyes.

Marianne rubbed her stomach in slow circles. "*He* definitely acts like his father. He's never still."

Sally set the rice aside and picked up a platter for the chicken that was grilling outside. She crossed the kitchen toward the French door that led to the deck. "All I know is the two of you are very brave—having two babies in a little over two years."

The look that passed between Jack and Marianne was warm and intimate, as if they were both recalling a private, pleasant memory. Laying one cheek against Jessie's dark curls, Jack grinned at his wife as he said, "Sally girl, I'm not sure bravery had a thing to do with either pregnancy."

Sharp envy sliced through Sally. But it passed quickly. And for that she was glad. Experience had taught her nothing was gained by wasting time on what you couldn't change.

Before acquiring such knowledge, she had wasted several years thinking she was in love with Jack Dylan. They had a lot in common—two misfits who dared think they could make something of themselves in a town that judged its own with particular harshness. Jack Dylan was the sort of needy soul Sally always tried to rescue. But he had never loved her. Despite what half the town thought, they had never been lovers. For him, it had always been Marianne.

He had grown up a rowdy farm boy, certainly not a fitting mate for Marianne, descendent of the town's founding fathers. Years ago, she married someone else, moved away, had a daughter, forged a successful career as a newspaper columnist in Washington, D.C. Meanwhile, Jack finished his education and went into practice with Marianne's uncle, Jeb Hampton. The one-time rebel became an unlikely success, a firebrand attorney known for winning the tough cases. Two summers ago, after her husband died, Marianne and Laura had returned to Willow Creek. That's when she and Jack had found each other again.

Sally was genuinely pleased at their happiness. She had realized long ago that her feelings for Jack were more brotherly than passionate. They both would have been cheated if things had turned out differently. Marianne was his soul mate.

She and Marianne had known each other in school, although they certainly hadn't run in the same crowd. Now their daughters were best friends, and the two women spent a good deal of time together. If Marianne sensed how Sally had once felt about Jack...well, she was secure enough in her relationship with him to be at ease with Sally. Perhaps that, above all, was what Sally admired and liked about her.

Tonight wasn't the first time they had all gathered in this kitchen for a casual meal. Sally was equally at home in the big, old Victorian where Jack and Marianne lived. Sally and Marianne were aware that their friendship was the subject of endless gossip. After all—the supposed ex-lover and the wife as best friends? It was a hot topic in Willow Creek. The two of them had shared many a laugh over the speculative looks and stage whispers they prompted when together.

Smiling at those memories, Sally was pushing open the door to the deck when Betsy said, out of the blue, "I heard two babies in two years wasn't proper."

Though all of them were used to the child's pointed and rather adult observations, Sally demanded, "Just where did you hear a thing like that, Miss Betsy Michelle Haskins?"

The use of her full name made Betsy roll her dark eyes. "Oh, Mom, just get hold of yourself, all right?"

"Excuse me?" Sally said, glaring at the ten-year-old.

"We did hear it," Laura put in. "Last Saturday, down at the mall. Some lady told Mom she was big as a house. When Mom walked away, the lady told her friend that she didn't think it looked proper to be having two babies so fast. She said Dad ought to learn how to control himself."

Jack looked ready to burst out in laughter, and the corners of Marianne's mouth were twitching as she said, "That lady really ought to just mind her own business. How many babies your Dad and I have are no one's concern but our family's."

"And you..." Sally caught Betsy's eye. "You should know by now not to repeat everything you hear." It was a useless statement since she knew Betsy was going to continue repeating bits and pieces of everything she heard, but Sally felt duty bound to issue the rebuke.

Flipping her long, dark hair over her shoulder, Betsy said, "Mom, I said I *heard* it wasn't proper. I didn't say I didn't think it was proper." Mischief danced across her features. "In fact, I wouldn't mind at all if you had two babies in two years. But I do want you to get yourself a husband first."

Sally was momentarily immobilized by her daughter's blunt directive.

Jack had started laughing. And Marianne wasn't doing much better. "Got anyone in mind for the job?" she asked Betsy. Her sparkling gaze captured Sally's. "'Cause if you don't, I just might know of a candidate."

"Oh?" Jack managed to ask in between guffaws. "Does Sally have a new beau?"

"Cotter Graham," Marianne announced.

"I've met him," Jack said, sending Sally a speculative look. "Seems like an all-right fellow."

"More than all right, I think," Marianne put in. "I caught him and Sally picnicking at the park today."

"Marianne..." Sally said in warning. Betsy was listening with avid interest. The child was so eager for Sally to marry that it didn't do to say anything about any man in front of her. Thankfully she was saved from a fullblown discussion of Cotter by the bell. Two bells, in fact—the telephone and the door.

"You go see who's at the door," she directed Betsy. And she pointed Jack toward the phone. "You get that. I'm going to get the chicken so we can eat."

Out on the deck, she quickly transferred chicken from grill to platter and offered a small prayer that Marianne might keep her mouth shut about Cotter.

"Mom?"

She turned to find Betsy leading the infamous Miss Louella and her equally notorious sister, Miss Clara, around the corner of the house and onto the deck. Clara was as tall and thin as Louella was short and stout, but they were equally matched in their lust for knowledge about everyone else's lives. Louella had run the downtown diner ever since the death of her husband more than thirty years ago, while Clara had only recently retired from teaching school. Though both had been married, they had always been referred to as "Miss."

Right now, Miss Clara's thin nostrils flared as she looked about the deck Sally had just added to the house. "I see you're making a lot of changes around here, Sally Jane."

"Yes, ma'am."

"That's why we're here," Miss Louella added, with the titter that accompanied most of her remarks. "As members of the Historical Preservation Society, we were taking a walk down this block to see what the neighborhood was up to. We saw that you were working on your house and wanted to talk to you."

Miss Clara adjusted her rhinestone-studded glasses as she paused beside a redwood planter filled with pink petunias. "This is a very historic structure, Sally Jane. We hope you'll be maintaining its original character."

Sally gazed helplessly at the platter of chicken she held. How like the two busybodies, who professed to be such ladies, to show up unannounced. "I'd be happy to discuss that with you, ma'am, but right now we're getting ready to eat. You could join us, if you like..."

Miss Clara sniffed. "We are sorry about interrupting your dinner. Most folks are usually through with their meals by this time on a weeknight."

Most decent folks, is what she meant, Sally thought, biting her lip in irritation. Looking up, she found Marianne standing in the door to the kitchen, the cordless phone in her hand. She didn't miss the pointed look that passed between the two sisters as they caught sight of Marianne.

Marianne greeted the two ladies, then held out the phone to Sally. "This call's for you."

"Take a message."

But Marianne shook her head and covered the phone's mouthpiece with one palm. "I think you'll want to take this call."

"Marianne—"

"Sally," Marianne said with false sweetness. "*I* want you to take this call."

"For crying out loud," Sally muttered, puzzled by Marianne's insistence. Instead of arguing further, she swapped the platter of chicken for the telephone.

"Sally?"

The unmistakable voice took her by surprise. "Cotter?" she said without thinking.

Misses Louella and Clara traded another eyebrow-raised glance.

If Marianne weren't great with child, Sally thought she might have heaved the platter of chicken at her head. Why in hell's name hadn't she taken a message?

"You're obviously involved in something," Cotter said, his voice deep, disturbingly masculine and undeniably sexy. Even with the audience Sally had looking on, she experienced a warm rush of excitement at just hearing him.

She turned her back on the onlookers and managed a small laugh. "You could say I'm involved, yes."

"When I went through conversations with both Jack Dylan and his wife to get to you, I realized this was a bad time."

"Pretty bad, yes."

"Well, I just wanted..." He paused, and Sally heard him clear his throat. "I was just thinking we might get together this weekend."

"This weekend?" Sally repeated. Out of the corner of her eye, she saw Betsy lead Miss Clara and Miss Louella down into the yard. The child was pointing up toward the second floor of the house. God only knew what she was telling them.

"Sally?" Cotter said, a hint of wariness in his voice.

"How about Saturday?" Sally said quickly. "We could take the kids with us."

There was a pause. "The kids?"

"There's a country fair out at Foggy Bottom Farm," Sally said, keeping her gaze firmly fixed on Betsy. "They've got an antique working mill, canoeing on the river, lots of music. Betsy and I always go. I bet you and Jamie would love it."

"I don't—"

"I promise you'll love it," Sally said. "You and Jamie can meet us at the Dairy Bar at one or so, okay? I can take Saturday off, but I have to check things out at the restaurant first."

"At one?"

"I'll see you then," Sally said quickly as Betsy started to lead the two women into the house. Much as she would like to talk to Cotter, she smelled a disaster in the making. "Bye, now," she murmured, clicking off the phone just in time to hear Betsy say, "Mom said she'd like to rip up half the kitchen floor."

In his own kitchen, Cotter stood, phone receiver in hand, wondering how his plans for an evening alone with Sally Jane Haskins had turned into a family outing. The woman just had a way of taking control. "Damn," he muttered, finally slipping the phone back into its base.

Moments later he had it in his hand and was about to call Sally again when Jamie jogged into the kitchen and plucked an apple from the basket of fruit on the counter.

"Something wrong with the phone, Dad?"

Cotter shook his head, hung up the phone once more, looked at his son and took a deep breath. If Jamie didn't want to go this Saturday, he would be off the hook. "Sally Haskins just asked if you and I would like to go to a country fair with her and her daughter this Saturday."

Jamie looked uncertain. "A country fair?"

Though Cotter wasn't sure why he was trying to convince Jamie to go, he added, "She said something about canoeing on a river."

The boy's interest appeared to be caught. "That might be okay."

"So you'll go?"

"Sure. Sally's cool. It could be all right."

Cotter let out his breath. He had expected some resistance from Jamie. But the boy was unconcernedly crunching into his apple. Cotter didn't think he would be so nonchalant if he was still laboring under pangs of lust for Sally. Those pangs had no doubt been replaced by somewhat similar feelings for the red-haired waitress whom Jamie now spent half of every evening talking with on the phone.

As if on cue, Jamie asked, "Are you done with the phone?"

Cotter spared an uncertain glance for the instrument, still thinking he might call Sally again. He didn't, however, know what he might say. "I'm through," he said.

"Great." There was an unexpectedly teasing light in Jamie's eyes as he grasped the phone and looked at Cotter. "Now that you've got your date for the weekend lined up, maybe I can do the same."

"It isn't a date," Cotter said quickly, although that's what it would have been if Sally hadn't thrown a curve at him.

Jamie just smiled. "I have to commend your taste, Dad."

There passed between father and son a rare moment of masculine understanding. Once again, Cotter realized Sally Haskins had drawn him and Jamie together. That was fine. In addition, however, Cotter wouldn't mind getting together with her. Very together. As in close. As in intimate.

Stifling a curse, Cotter left his son to his phone call and banged out the back door, eager for a run. He needed the exercise. He needed to work out some of the tension he had been feeling ever since lunch with Sally.

He had thought about her all afternoon. Thought about her skin. About the full curve of her breasts. About how she would feel moving against him. Even as his running shoes slapped against the pavement of the quiet, tree-draped street where he and Jamie lived, Cotter knew this workout wasn't going to exorcise those thoughts of Sally. Just as a day at a country fair wasn't going satisfy the urges she aroused in him.

He turned east, running hard, trying to get this woman out of his head.

Hard.

By Saturday, Cotter realized that was a word that just naturally applied to him when Sally was in the picture. He stood beside her on the bank of a river while Jamie and Betsy pushed off in a canoe. Sally was laughing. The sun was shining on her face. There was so much life in her pretty features. So much unfettered joy. Such qualities hadn't always been turn-ons for Cotter. But at this moment, looking at her, he found his body quickening in response. He realized he hadn't been this consistently aroused by any woman in a long, long time.

Something was going to happen between them soon, he promised himself. Somehow they were going to be alone, and he was going to kiss Sally Jane Haskins senseless.

Chapter Three

"This was the best day."

Betsy's statement made Sally smile as she drew the bed covers up to her daughter's chin. Ten and a half was perhaps a bit old to be tucked in, but it was a ritual both mother and daughter were reluctant to end. She perched on the edge of the bed and stroked Betsy's hair back from her face. "So you liked the fair, did you?"

"And Cotter and Jamie, too." Framed by the light spilling from the frilly-shaded lamp on her bedside table, Betsy's face was wreathed in smiles.

Thinking of the man who was waiting for her in the kitchen, Sally leaned close to whisper, "So do I."

"Enough to marry him?"

Sally was used to her daughter pairing her off with men, so she didn't take the statement too seriously. "Since I barely know Cotter, I don't think you should start planning the wedding just yet."

"But would Jamie be my brother?" The teenager had been exceedingly kind to Betsy all day, attentive and fun, acting the part of an older brother to the hilt. Betsy had nearly cried when, after dinner at the Dairy Bar, he had elected to stay behind with Lana and a group of friends.

But Sally wasn't going to encourage Betsy's hopes for a ready-made family. "Go to sleep," she said, with as much sternness as she could muster when her irrepressible daughter looked this cute and cuddly.

It was nearly eleven, and Betsy had already conned her into staying up an hour later than normal. Even then, Sally had been forced to interrupt the heated video game Betsy had been playing with Cotter. He said he had never played it before, which made Sally wonder exactly what he and Jamie did do together. There was a wariness between the two of them that she hoped never existed between her and Betsy.

Eyes at half-mast, Betsy was still talking weddings. "I want to be a bridesmaid and wear a purple dress."

Sally pressed a kiss to her forehead. "Close your eyes and dream about it." She started to stand, but Betsy caught her hand.

"Sing to me," the girl said around a giant-sized yawn.

"You're already almost asleep."

"Please." Her voice held just the right amount of sweet entreaty to ensure Sally's compliance.

"What song?"

"Mom, you know. The best one. The one you sang the first night I was your baby."

Grinning, Sally shifted so that her back was against the headboard and her arm was curved around Betsy. Then she launched into an unlikely lullaby, The Eagles' classic "Best of My Love." Betsy's features quickly relaxed into sleep.

But long after she knew her daughter was asleep, Sally kept on singing, the wistful words reminding her of that first night alone with Betsy. It had been a summer night, and they had been living in a small rented trailer without an air conditioner. The air had been humid and distinctly uncomfortable. Betsy had awakened several times, unsettled by her strange surroundings and suffering from heat rash. She quieted only when Sally sang. And this song had remained a favorite through the years, a comfort to them both.

A familiar feeling of peace settled over Sally as she sang the last few bars. She and Betsy had come a long way from those early days. The journey hadn't been easy. But she never regretted the decisions she had made about this precious little girl. *Her* little girl. Once more she touched her daughter's cheek and smiled.

"So you sing, as well."

She looked up to find Cotter standing in the doorway. In well-worn jeans and a casual white knit shirt, he exuded masculine appeal and seemed to dwarf the pink-and-white prettiness of Betsy's room.

"I hope I'm not intruding," he whispered. "I heard you singing and couldn't resist."

Edging away from her sleeping child, Sally said, "You're not intruding."

But Cotter felt like an interloper. He should have remained in Sally's cozy kitchen, sipping coffee and enjoying her song from afar. But her strong, true voice had drawn him down the short hall to Betsy's bedroom. He had stood outside the room for most of the song, watching the tender emotions flicker across Sally's vivid features. Motherhood apparently came as naturally to her as did talking to teenagers and making great cheeseburgers.

And turning him on.

Before Cotter could dwell on that, Sally tucked the covers around Betsy again, snapped off the bedside lamp and tiptoed across the room, the well-worn floorboards creaking beneath her feet.

"From the sound of this floor, you'd think the whole place was about to fall down," she said once they were out in the hall.

"It's a great house," Cotter replied, admiring the hall's high ceiling and simple, broad-planed moldings.

Sally chuckled as she eased Betsy's door halfway closed behind her. "It is great. And it's in pretty good shape structurally for being a hundred years old and having gone through so many owners. I'm redoing it in sections." Her smile was rueful. "What I should say is that I'm redoing it as money permits."

He glanced about with approval. "You're doing well so far."

This hall was really more like a small, rectangular room, with walls painted a peachy cream in harmonious contrast to the woodwork's dark mahogany stain. The only furnishing was a narrow table topped by an antique-looking water pitcher filled with fresh daisies. The kitchen and family room lay just beyond an arched doorway to Cotter's right. Betsy's room was to his left. A bathroom was behind him. Through an open door at the opposite end of the hall, soft lamplight illuminated another bedroom on the front of the house. White ruffled curtains were tied back at either side of a broad window. The bedspread was a patchwork quilt. Trailing over its side was something red and silky-looking. A gown, perhaps. Sally's gown, most likely.

Cotter's mouth went dry. He turned quickly away from that invitingly open door. It was too easy to imagine Sally in a red gown, sliding down onto that homey quilt while he slid down and into her lush, tempting body. But with her daughter sleeping a few feet away, that wasn't likely to happen. Even without Betsy here, he didn't trust his take on this situation.

This woman fueled his libido like no one had in a long time. But he wasn't sure if his feelings were returned. Though she flirted, he couldn't tell how much of that was serious and how much was just her natural warmth. Today at the fair, she had played the coquette with a ninety-year-old retired farmer as well as with him. She was charming and outgoing to most everyone, and Cotter didn't want to misinterpret her signals. Maybe he was just Jamie's father to her, a fellow single parent.

What he knew for certain was that nothing about this day had been what he had envisioned when he asked her out. His thoughts had centered on bed. Simple, straightforward physical pleasure. Strange how he had thought through the whole seduction, though he had yet to kiss her.

Kissing her. Kissing that pink, irresistible mouth. He wanted it. Badly. He hadn't put this much thought into a kiss since college.

Right now, Sally was clearly oblivious to his inner turmoil. She led him into the family room and kitchen, still talking about her house. "There's a whole second floor that I haven't touched. Someone put in a bathroom up there that I'm going to have to gut." She pointed to the foyer that ran from the family room to the front of the house. "The floor in there needs resanding, and I haven't touched the front parlor or the dining room beside it."

Cotter tried to concentrate on what she was saying. Remodeling was a far safer subject than any that sprang to his mind.

"More coffee?" Sally asked as she crossed the family room to the kitchen.

Though further stimulation of any sort was the last thing Cotter needed, he picked up his mug from the dining room table and trailed Sally to the tile-topped island in the center of the kitchen. "I like this," he said, gesturing to their surroundings, even though what he really liked was the saucy wiggle of her curvaceous hips in her blue denim shorts.

The family room and kitchen were really one large room that stretched across the back of the house. The kitchen area was tucked into a U-shape at one end. In the center, a windowed nook had been "bumped" out of one wall, making room for a dining table. At the end near the bedrooms they had just left, a couch, love seat and chair were clustered around a small brick fireplace and a television set. The cumulative effect was one of comfortable clutter.

Sally wrinkled her nose as she filled his mug. "From everything I've been able to read about the house, mainly newspaper articles about parties the original owner held, this room started out as a detached kitchen and a porch. And let me tell you, the brick underfoot can be really cold on winter mornings, even with rugs on top."

"Can't you change it?"

"Change a brick floor that is original to this house?" She rolled her eyes. "I'd have the Willow Creek Historical Preservation Society down on my head."

"The house is that important?"

"It was built for Mrs. Clementine McAllister, a local legend who came to Willow Creek right after the Civil War with her husband. He was a minister. She had family money. And after he died, she carried on his good works, pushing for public schools, founding the library, that sort of thing. Her only child died without marrying, and the house passed from owner to owner, finally falling into disrepair, like a lot of the houses on this street. Things have begun to turn around since I bought this, though."

Cotter cast another glance around the room. "It seems to me that if this house is so important to the Historical Society, they would have bought it themselves, made it a museum or something."

With a laugh, Sally leaned against the kitchen counter. "Last summer, when it went on the market, I snapped it up first thing. The Society offered to buy it later, and I thought Miss Louella and Miss Clara were going to have a stroke when I refused to sell."

He chuckled, shaking his head. "That Miss Louella is something. She cornered me at the diner the other day to introduce me to her sister, Clara."

"*Miss* Clara."

He grinned. "Well, whatever. I spent an hour trying to get away from them."

Sally toyed with a crystal sugar bowl, not looking at him. "Did either of them say anything about me?"

"No, should they?"

"Well, they..." Voice trailing off, she straightened from the counter. "Never mind. Why don't you take that coffee out on the deck? It'll be nice out. If the mosquitoes don't eat us alive, that is."

The night was warm. Quiet, save for the songs of insects and the click of their bodies as they made suicidal dives against the wrought-iron gas lamp at one end of the deck. The house was only a block from the downtown courthouse square, but the silence was such that Cotter thought they could have been miles out in the country.

Absorbing the peaceful atmosphere, he took a seat beside Sally in a cushioned redwood glider and set his mug down on a small side table. "I'm adjusting to almost everything about small-town life. But the quiet at night continues to amaze me."

"It seems plenty noisy out here to me."

"What do you hear?"

Sally turned to face him, drawing one knee up to rest on the cushion between them. The other leg set the glider in motion. "I hear the crickets, of course. And the radio from the Turners' house next door..."

Cotter cocked his head to the side, suddenly aware of the music humming in the background.

"And there's Paul Martin's car. He's coming home from his part-time job at Wal-Mart."

Right on cue, a car chugged up the street and shuddered to a halt several houses down.

Sally tsk-tsked. "It sounds to me like Paul should have bought that new truck instead of having a new baby."

"You certainly hear more than—"

"Wait a minute," she cut in, leaning forward with her hand upraised. "Listen. The clock's about to strike."

The clock on the courthouse tower struck eleven times.

"How did you know?" Cotter asked.

She shrugged, settling back against the cushions again. "There's just this sound, a little hush, or something, just before the hour is struck."

"It must be something only a native can hear."

"It's one of my favorite sounds. Don't you like it?"

"The first night Jamie and I moved in, it was cool enough to leave the windows open. The clock woke me up three times."

"If you want small-town charm, you have to pay the price."

"I just closed the window."

"And spoiled the ambience? My, my, the Historical Preservation Society would be appalled. They're very proud of that old clock and the way it keeps time. Your shutting it out is like me ripping up my brick floors."

"This house isn't on the historic register, is it?"

"Not yet."

"Then why do you let them dictate your kitchen floor?"

"Well, the truth is," she said, her voice dropping to a confidential tone. "I really like the historic significance. But don't tell that to Miss Clara and Miss Louella. I like to keep them off-balance about such things. If they didn't have me and folks like me to worry about, what would they fill their golden years with?"

He couldn't imagine why she cared so much about two old biddies, but he supposed that was another of the small-town features that, like the quiet, he would adjust to in time.

"Did you buy the house because of the historic significance?" he asked.

She shook her head. "I bought it because... well..." She brought the motion of the glider to a stop and stood. Arms folded and head tipped back, she walked across the deck while looking up at the house. "I always wanted to live here," she said, her voice dreamy. "I used to ride past here on my bicycle in the summer, and even though the paint was peeling and the shutters were hanging off and the roof was going, I thought living here would be like living in a palace."

Cotter stood, as well, and followed her gaze. The house was only a shadowy outline against the summer night sky, but he wanted to see what it was about the big brick-and-frame structure that had once captured her little-girl imagination. "Is living here the way you thought it would be?"

"Does anything ever turn out the way you thought it would as a kid?"

There was something in her voice, a hint of melancholy, perhaps, that touched him. He crossed the deck and stood beside her, his back braced against the railing, his gaze now on her.

She perched atop the railing, still looking up at the house. "I can't redo the inside to be completely authentic. We do have to live here, and this isn't the 1890s. But I want most of the outside to look just as it did when Clementine McAllister moved in."

"The outside looks fine now. Just painting the trim and the upper floor must have cost a fortune."

"I did it myself."

"What?"

She laughed. "Don't look so shocked. I learned how to paint and hammer and nail and sand and stain from my father. He was a carpenter, and he used to make my sister and I work with him a lot. I hated it at the time, but all I learned came in handy when I redid the Dairy Bar and bought this place."

Cotter took a second to adjust to the thought of this very feminine woman wielding a hammer and paintbrush. But it fit, he realized. Sally had a no-nonsense, I-can-handle-it-all air about her. "All I can say is that your father taught you well. He must have been a good carpenter."

She shrugged. "Oh, he was. When he wasn't flat-out, falling-down drunk, he was the best carpenter in town. That worked out to about four months of the year."

Her voice held the same carefully careless unconcern Cotter had heard the day in the Dairy Bar when she had

mentioned Betsy's absent father. Such studied nonchalance must mask a world of hurt, he decided. Unlike that
day at the restaurant, he couldn't let the comment pass
without a reply. But "I'm sorry" was all he could come
up with.

"Oh, don't be," she returned, her tone even and bright.
"It's ancient history, and Daddy's dead, and I can't
change a thing about him or the way he was. Maybe his
ways made me realize the way I wanted to live my own
life."

Cotter could appreciate her acceptance of the hand life
had dealt. When Brenda was dying and he realized all the
many ways their marriage had failed, all the ways in which
he had been at fault, he had faced his own limitations,
accepted them and made new plans to forge ahead. Like
Sally, a bad situation had taught him some invaluable
lessons about himself and would keep him from making
the same mistakes again.

"What about the rest of your family?" he asked now.
"Still living in Willow Creek?"

"All gone" was Sally's noncommittal reply, leaving
Cotter to wonder if they were dead or had just moved
away.

"Betsy's the last of the line," she continued. "And I am
sure she will grow up to make the Haskins name something to be proud of. God knows, the rest of us didn't."

"But that's not true."

"Believe me," she retorted. "You don't know much
about the family. We were always just a no-account bunch
from the wrong side of the creek."

"But look at you."

"Me?"

He faced her, and with a gentle touch lifted her chin so
that their gazes met. "I don't know much about this town,

or about what side of the creek produces the best citizens, but from where I'm standing, you turned out just fine."

"There are folks who would disagree."

"They don't matter," he murmured, lost in the vibrant beauty of her features.

Now that he was touching her, was close enough to kiss her, he wanted to draw out the anticipation. Spreading his palm upward against her cheek, he stroked his thumb across her lower lip. Soft and yielding. Delicately curved. He could almost taste those lips against his own.

"What's it gonna be?" she whispered, eyes wide, voice husky.

"Be?"

"Who's gonna kiss who?"

The question caught him off-guard, made him laugh as he drew her off the railing and brought her close. But the laughter died when they kissed. Two weeks of anticipation hadn't prepared him. His fantasies hadn't come close to the reality. Kissing Sally Jane Haskins was like experiencing his first shot of straight bourbon. It was hot. It burned. And the sizzle spread straight to his belly like a streak of wildfire. He couldn't even call it pleasant. It was too intense for that. But one shot wasn't enough. He whispered a protest when she moved away, and with his hand on the back of her neck, tangled in her hair, he brought her mouth to his again.

Murmuring a soft sound of acquiescence, she gave herself over to the kiss, lips parting, arms slipping around his shoulders. Cotter could feel her full breasts pillowed against his chest, could feel the pounding of her heart. Or was that his own heart? They were pressed so close together, were so intent on the endless rapture of this kiss, that he couldn't tell and he didn't care. All that mattered was kissing Sally. Touching her soft hair. Fitting his growing erection against the yielding heat at the juncture of her thighs.

But when the liquor that was Sally was streaming through his blood, sending him close to intoxication, she pulled away again.

"I guess I've been wondering how that would be," she murmured, a trace of laughter in her voice.

"And?"

"You kiss very well for a city boy."

He brought her hand to his lips, just grazing her knuckles with the tip of his tongue. "And for a small-town girl, you pack quite a wallop, Miss Sally Jane Haskins."

Her lashes swept down, a flirtatious gesture he had seen her use to perfection with young and old all day. "Do I?"

In answer, Cotter drew her tight against him once more. He liked the way she flirted, but he didn't want that now. He wanted an honest reaction. As honest as the pointedly physical, undeniable reaction he had to her. Against her ear, he whispered, "I think you can feel what you've done to me."

She stepped backward, quickly, but with her patented smile in place. "You're turning my head, you know. All these kisses in the moonlight."

"Sally..." he began.

But she moved away, with an adept movement that made him think she had practiced it many times before now. She said something about mosquitoes and the time. And while Cotter tried and failed to come up with a suitable protest or a pretext for getting her back in his arms, she maneuvered him around to the front of the house and into his Bronco. She did it all with such charm, such laughter, that he wasn't angry. He didn't feel as if he had been led on. He was smiling as he drove away.

Yes, they had shared the sort of kiss that could knock a man off his feet. But she had ended it quickly. She hadn't made promises she didn't deliver on. He didn't feel teased.

He was exhilarated.

He hadn't laughed the way Sally made him laugh for years. Thinking back over the entire day, Cotter rolled down the car window and breathed in the humid September air. There was a distinct possibility that he hadn't ever laughed as much as he had this afternoon and tonight. A scary thought for a man who had decided, quite firmly, never to become involved with a woman again. He had started out looking for sex with a luscious, sensual woman. He got laughter and talk. A day spent with their children. And only a good-night kiss. He frowned, realizing how far he had strayed from his original goal.

Damn it, he should be feeling teased. He should be angry because she was being as elusive as sin.

But he wasn't angry. Horny, yes. But angry? No.

Because she wanted him, too. He knew he was reading the signals correctly now. His grin returned as he wheeled his vehicle to a stop in his driveway. Sally Jane Haskins could flirt and charm and evade the issue. But she had kissed him with a power and a hunger that matched his own. She couldn't fight it forever.

Sunday morning, Sally woke before her alarm, as usual. The house was quiet as she waited for the town clock to chime six times. She got up and made coffee and made plans for her day. Laundry and housework this morning. Noon to six at the restaurant. Dinner at Jack and Marianne's. Most likely, the normal Sunday night bedtime tussle with Betsy. It would all be very familiar. It was the secure life she had built for herself and her daughter. If she concentrated on that, she wouldn't have to think about Cotter.

About that kiss.

About what he made her want.

But in her safe and silent kitchen, she finally gave up the pretense of not thinking about him and sank down at the table. What was happening with Cotter was more than just that kiss, more than the friendly and fun flirtation she had intended it to be, more than sex. Since her wilder days, she had been able to walk away from sex with little problem. She laughed, thinking how that news would shock and disappoint some of the people who regarded her as a scarlet woman.

Through the years, town gossip had placed her in bed with at least a dozen men. The actual number was much, much fewer, but Sally had long ago given up trying to change mistaken impressions. She supposed she was the sort of woman most small towns had. Her body had developed early. She had attracted the attention of men and boys early. And she had made her share of mistakes early. She had paid the price, too. But after her mistakes were over and done with, everyone assumed she would repeat them.

When she was much younger, she had tried to change the way she was thought of. She adopted a more modest style of dress. She curbed her natural impulse to smile or flirt or to reach out to people. But she found that no matter what she did, those early, youthful mistakes had labeled her.

Easy, sexy Sally Jane Haskins.

Around the time Betsy was born, she had said a mental, "To hell with you all," to the town. She stopped trying to hide her body behind dowdy clothes. She stopped trying to be someone she wasn't. She flirted. She even learned to enjoy feeding the rumors about her, though she had tempered that inclination a bit as Betsy had grown old enough to hear what others might say about her mother. Nowadays, she confined her rumor-fostering efforts to dropping in at the local dress shop, picking through their limited selection of lingerie and choosing the most scandalous lace and silk they had to offer.

The truth was that Sally had dated her share of men. But few got close. Oh, for a long time she had been caught up in thinking she loved Jack Dylan. But even Jack hadn't touched her, down deep, not in the way Cotter Graham, a virtual stranger, did. She didn't know why he should be so different. With little effort, he made her wish for things she had set aside long ago, the forever kind of things she could never have.

She could have Cotter in her bed. For a night. Or a month of nights. Miss Louella and Miss Clara were probably already spreading word of their torrid affair. Last night she had expected Cotter to say the two women had warned him against her. She supposed it was only a matter of time till they did.

His car parked outside her house until nearly midnight last night would most likely be a topic of conversation at churches this morning or at the hospital tomorrow. Some bozo she had rebuffed at one time or another would no doubt soon slap Cotter on the shoulder and ask him how he liked the taste of hometown sugar.

But Sally didn't want one night with Cotter. Being with him and Jamie and Betsy yesterday had raised the specter of dreams she had thought long dead. Dreams women like her should never have. Of living on a quiet, tree-shaded street, in a cared-for brick home, with a husband and children. Of going to sleep every night knowing that you had dignity and respect. That you were safe. That you were loved.

When Sally was a little girl in a four-room house with paper-thin walls and a drunken father and a mother who instructed her daughters with the back of her hand, those were her dreams. Those were the dreams in her head when she used to bicycle past this house. Those were the dreams she thought had died with her innocence, with her family troubles, with her struggle to raise Betsy on her own.

She thought her dreams had changed. She had the child and the house. And if she wasn't considered a lady by some in town, well, she had self-respect. Like everything she possessed, that respect was hard won and treasured. She had decided she didn't need the husband, didn't need any man.

She didn't need Cotter Graham to make her ache and want and dream of what could never be.

But was she strong enough to stay away from him?

Of course not.

But she wasn't so weak that she would succumb to moonlight and kisses and the promise of hot sex and little else.

So when the phone rang later that morning and it was Cotter, suggesting dinner, she invited him and Jamie to the cookout that night at Marianne and Jack's. He grumbled a bit, said he had something a little more romantic in mind, but she held firm and he showed up.

And for a week, Sally played a game of dodge and deflect, with him and with herself.

Wednesday night he dropped by the Dairy Bar just before closing time. There was a gleam in his eye when he suggested coffee and a drive. Sally asked him to run Lana home instead.

Friday night he went to the high-school football game with her and Betsy. They laughed and cheered themselves hoarse over a hard-fought battle. But with Betsy underfoot, she could avoid being alone with him.

Saturday it rained. Sally worked all day, watching the door in vain for Cotter to appear. He called late that night. And there was something intimate and almost dangerous about talking with him in her silent, darkened bedroom.

Sally got hold of herself the next morning. That night, they had dinner with their children again. And, though Cotter watched her like a man in heat, though she felt a tingling superawareness whenever he was near, she held him at arm's length. Nothing was going to happen with his son and her daughter dancing attendance on their every move, but she did her best not to give him any ideas, anyway. His mouth was set in a hard line when he and Jamie climbed into his Bronco and left.

On Monday he didn't call.

She told herself it was for the best. She told herself the man was dangerous to her emotional health. She told herself to tuck her silly girlhood dreams in a place where they couldn't be summoned by a pair of beautiful hazel eyes, a set of broad shoulders and a kiss that stirred more than her senses.

But all day she answered the phone on the first ring.

Carrying his tray through the crowded hospital cafeteria after lunch on Tuesday, Cotter nodded to people who were rapidly growing familiar. He had been on the job for three months, and after swimming in paperwork and immersing himself in policy and procedure, he was finally getting into the day-to-day operation of this big, regional facility.

To him, health care was the ultimate people business. And first and foremost, he liked getting in touch with those who provided the care. He demanded a lot from his staff, but he wanted them to see him as involved in daily operations as they were, not just as a suit behind a desk. He had just come from an informal round-table discussion with a group of nurses in one of the small, private dining areas set aside for such purposes on the other side of the cafeteria.

When Brenda became ill, she told Cotter that his staff had seemed to be his first priority, above her and Jamie. Cotter was trying not to make that mistake again, but he also knew of only one way to run a hospital—with total dedication.

He had gone into health care management straight out of college. Not only had it been a growing industry with good opportunities for an ambitious person, it also felt like important work, like his contributions made a difference in others' lives. His mother had raised him and his sister, Susannah, to believe such contributions were important.

Last year, when he had decided moving away from Atlanta might be best for him and Jamie, he had looked for a position where his talents would be put to good use. Willow Creek had been his first choice. This hospital was new, and had been designed to serve a three-county region of small towns and rural communities where competent health care was in desperate need. They were facing a lot of challenges. Yet Cotter was excited by the possibilities.

With so many challenges at work and with Jamie to worry about, he didn't have room for complications like Sally Haskins.

He frowned as he dumped his paper napkin and cup in a trash bin and set his tray on a nearby conveyor belt. Last week he had grown increasingly confused about Sally. He didn't have the time or the patience for games, and that was what he thought she was playing. So he had decided to back off, though it wasn't proving easy to get her out of his mind.

"Cotter, wait up."

He turned to find one of the doctors he liked best bearing down on him. Tall and thin, with a shock of carrot-red hair and thick, perpetually askew glasses, Dr. James Kincaid reminded Cotter of a cartoon woodpecker. He was always in motion, his head bobbing as he strode through the hospital corridors. Like Cotter, he wasn't a Willow Creek native.

"You in a hurry?" Kincaid asked as he pushed through the cafeteria's glass exit doors beside Cotter.

"No more than you," Cotter retorted with a laugh. His legs weren't short by any means, but he was hard-pressed to keep up with Kincaid's strides down the hall toward the elevators. "Something you want to talk about?"

Kincaid's head bobbed in response, but he didn't slow down. "Just wanted to say I like those new emergency-room regulations you pushed through."

"Thanks." Cotter was pleased. Even though this was a new facility, there was some outmoded thinking among local doctors. He was pushing for changes, and the support of a respected physician like Kincaid was invaluable.

At the elevator, Kincaid punched the "up" button with a long, bony finger. "I was also instructed by my wife to invite you to a dinner party a week from Saturday. She said to tell you that refusing is not an option."

Having been invited to James and Deanna Kincaid's warm and hospitable home earlier in the summer and knowing a gourmet dinner was most likely in store, Cotter said, "No is not a reply I would consider."

"You should bring Sally Haskins, of course."

Cotter's surprise was covered by the opening of the elevator doors. Once inside, however, he said, "Sally?"

"Well, yes," Kincaid replied. "Deanna and I saw the two of you at the football game Friday night. The friends we were with said you were dating." His eyes fairly danced behind his glasses. "I suppose you saw my son score the winning touchdown in that game?"

"Of course," Cotter said, giving his friend a congratulatory slap on the back. But his mind was on what Kincaid had said about him and Sally. *Dating?* It wasn't a word he would use to describe their relationship.

The elevator doors opened, and Kincaid stepped out, sparing a brief, "Dinner at seven next Saturday," over his shoulder before his long strides carried him away.

Cotter nodded, but as the elevator rose to the third floor, he couldn't stop focusing on that one word. *Dating.*

It simply didn't apply. He and Sally had been on family outings, not dates. He had never really wanted the outings, never intended to date her. He had wanted an affair—fierce and hot and over quickly, with no emotional excess to worry about. Damn it, he still wanted that.

Didn't he?

Scowling now, he stalked off the elevator and through the outer rooms of the executive suite, nodding at the two clerks who shared one of the offices. His administrative assistant, who occupied the desk just outside his office, scurried after him.

"Mr. Graham," she said, hesitating on the threshold to his office.

He wheeled to face her with a deepening frown. Jackie Bryant seemed to be a competent woman, but she scurried around the office like a mouse, always worried about things that Cotter didn't think mattered. Small, usually impeccably though rather conservatively dressed, she reminded Cotter of the girls who used to work in the principal's office when he was in high school. They had always seemed just a little too good to be true, a little bit holier than thou and a whole lot irritating.

Cotter needed someone strong in this position, someone unafraid to stand toe-to-toe with him. Unfortunately the only time Jackie showed any backbone was when she was defending or explaining some antiquated custom or procedure that Cotter thought needed to be changed. Appearances were all that concerned this woman. It had become clear to him that they were incompatible. But Jackie's father-in-law was a prominent physician and chairman of the board, so it wasn't politically correct for Cotter to replace her just yet. He was trying to give her a chance.

"Jackie," he said now with ill-disguised impatience. "I've told you to drop the Mr., okay? It's just Cotter."

"Yes, sir, um, yes, Cotter."

"Good. Now what is it?"

She waved a stack of pink message slips. "Some of these are important. Your son called from school—"

"Jamie?" He took the message. "It says here that he's ill?"

"Yes, the school nurse—"

"Nurse?"

"He was in her office—"

"Why didn't you page me at lunch?"

The woman blinked big, frightened brown eyes. "I didn't know... I mean, I didn't think it was that..."

Suppressing a curse, Cotter turned his back on her and snatched up the phone, dialing the number on the message. The school nurse informed him that Jamie, who had the stomach virus that had been making its rounds at school, had been picked up.

By Sally Jane Haskins.

Cotter didn't attempt to mask his fury. "You mean you allowed my son to be taken from school by someone other than me?"

"We tried to reach you, Mr. Graham," the nurse replied calmly. "Jamie was feeling very sick and wanted to go home, and he is the one who suggested calling Sally Jane. And since I know you and Sally are seeing each other—"

"Seeing each other?"

"*Dating.*"

The word slammed Cotter right between the eyes.

The nurse's voice took on a chatty tone. "My husband and I were at the Dairy Bar last Wednesday night and saw you together. In fact, Sally introduced us. She and I were in school together. My husband runs the downtown hardware store with his father—"

"Yes, yes," Cotter cut in. Damn these small-town gossipy ways, he thought to himself.

"Well, I was just sure you wouldn't mind Sally getting Jamie. I mean, Sally is Sally and everyone knows that—"

"What does that mean?"

The nurse stammered a minute, but continued. "What I mean is, she has her own way about her, but unlike some people, I've always liked her, and I know she's a good mother, and I just couldn't see what was wrong with letting her come and get a sick boy." There was a faintly defensive note in her voice. "We did try to reach you first."

Cotter turned to glare at Jackie, who was hovering uncertainly on the other side of his desk. "Yes," he said dryly. "I'm sorry you didn't reach me. If Jamie is ever sick again, you can be assured that I will be available. Okay? If you have to call me again, don't take no for an answer."

"Well, sure, but—"

Not interested in anything else she had to say, Cotter said a terse goodbye and put down the phone. He was punching in his home number when Jackie poked the rest of the message slips in front of him. On top was one from Sally, saying she had taken Jamie home, where she would wait with him until Cotter could get free.

He placed the receiver in its cradle and glared up at Jackie. "Did it occur to you to give me this message from Sally before I called the school?"

The woman flushed, but for once she didn't cringe when Cotter questioned something she had done. "You didn't give me a chance."

Cotter started an angry retort, but then took a deep breath instead. "You're right, Jackie. I'm sorry for biting your head off. But in the future, my son has to come first."

"I'm sorry, too," Jackie replied. "I guess since you don't mention your son very often...well, I didn't...I just didn't think, I guess. You've told me before not to interrupt you when you're having these round-table luncheon discussions."

Cotter couldn't see that how much he talked about his son made any difference, but as he had yet to figure out the workings of this particular woman's mind, he didn't argue. All he did was pluck his car keys from the top of his desk and start toward the door. "Cancel my afternoon meetings, okay?"

"But what about the representative from the governor's office?"

Cotter wavered in the doorway. This meeting to talk about a state services tax on hospitals was an important one and had been set up for weeks. He turned back to Jackie. "The meeting's at three-thirty. Unless Jamie can't be left alone, I should be back. Stall him in case I'm not."

At home, he came in the kitchen door to find Sally stirring a pot of something on the stove in his kitchen. She wore a checked gingham apron over her pink polo shirt and jeans. One of Brenda's old aprons, Cotter thought, oddly disturbed by the sight.

Sally turned from the stove and smiled as he crossed the room. With her dark hair tied back in a pink ribbon and her face glowing, she looked young and fresh and damned appealing. But Cotter tried not to focus on any of that.

She said, "I see you got my message."

"Is he okay?"

"He's upstairs. I think he had the worst of it at school this morning and right after we got home. He's actually asking for food now. I don't think it's a great idea for him to eat much, but I'm heating up some chicken broth."

"Thanks." Cotter draped his coat over a chair at the dinette and loosened his tie. "I'm sorry Jamie called you."

"I didn't mind."

"Well, I do." His tone was sharp, sharper than he intended, but he cleared his throat and continued. "He shouldn't have inconvenienced you."

Sally looked surprised. "He was sick, and he couldn't find you, and we're friends. I don't feel inconvenienced."

"That's not the point."

She was quiet for a moment as she continued to stir the contents of the pot on the stove. Then she faced him. "I feel like you're angry with me about this, and I'm not sure why."

"This isn't your place."

"Excuse me?"

"Jamie is my responsibility."

Twin spots of color appeared in her cheeks. "You couldn't be found."

"That won't happen again."

"That's fine and dandy. But today you weren't around, and even though he's almost sixteen years old, he was sick and he wanted to come home. I thought I was helping out."

"You did help, but I just...I just wish Jamie hadn't called you."

"But we're friends—"

"Are we?"

She looked uncertain. "I thought—"

"Your friendship isn't exactly what I've been looking for from you, all right?" Cotter said with brutal frankness.

The kitchen clock over the sink, a copper and ceramic rooster Brenda had found at a yard sale, ticked noisily in the ensuing silence.

The color disappeared from Sally's face. "I see."

Cotter hadn't set out to hurt her. He wasn't sure why he was attacking her this way, except that twice in the space of half an hour, people had coupled his name with Sally's as if they were a done deal, as if there was something more between them than a powerful sexual urge.

He didn't want more between them. He didn't want to know about her alcoholic father, or to think of Sally as she had looked when she sang Betsy to sleep. Hell, he didn't even want to know Betsy, to play games with her, to laugh at her very adult pronouncements. He didn't want to see Sally in his kitchen, making herself so perfectly at home.

He realized now that simply having an affair with her had been out of the question for a long time. There was something more than sexual chemistry going on between them. The simplicity was gone. He now knew too much about her, and she had invaded his territory, as well. What he had decided to pursue for purely physical and sexual reasons was now complicated by emotional involvement. He didn't want it. Furthermore, he couldn't handle it. His empty marriage had proven that point once and for all.

"I suppose I should leave," Sally said, her voice tight.

"I think so."

Sally didn't pause to debate anything with him. She whipped off the apron, mumbled, "Say goodbye to Jamie," and was gone. Dishes rattled in the cupboards as she slammed the kitchen door behind her.

"Dad?"

Cotter wheeled to find his pale, gaunt-looking son in the doorway from the hall with his dog at his side staring at him in confusion. "Why did you say that to her?"

How much had he heard? Cotter wondered, stricken. He took a step forward, hand outstretched. "Son—"

Jamie's voice rose. "Why would you ask her to leave?"

"You don't understand—"

"She didn't deserve to be asked to leave."

Cotter felt a pinprick of anger. "Jamie, this is none of your business."

But the teenager wasn't listening. "Man, I thought you were only a selfish bastard when it came to me and Mom. Now I see that you don't discriminate."

Fury sent heat scalding up Cotter's neck. No matter what the boy thought, he wasn't going to talk to him this way. "Go to your room."

"Gladly."

Jamie disappeared, and in a moment the house shook from the force of another slammed door.

Cursing his awkward handling of the situation, Cotter watched the broth boil over on the stove.

Chapter Four

For two days, Sally didn't allow herself to think about what had happened with Cotter. The restaurant was busy, the bathroom plumbing went on the fritz at home, and with Betsy there was always plenty to think about and do. But on Thursday evening, just before closing time at the Dairy Bar, when the last customer had left, when the place was clean, when she couldn't avoid the facts any longer, depression set in. Depression and anger.

She was angry because she had allowed herself to think Cotter might be different from other men. Of course he didn't want her friendship. And of course he didn't want anything deeper, either. Those girlhood dreams of hers, about a forever kind of love with a forever kind of man, had been resurrected just long enough to be killed off again. Cotter Graham wanted only what most of the men in Sally's life had ever wanted from her. A roll in the hay.

A trip around the world. An easy lay. There were a hundred euphemisms for the act, but it boiled down to sex.

She had done everything to avoid the truth. She had dodged and ducked the issue. She had fooled herself into believing that if they got to know each other, he would see her as more than a collection of female body parts assembled for his pleasure. But that wasn't to be.

Damn him, she told herself. And damn me for forgetting everything I learned long ago.

"Sally?"

Frowning, she turned from the counter to look at Lana, who was cleaning the restaurant grill.

The redhead was eyeing her with concern. "Are you feeling okay, Sally?"

"Of course."

"You look kind of pale."

"My summer tan's fading."

"Lots of people at school have been sick. Like Jamie was."

"Is he doing okay?"

"Oh, yeah." Lana applied herself to the grill once more, with a vigor that seemed overly enthusiastic to Sally. Her voice was a practice in nonchalance as she said, "Jamie said you picked him up at school."

Sally studied the girl's profile, wondering if Jamie had told her something else. Perhaps the teenager knew something of what had transpired between her and Cotter. Sally hadn't seen Jamie since Tuesday, so she had no idea whether he had overhead what she and Cotter had said to each other. Whatever the case, the best course of action was to change the subject. This was none of anyone's concern, least of all a couple of kids.

She opened the cash register and began preparing the deposit for the night. "You and Jamie going to the game tomorrow night?" she asked casually.

"I'm going," Lana replied. "They say it could be the best game of the year. Aren't you going? You and Jamie's dad went last week."

Sally remembered last Friday night, sharing popcorn with Cotter and Betsy while they cheered Oxford County High School's last-minute victory. "I think I'll give Craig a Friday night off," she said, referring to the local junior college student who lived in the apartment over the Dairy Bar and acted as manager when Sally wasn't there.

"Craig?" Turning from the grill, Lana rolled her eyes. "What would he do with a Friday night off?"

"Go to the game?"

"I doubt he's ever seen football played. He spends all his time with his head stuck in a chemistry book."

"As I recall, you've spent plenty of time with your head in a chemistry book yourself. Until this year, I can't remember you ever being so interested in football."

Lana flushed and turned away. "It's because we've got a good team, you know."

"And because it's something Jamie likes to do?" Sally couldn't resist teasing.

"Jamie? He cares less about football than I do."

Sally was surprised, although she did remember Jamie mentioning that he wasn't much of a sports fan. "So why do you go?"

Scrubbing harder than ever at the grill, Lana shrugged. "Everybody goes."

Since this girl, with her distinctive fashion sense and brilliant mind, had never been one to follow the crowd, Sally was even more confused. But she had been around teenagers enough to know better than to try and understand. She returned to her deposit, merely commenting, "Jamie's pretty cool, isn't he?"

"I like him."

"The two of you going to the Homecoming Dance?"

"Of course not."

"Why not?"

"Jamie's not really into dances, you know. But if he goes, I imagine he'll ask that girl in English Lit who's been flirting with him all week."

Sally set a stack of dollar bills to the side and looked at Lana again. "Why would he go out with someone else?"

"Jeez, Sally, Jamie and I aren't dating or anything."

That was real news considering they seemed to spend an inordinate amount of time in each other's company. "I guess I'm lost," Sally said. "Because I could have sworn that not three weeks ago you told me he was the cutest guy you had ever seen. And you're going to tomorrow night's game with him."

"If you'll think about it, you'll realize I never actually said I was going to the game with him," Lana said, grinning over her shoulder at Sally. "Although I might see him there."

"But what about him being the cutest guy in the world?"

Lana shrugged again. "He is cute. And we like the same music. And the same books. And he doesn't think it's weird that I make good grades. He sees a lot of stuff differently from the boys around here."

"So why aren't you madly in love with him?"

"Oh, puh-lease." Lana again rolled her eyes. "Jamie's a little young for me to be in love with."

"What are you, maybe six months older than him?"

"It makes a difference."

"Really?"

"I'm getting into older guys."

"Like who?"

Lana really blushed this time. "Just someone." She stepped back from the grill with a flourish. "I'm all done here. Can I go?"

"Of course."

The girl raced to the office, ostensibly to retrieve her purse, but Sally also heard her dialing the phone and talking with someone. She was probably calling Jamie, her "friend." Chuckling, Sally finished tallying the deposit. She might not understand Lana, but at least this conversation had shaken her out of her doldrums over Cotter. For the moment, anyway.

A few minutes later, Lana paused beside the counter once again. "Don't give Craig the night off tomorrow," the teenager said. "Come to the game with me."

"With you?"

"Yeah, send Betsy off somewhere and come with me."

"I'm sure you'd rather be with your friends. Or with that older guy."

Lana laughed. "I'd rather go with you. Please say you will."

Sally thought about it for a moment. Betsy was already slated to spend the night with Laura. Sally could either sit home alone, fretting over Cotter and feeling sorry for herself, or she could get out and enjoy a rousing football game.

"All right," she agreed. "I'll go."

"Great. I've already got tickets in the reserved section."

"Not the cheering section?" Sally asked, puzzled. When she had been in school, all the kids liked to sit beside the band and in front of the cheerleaders.

"Nope" was all Lana said, with a strange smile on her face.

Just as she hadn't tried to understand Lana's relationship with Jamie, Sally didn't try to analyze that smile.

But the next night, when their reserved seats turned out to be right beside Jamie's and Cotter's, Sally wished she had paid a little more attention to Lana's attitude.

Sally stood at the end of a row of seats near the bottom of the football stadium's concrete aisle and stared at Cotter. He stared back. Then he glared at Jamie, who was grinning at Sally.

"I'm going to kill you," Sally whispered to Lana.

The girl didn't even flinch. "What's wrong?"

"You and Jamie set me up."

"I told you I'd probably see Jamie here."

Sally gripped the girl's arm, while she hissed in her ear. "I'm going to fire you and *then* I'm going to kill you."

Smiling like a well-satisfied cat, Lana just waved and said, "Hi, Mr. Graham," as she slipped past him and into the seat on the other side of Jamie.

That left Sally standing in the aisle while people grumbled and mumbled as they pushed past her on their way to their seats. Since the entire town of Willow Creek was football crazy and this was the biggest game of the year thus far, the stands were packed. It was a big stadium, carved out of a natural bowl near the high school. Sally felt as if half the crowd was staring at her while she hesitated to take her seat. She could count at least a dozen familiar faces in the people who were seated nearby. Cotter looked as if a thundercloud could appear above his head at any time. Jamie and Lana, like good little conspirators, had their heads together.

When Sally continued to hesitate, Cotter got to his feet and gestured to the seat beside him. "Aren't you going to sit down?" was his less than gracious invitation.

So she sat. She folded her arms across her middle. And she didn't say a word.

Cotter braced his hands on his denim-clad thighs, his gaze on the football field but in reality seeing nothing but red. He turned once, to glare at his son and his red-haired partner in crime. They gazed back with wide-eyed innocence. What in the hell were these two trying to prove with this stunt?

He darted a look to his other side. In her snug black jeans and ruffled red blouse, Sally sat beside him like a statue, back straight, eyes trained dead ahead. And no wonder. After what he had said to her Tuesday afternoon, he was probably the last person she wanted to see, much less sit beside.

And this was Jamie's fault. Cotter realized now that he should have seen something like this coming.

Tuesday afternoon, following Jamie's angry outburst, Cotter had rescued the broth from the stove and gone back to the hospital. Jamie hadn't looked as if he was dying from the stomach virus, and Cotter did have an important meeting to return to. But he came home early and found Jamie, still looking pale and ill, in the den with his dog in attendance. He was still upset. He got up and looked Cotter straight in the eye and demanded once again to know why he had asked Sally to leave.

Cotter had walked across the room, snapped off the television set and said, bluntly, "What happened between Sally and I this afternoon is none of your business."

"I thought you liked her."

"I did."

"Well, so do I, so what—"

"You shouldn't have called her today."

"I was puking my guts up, Dad—"

"You could have stayed at the nurse's office."

"Yeah, and waited till you found the time to come and get me."

He had a legitimate complaint, which Cotter tried to address. "I didn't get the message that you were sick. I can assure you it won't happen again."

Jamie's jaw was set in a stubborn line. "I still don't see what was wrong with calling Sally. She said she didn't mind."

"Maybe I mind."

"But that's stupid—"

Cotter raised his eyebrows at that, and Jamie backed down, turning away to fling himself down on the plaid-upholstered couch once again.

"I still don't get it," he grumbled. "Sunday night we had dinner with her and today you act like you're totally pissed at her. What happened?"

After casting about for a reason which he wanted to share with his fifteen-year-old son, Cotter settled on, "It's no big deal. I just don't think I'll be seeing her anymore."

"But why?"

He tried to sound casual. "It's just one of those things. I'm not interested, I guess."

Jamie snickered. "That's a good one, Dad."

Cotter frowned. "What do you mean?"

"I'm not stupid enough to buy that you're not interested."

"I don't care if you don't buy it or not. The subject is closed." Cotter turned on his heel, ready to leave.

Jamie's voice stopped him. "I hate it when you do that, you know."

"What?" Cotter faced him again.

The boy's pale face was now washed with color. "I hate it when you dismiss me like that. Like I'm one of your flunkies down at the hospital. I'm not an employee, Dad. You may like treating me that way, but I'm not on the payroll."

For a moment, Cotter had no answer. He just stared at his son, astounded. Jamie never talked to him this way.

"You can't lie to me and expect me to believe you because you're the big boss."

Cotter held up a hand to stop him. "I don't lie to you, Jamie."

"This crap about not being interested in Sally is a lie and you know it."

"Son, I'm warning you—"

"Warn away," the boy retorted. "I don't care. I still won't believe you. And I still won't understand why you were so rude to her today. If I had talked to someone the way you talked to her, you would have chewed me out."

The sad fact was that Jamie was right. Cotter had been unforgivably rude. But today, with everyone assuming he and Sally were involved, with her standing in his house like she belonged here, he had felt so damn threatened. She stirred something in him, something he didn't want to face. He wanted to untangle himself from her as quickly as he could. He had to explain that to Jamie in a way that the boy would understand. And perhaps the truth was a good place to start. Maybe he should tell Jamie right now that marriage or a serious involvement with anyone weren't on Cotter's agenda.

"All right," he began, measuring his words with care. "I'll admit I like Sally, but the fact is, Jamie...after your mother died, I decided . . . well, I didn't want—"

"Do you think I mind you going out with Sally because of Mom?"

Jamie's question knocked Cotter off-balance. "What?"

"If you told her to leave today because you think I mind you seeing her, you're crazy."

Cotter sank down on the edge of the couch. Jamie had totally misunderstood. "Son, that isn't—"

"I think she's totally cool."

"But, Jamie—"

"And she's beautiful."

"That's not—"

The boy waved him off. "I know, I know, that's not like a major consideration for someone your age."

Drawing himself up, Cotter repeated, "My age?"

"And I'm not hung up on looks myself."

Recalling their earlier conversation on the definition of "babes," Cotter managed a wry smile. "So you told me."

"So you can start seeing her again. Call her up and apologize for this afternoon."

"It's not that simple."

"Why?"

Cotter stood and tried to take control of the conversation again. All at once the truth seemed a bit too complicated to explain. "It's just not simple, all right? Let's leave it at that."

"But, Dad—"

"Hang it up, Jamie."

And Cotter actually thought that was that. Later he was even pleased when he went over the conversation in his mind. Sally might have been the catalyst for yet another real exchange with Jamie, but he didn't think it mattered so much why they talked, as long as they did. When Jamie had come to him late Thursday night with an invitation to the football game, Cotter had been extraordinarily pleased, thinking they had made real progress.

But as the band played the National Anthem and Cotter stood with a stiff and miserable Sally to his left and a smirking son to his right, his pleasure was minimal.

The teams took the field and kicked off, but Jamie got to his feet before the first series of plays were called. "Me and Lana are going for popcorn, okay?"

With restrained but reasonable force, Cotter pulled the boy back into his seat. "No, you're not. You're going to sit here without moving for this entire game."

"Dad—"

"You chose the seats. Now enjoy them."

"Oh, for heaven's sake," Sally exclaimed. "Why don't I just leave? Would that make you happy?"

"No!" Lana and Jamie protested at once.

"Shut up!" Sally and Cotter shot back at them in unison.

Muttering something angry under her breath, Sally swung out of her seat.

Obeying an impulse he couldn't name, Cotter followed her.

Halfway up the vertical concrete aisle, she rounded on him. "Just go back to your seat, will you?"

"I want to talk to you."

"Too bad."

Cotter knew that heads were turning in their direction. "Can we go somewhere and talk about this?"

"No." She swung back around.

He caught her elbow.

She jerked away. "Would you just stop it!"

"Everyone is staring at us," he muttered.

"Who cares?" she said in a voice loud enough to vie with the noise of the crowd. "I'm used to being stared at." She twisted away from him and took the remaining stairs two at a time.

But Cotter followed. And his legs were longer, so he reached the top of the aisle right behind her. He was aware of the ripple of sound and interest following their progress and trailing in their wake as he pursued her through the crowd that had gathered around the concession stand.

Sally pushed her way through a group of kids near the entrance gate. Cotter was still only a step behind her when she reached the parking lot.

She turned on him again. "Would you please go away?"

It wasn't until that moment, when he stared down into her angry, beautiful features that Cotter realized why he was chasing her this way. It was because he was afraid that if he let her go, she'd be gone for good. What a shock. On Tuesday and yesterday, and even tonight when he looked up and saw her standing in the aisle, he had told himself that being rid of her was what he wanted. But it wasn't true. May God save his soul, it wasn't true at all.

"I've got to talk to you about what happened the other day," he told her.

"I'm not interested."

"Jesus, Sally, just give me a minute, okay?"

But she was in motion again, cutting a zigzag path through the parked cars, not pausing until she reached her blue Toyota Corolla. She jerked her keys out of her purse, but dropped them before she could get the door unlocked. Cursing, she bent over to pick them up, but Cotter was there before her.

"Give me my keys," she demanded, straightening up to face him.

"I want to talk."

She was visibly trembling, her face white with rage. "Give me my keys or I'm going to scream and scream and scream until somebody in this damn place decides to call the cops."

Admitting defeat, Cotter caught her hand and pressed the key chain into her palm.

Sally turned, fumbling with the door key, trying to fit it in the lock. But her hands were shaking, and her eyes were blurred with angry tears that she had to dash away. To make it worse, Cotter was still standing beside her. Tall and silent and watching her every move, making her so nervous she couldn't do anything right. "Damn it," she muttered, continuing her struggle with her keys. "Double, triple, quadruple damn it."

"Let me." Once again, Cotter's fingers folded around hers. She wanted to hit him, to scream and rage and give full rein to the agitation thrumming inside her. But all she could do was stand, immobilized by her whirling emotions, while Cotter helped her fit the key into the door lock.

But he didn't turn it. And she didn't pull away.

They just stood there, his hand over hers, his body close enough for her to catch the spicy scent of his after-shave and feel the warmth of his bare arm resting against hers. She didn't want to react to him, to be so aware of him. But she couldn't help it. She wasn't looking at him, but she could imagine the expression in his eyes, the way the lines bracketing his mouth would be deepening, the way...

"Sally." The sound of her name, a low, gravelly, sexy plea, cut into her thoughts. "Sally, I'm sorry."

She kept her head averted. "That's good. Now let me go."

"I'm not keeping you." His hand fell away from hers. But she still didn't open the door.

"Couldn't we just talk for a minute?"

If she was smart, she knew she would say no. She would open the car door, get in and drive away without looking back.

Before she could follow her head's advice, Cotter's voice, steady and calm and reasonable, broke in. "Sally, I feel rotten about what happened the other day."

Rage boiled up inside her again. She twisted to face him. "Oh, don't tell me that. You were just being honest the other day. Admit it."

To his credit, he hesitated only a moment. "Maybe I was."

"Then don't apologize."

"But the truth is beside the point. I still shouldn't have treated you the way I did, ordering you out of the house after you had been so kind to Jamie. It was inexcusable."

"All right, I'll excuse you," she bit out. "You're forgiven for your breach of etiquette. Does that make you feel better? Does it ease your conscience?"

His jaw squared. "No," he retorted, his voice rising. "It doesn't make me feel better at all. To tell you the complete truth, I haven't felt like myself since the minute I met you."

"That's your problem."

"You're right," he said, tapping himself on the chest in an impatient gesture. "It is my problem that I'm half out of my mind over you. It's my problem that every time I come near you I want to touch you, That I think about you in pretty much the same terms that Jamie put in that goddamn poem he wrote. It's my problem that you...you make me feel…" He broke off, shaking his head. "Those are my problems, Sally. But you've got a few of your own."

The raw emotion in his voice and his expression tugged at her heart even as she repeated, "I've got a problem?"

"Because you're hiding."

"Hiding what?"

"Not *what*," Cotter said. "You're hiding *from*."

"And you're talking in riddles," she accused, finally finding the fortitude to turn the key in her car door. It was pointless to stand here arguing with him. She was going home. She was going to forget Cotter Graham.

But she didn't get the door open. Instead, he turned her around, brought her tight against his body as he insisted, "You're hiding." Before she could protest, his mouth lowered toward hers. "Hiding from this."

The kiss was a rocket. An explosive start and a fast ride. It took Sally by surprise, took her breath, took every ounce of fight out of her. The heat melted her paltry resistance.

He's wrong, Sally told herself. *Wrong about my hiding from this. I haven't been hiding. I've been waiting. Hoping that this passion isn't all he's offering. Waiting and hoping against hope.*

Shouts and whistles from a passing car tore them apart. Cotter surprised Sally by pulling her back against him, shielding her from the view of a carload of rowdy teens.

"Get in the car," he told her when the car was gone. "Get in and let's get out of here."

Mutely she obeyed, climbing in the car and over the gearshift while he took the driver's seat.

He started the engine, not looking at her, his face set in harsh lines. "I want to go somewhere, Sally, someplace where everyone in this damned town won't be looking on."

She wasn't taking him home. She wanted neutral ground. So she directed him to a hill on the outskirts of town. Cemetery Hill.

The lingering twilight was fading to evening when Cotter finally pulled her car to a stop and killed the engine. There was still enough light for Sally to read his expression as he looked around and then looked at her. "I guess this will be convenient in case you decide to kill me."

"It's the town's favorite makeout spot. But every kid in Willow Creek is down at that ball game, so I figured we'd be alone."

"Just me and you and a couple of hundred graves." He turned to gaze out the window, the corner of his mouth curving into a grin. "Since these are all Willow Creek folks, I'm not so sure they won't rise up and try to listen in."

She was still too angry and upset to be cajoled into a smile by his meager attempt at a joke. Instead, she got out of the car, taking deep, calming breaths after she slammed the door and leaned against it. She could smell autumn on the breeze. Dying leaves. A hint of coolness. Summer was finally fading. Another summer of her life gone for good. And what had she to show for it? Another interlude with another man who didn't want what she was willing to offer. Another man who wasn't interested in her heart.

Though she heard Cotter get out of the car and walk around to her side, she didn't look at him. She concentrated instead on the glow of lights from the town below.

"We need to talk," he said after a few minutes of silence had passed.

"About what?" she retorted with a careless shrug. "You want to jump my bones, and I want..." Just in time, she bit back the traitorous words.

But Cotter wasn't easily put off. He stepped in front of her, lifted his hands to her shoulders as he asked, softly, "What do you want, Sally?"

"More?" The answer escaped without much thought and came out as half question, half plea, and she wished with all her heart that she hadn't spoken.

The word hung in the air between them, heavy with meaning.

Gaze intent on hers, Cotter slipped his hands from her shoulders, down her arms, to the hands she had balled into fists at her side. He gripped them tight.

"I'm not sure I have more to offer," he admitted.

Sally managed a brittle laugh. "At least you're staying true to form and remaining honest. Most men just make promises they don't mean in order to get what they want."

"I used up my quota of promises with someone else."

A hard, painful ache started in Sally's chest. "Jamie's mother?"

He nodded. "She showed me..." Cotter hesitated, wondering how best to express what he had learned from his marriage.

"Love?" Sally supplied.

"Yes, Brenda loved me—"

"And there can't be anyone else?" Sally cut in again, mistaking his meaning, just as Jamie had done when Cotter tried to explain this to him. "Because of what you had with her, you're not willing to try with me or anyone else?"

That was exactly what Cotter meant. Only it wasn't love between him and Brenda that had shown him he couldn't embark on another relationship. It was the emptiness they had shared. The emptiness with which he had greeted the love and the care that Brenda had so freely offered. And she had been free with that love. In that respect, Jamie was so right in comparing Sally to his mother.

Like Brenda, Sally was an open, warm and welcoming woman. And he knew, down in his heart, that he didn't have what it took to make a woman like that happy. He would have given anything for Brenda to have died happy. But she hadn't. And it was his fault.

He didn't want to commit himself to another person, only to one day look at her and realize she was a stranger, a familiar stranger who merely shared his house and his bed, who needed something that he didn't have within him to give. Brenda had wanted that elusive something. She had deserved it. And he had failed. Miserably. He wouldn't risk the same mistake again.

So why had he chased Sally out of that football stadium? Why was he here with her now? Why had the thought of her walking away for good filled him with such pain?

Cotter had no firm answers. He only knew that when he was with this woman, there was a part of him, a deep-frozen part of him, that came to life. He hadn't felt this way since long before Brenda fell ill, long before he realized there was something missing from the marriage that had looked so picture perfect on the outside.

Sally had roused something inside Cotter. With sudden, startlingly clear insight, he put a name to the emotion. It was hope. That was why he hadn't wanted her to walk away tonight, why he hadn't been able to get her out of his mind. There was something in her bright, disarming manner that gave him hope. He barely recognized the feeling. For a long time now, he had lived without the hope of anything more than a narrow life of work and responsibility to his son. After Brenda died, he felt that was all he deserved. But Sally made him hope there was something else.

She was looking up at him, her expression shadowed by the deepening twilight around them. But her voice shook as she said, "I wasn't looking to replace your wife, Cotter."

"I wasn't looking for a replacement."

"No. You weren't looking for anything."

His fingers tightened around hers again, while he managed a rueful smile. "I think we've already established that what I was looking for isn't what you're interested in giving."

With a sound that was equal parts sigh and groan, Sally stepped closer. She rested her head on his chest and tightened her arms around his waist. Cotter drew her tight against him, his face pressed into her ebony hair, drawing in the sultry, female scent of her. If he gave in to the impulse raging inside him right now, he would say to hell with honesty and indulge in another kiss. And another. All in hopes of laying her down somewhere and burying himself in her ripe body. He wanted to forget doing the right thing, at least until he knew what it was like to have Sally Jane Haskins in his bed.

"I don't understand," she murmured. "I keep proving that cliché about the right guy at the wrong time."

"I've never been a right guy."

"Then why do I feel as if you've kicked a hole right in the center of my chest?"

"Ah, Sally." He held her away from him. "I never meant to hurt you. That's why I'm being honest. Believe me, if I followed my true inclinations, I might just tell you what you want to hear." He smiled, and this time the impulse to kiss her was just too hard to resist. He touched his lips to hers, lightly, resisting the urge to deepen the caress. She didn't pull away, but Cotter made himself stop.

But now he was the one who groaned. "Every male instinct I have, every piece of my anatomy, is telling me to take advantage of you, you know."

"But you aren't," Sally murmured, her gaze still on his. "That's why you're a right kind of guy."

He had to force his voice around the sudden constriction in his throat. "I'm going to forget that if you don't stop looking at me that way."

"What way?"

He reached up and drew his fingers through her hair, then slipped his hand down her face to cup her chin in his palm. She was still looking up at him, lips trembling, eyes framed by thick lashes. "That way."

"Goo-goo eyes?" she teased, though her voice held the same breathlessness he felt.

"Exactly."

She didn't stop looking at him. He forgot all his noble intentions and kissed her.

It took maybe half a second for that kiss to go from sweet to sinful. And only a few seconds more for Cotter's body to go from pleasant arousal to full erection. God, how he wanted her. With a ferocious, unfaltering ache.

And for all of Sally's talk about wanting more than this, she matched his ardor. She met his kiss with strong, straight-ahead passion. Her hands moved to his face, then downward, tugging until his blue cotton shirt was freed from his pants, then upward again. It was her touch on the bare skin of his back that shattered his last vestige of hesitation.

He turned them around so that her back was pressed against the side of the car. She put her head back, sighing his name as he trailed kisses down the side of her neck. Only when his hand settled on her breast did she protest.

"We shouldn't," she whispered. "You know we shouldn't."

"Then stop me," he growled, with his lips at the base of her throat. "I'll stop if it's what you really want."

But she said nothing. Instead, she brought his mouth back to her own, kissing with openmouthed, hot greed while he fumbled with the buttons of her blouse. At the same time, he snaked his leg in between her own, pressing upward to the source of her feminine heat. She met his questing motions with gentle, downward rotations of her pelvis.

Impatiently he undid the last button of her blouse and dispatched the front hook of her bra with an aplomb he couldn't recall ever having before. He looked down and, in the velvety, remaining light, watched her breasts fall forward and into his waiting palms. Sweet, temptingly pale globes crowned with peaking tips. Full and taut and proudly thrusting. She was silk and cream and more than he could resist.

"Perfect," he whispered before he bent to taste one and then the other turgid nipple.

Sally's breathing came in gasps. Her hands laced together behind his neck, holding him at the breasts he bathed with strokes of his tongue. When he broke free and claimed her mouth with his own once more, he swallowed her soft murmur of protest.

The evening air, so cool only a moment before, felt sultry now, charged with an electric, fundamental heat. Sally's skin was damp as Cotter kissed the pulse that beat in double-time rhythm at her throat. His mouth returned to the valley between her breasts, where he tasted the salt of her perspiration. The same moisture was dampening his forehead and back.

From knee to torso their bodies ground together, her denim-clad legs spreading to accept the weight of his hips. He pushed her hard against the side of the car. The friction of his clothes combined with the sinuous movements of Sally's body created an unbearable yet exquisite torture.

Dimly, Cotter could remember moments like this when he was a teenager. They'd had a term for this simulation of lovemaking. An ugly, *dry* term. The memory curbed his movements, reined in his primitive drive toward completion. He realized with sudden blinding clarity that he didn't want it to happen this way. He didn't want to grope Sally like some awkward teen. The alternative was taking her right where they stood or in the back seat or on the damp, uninviting ground. All those options were erotic and exciting. None of them felt right. But neither did waiting for a better moment.

Yet waiting was the option he chose.

Summoning every ounce of control he could muster, he found the strength to push away from her, to step back and out of her embrace.

Eyes wide, blouse hanging open, she stared at him with a question on her lips.

His hands weren't quite steady as he brought the two gaping sides of her blouse together. Then he bent his head close to hers to make a promise. "When you and I climax together for the first time, I'm going to be inside you."

She drew in a sharp breath.

He kept his gaze steady on hers. "I may not be offering exactly what you're looking for, Sally Jane Haskins, but I know for a fact that you deserve something more than a screw against the car door.''

Sally thought of all the men she had known who would have taken just that, without half the encouragement she had given this man. She remembered one who had insisted on worse. If Cotter knew about that, would he still have stopped? If he knew everything there was to know about her past, would he be turning away, running a hand through his hair, getting himself under control as he set his clothes to rights?

She wanted to think so.

She had been falling for him since the moment he strode into the Dairy Bar, waving Jamie's poem in her face, some three weeks ago. She had been dodging that knowledge, fighting it. But it was true. From the start, her dealings with him had felt like more than just a lark, more than a flirtation to break up the stagnant rut of her life. She had been falling all along. Tonight had sealed the deal. So she wanted to think nothing she had ever done would make a difference in what he had just chosen to do and say.

"You deserve something more..."

The words swelled in her heart. Sally realized that even if she never had anything else from this man, she would have those words. She knew of only a handful of people beside herself who had ever thought she deserved anything but the worst the world could offer. But Cotter thought she deserved more, deserved better. Earlier, he had told her he had nothing more than passion to offer her. But he was wrong. He might not even realize it, but he was wrong.

He turned from tucking in his shirt, a teasing note in his shaky voice. ''Hey, I'm a nice guy, you know, but if you stand there like that...''

She looked down, only then aware that her blouse was still unbuttoned, the shadowy outline of her cleavage still bared to his gaze. Flushing, she turned around. Her unsteady hands worked at the clasp of her bra. But just like the keys she had been unable to fit into the lock earlier, the small plastic link wouldn't cooperate.

And just as before, Cotter took over.

Gently he turned her around to face him. His hands pushed hers aside as he hooked the bra and fastened the buttons of her blouse from the bottom up. For Sally, it was an act that felt more intimate than any that had transpired between them thus far. There were other men who had tried to take her clothes off. No one but this one was kind enough, sweet enough, to try and reverse the process.

When he neared the top button, Sally put her hands over his. "I can do it now," she whispered.

His smile flashed in the shadows. "But I was enjoying it so much."

She managed to laugh, as well. That was a revelation. The other men Sally had known in this way hadn't inspired laughter. At this point with any one of them, the atmosphere would be deadly serious.

As serious as the expression that now replaced Cotter's smile. He reached out and touched her cheek. "Sally, I wish I could say this has changed everything about the way I feel."

She wasn't surprised, and she wasn't hurt. Just because Cotter hadn't taken what she had offered didn't mean he was ready to indulge in an old-fashioned courtship, either. But did that mean it had to end like this? Hadn't something between them changed here tonight?

She caught his hand and held it against her cheek for the briefest of moments. Then she turned away, smoothing her clothes and hair and daring to ask the hard question. "What do you want to happen now?"

He stepped close behind her, his chuckle a pleasant, deep rumble next to her ear. "I think you can answer that."

"I want that, too," she whispered with fervor as she turned into his embrace again. Hands braced on his broad chest, she tried to gauge his reactions. "I'm not trying to hide from what almost happened here tonight, Cotter. I'm not playing games, either. I think I've now been as honest with you as you've been with me. I'm not looking for someone to just have sex with."

"Just sex?" He laughed again, leaning his forehead against hers. "Sally, do you really think you and I are going to have 'just' sex?"

Flushing, she drew away. He meant it would be fabulous sex. Sally suspected he was right. But she also thought they might discover something else in the process. Maybe, if she gave this some time, if for now she would accept only the physical relationship Cotter was offering, maybe later his feelings would change. Time would also allow her to understand her own emotions, to see what it was that she felt for him. They had feelings between them. Not just sex, as he said, but something...*more*. That word kept coming up again and again.

Sally had stopped taking chances on men a long time ago. Bitter experience had taught her to exercise caution before involving her heart. But her heart had been in mothballs for years now. Another summer had passed. Soon another fall. Time would keep on moving. And if she risked nothing, her life really would became as predictable as Lana's much-hated saltshakers at the restaurant.

It was funny. Half the town of Willow Creek would say Sally Jane Haskins was a big risk taker. But they just looked at the surface, at the smoke screen she knew they had come to expect. Since Betsy had been born, Sally had done little more than pretend to live up to her scandalous image. Just pretending had landed her in trouble a few times, and her past had came back to haunt her on a couple of occasions. But for the most part, Sally had lived a staid existence. Nothing she had done had risked anything that was important to her—not Betsy and not her heart.

But with Cotter, she knew her heart had been on the line from the start.

"Sally," he said now, coming around to face her once more. "What happens next is up to you."

"Me?"

"I'm not going to push you for something you're not comfortable with. I've told you up-front that I'm not looking for marriage or long-term commitment. If you can't accept that..."

But her decision was made. "I want to see you again, Cotter. But I don't see why we can't be friends..." She hesitated, then slipped her hand in his. "Friends as well as lovers. Is friendship too much of a commitment for you?"

"I think we're already friends."

"That's not what you said Tuesday afternoon."

"Let's forget Tuesday afternoon ever happened."

She agreed quickly enough, though she knew without Tuesday there wouldn't have been tonight.

Cotter kissed her before she could say anything else. He didn't want to intellectualize this any further. Maybe he was afraid to think too hard about it. A little voice was whispering inside his head, telling him that he was a fool,

that Sally Jane Haskins was looking for a husband and
father for her daughter, that further involvement with her
would lead to the sort of complications he professed to
want to avoid.

He was ignoring that voice of reason. He was letting his
senses override his intellect. Because this taste of Sally's
passion wasn't enough. He wanted to explore it all. And
he wanted to see if the hope she created inside him was
real.

They drove in comfortable silence back to the football
stadium, where, from the level of noise coming from the
crowd inside, an exciting game was still under way. After
their emotional, passionate scene together, Cotter knew
the wisest thing he and Sally could do would be to go
home. But they stood in the parking lot, looking at each
other, then looking toward the entrance gate, until Cotter said, "What the hell." Hand in hand, they went inside and reclaimed their vacated seats beside Jamie and
Lana, who were now so engrossed in the game that they
barely spared them a glance.

They were in time for the final quarter of play, wherein
Oxford County High School kicked a field goal and won
by a single point. The ensuing jubilation gave Cotter the
opportunity to grab Sally up in his arms and kiss her in
full sight of his son, of God and of most of Willow Creek,
including a tittering Miss Louella and a scowling Miss
Clara, whom he glimpsed over Sally's shoulder just as he
let her go.

He ignored those old gossips and kissed her again.

And when he felt the buzz that went through the crowd
around them, he kissed her a third time, long and hard
and deep, a kiss not called for by even the most exciting
football victory in the town's history.

Sally looked up at him and laughed. "We're going to be front-page news, Mr. Graham."

"We're hardly that important, are we?"

"This is Willow Creek," she retorted, a serious look replacing her laughter. "And I'm Sally Jane Haskins. So we are news."

Chapter Five

After one of the best weekends he could remember in years, Cotter arrived at his office early on Monday morning. He sped through a mountain of paperwork in the hour before the rest of his office staff arrived.

He probably should be cranky and out of sorts, frustrated because he and Sally hadn't consummated what they had started Friday night. But he wasn't. Oh, the memory of what had almost happened had intruded on his thoughts and even crept with erotic ease into his dreams. However, he found he was enjoying the building anticipation between them.

Besides, they'd had no chance to be alone again. Her weekend help at the restaurant called in sick, so she had spent both days working. The closest they came to any kind of intimacy was late Saturday night when they sat together on her sofa, listening to Jamie, Lana and Betsy argue their way through a game of Hearts. But even that had been pleasant. Friendly. Comfortable. Cotter found it very easy to spend time simply looking into her beautiful, clear gray eyes. Such an unusual color, those eyes, like the mist on a winter morning... Yes, the hours could spin away unnoticed when a man was lost in her gaze.

The annoying little voice in his head kept whispering that this Saturday evening was a far cry from the affair he supposedly wanted. Cotter finally tuned the voice out.

The simple truth was that he liked Sally about as much as he desired her. Yes, *liked.* It was a basic description that suited how he felt without involving other more, complicated romantic emotions. Sally was funny and plainspoken. At ease with silences as well as animated conversation. And though he suspected she lacked any formal education beyond high school, she had an innate intelligence and a unique view of the world.

She was simply a joy to be around.

Saturday night had been very congenial. Jamie and Lana avoided out-and-out smugness, though they were free enough in expressing their pleasure over the way their plot to throw Cotter and Sally together had worked. Cotter, feeling he should exercise some parental authority, had asked Jamie to stay out of his personal life in the future. His son made no promises. Cotter took some pleasure in being able to laugh and talk so easily with his son. In fact, he and Jamie had spent Sunday alone together, making pancakes for breakfast, playing an unexpected game of touch football in the park. Cotter didn't know what surprised him most, his son's awakened interest in the sport or the ease with which they got along together.

So it had been a good weekend. Cotter felt up, happy, *hopeful.* His outlook dimmed only slightly when his administrative assistant appeared in his doorway, wearing the earnest expression Cotter had learned meant she was going to tell him something "for his own good."

Sure enough, Jackie opened with the phrase Cotter had learned to dread. "I'd like to talk with you about something."

Stifling a sigh, he set aside a half-written memo and waved her into the office. She closed the door behind her, a sure sign of trouble.

"What's on your mind?" Cotter asked in as friendly a tone as possible. He could only hope she was about to resign.

She took a seat in one of the chairs in front of his desk and folded her hands neatly in her lap. "I know we don't always see eye to eye, Mr.... I mean, Cotter."

"I don't expect to agree with anyone on everything."

Her small rounded chin lifted. "I also know that you have a big-city way of doing things."

"I don't know about that."

She surprised him with a forceful, "Believe me, you do."

"Is something I've done created a problem for you?"

"I think you should know a few things about this town."

He sat forward, unaccountably intrigued. "What about it?"

"People here talk."

"I'm well aware of that already."

"And right now they're talking about you and Sally Jane Haskins."

The leather upholstery of his chair squeaked in the sudden silence as he sat back. Eyes narrowing, he stared at the young woman across from him. "I don't think anything that Sally and I do is anyone's business but our own and our families'."

"But I don't think you understand about Sally."

"Understand?"

Pink tinted Jackie's cheeks. "There are a lot of very nice women in this town, any one of whom I know would enjoy going out with you. But Sally Haskins isn't...I mean, she's not..."

"Not what?"

Jackie took a deep breath, then said, with an incredible amount of dramatic intensity, "She's fast."

The outdated, hopelessly outmoded word left Cotter fighting back laughter. "Fast?"

"To be brutally frank about it, Sally Jane Haskins goes through men like some women go through... through...panty hose!"

The metaphor was too funny to let pass. Cotter laughed out loud.

But Jackie Bryant didn't share in his mirth. She drew her shoulders back, her face now flaming, and said, "You can laugh all you want. But I've lived here all my life. I went to school with Sally. I know what she's like. She's trouble, pure and simple. For your own good—"

"My good?" Cotter cut in. "Jackie, I wish you'd stop telling me these things for my own good."

"As your assistant I feel duty bound to try and help you."

"And I don't see how commenting on my personal life has anything to do with your job."

"But you're in a highly visible position."

"I don't recall being elected to this job."

"This hospital is important to this community. Whoever runs it is going to be in the public eye, whether they like it or not. I knew you were seeing Sally. I mean, she called here last week after she picked up your son. And I wasn't going to say anything, but Friday, when you chased

Sally Jane Haskins up the steps at the football field...well, half the town's population was looking on."

A slow burn had started in the region of Cotter's gut. He'd had about as much of this sanctimonious little woman as he could take. "I hope half the town enjoyed the show," he said, struggling to keep his anger under control.

"Oh, they enjoyed it all right. Some folks just love a scandal."

"And if there isn't one, they just make one up, right?"

Jackie had the grace to pause for a moment after that, but then she went right back on the offensive. "It's never been very hard for Sally Jane Haskins to cause a scandal."

"With folks like you just waiting for something to gossip about, I can understand why," Cotter retorted.

"Whether you believe what I'm saying or not isn't important. Other folks know Sally. And I don't think a scandal is what you really want. Despite how we've disagreed about some things here at the hospital, I do think you're serious about doing a good job. And I'd hate to see a woman like Sally mess everything up for you."

The burn in his belly became a full-fledged fire. "A woman like Sally?

"A tramp."

Cotter shot to his feet. "I hope you'll pardon me if I ask you to leave, Jackie. I'd rather you go now than have me say something you might not like."

She retreated only as far as behind the chair, gripping the back with a white-knuckled hand. She wasn't through with her attack on Sally. "I don't think you'd be so angry if you really knew about her."

"I know all I need to know, thank you." He deliberately broke eye contact with her and pretended to be rearranging some of the papers on his desk. "This discussion is over."

"Then you know Betsy isn't Sally's daughter?"

The statement hit Cotter like a tackle from the rear. He looked up. "Come again?"

Jackie sniffed. "I didn't think she had told you about Betsy. Sally's sister is that child's real mother. Only she went to prison for drugs—"

"Wait a minute," Cotter interrupted, trying his best to absorb all of this. "Sally's sister is Betsy's mother?"

"Renee's her name. She's about two years younger than Sally, the same age as me. She tried to get Betsy back a few years ago, but Jack Dylan, the attorney who's running for the state house of representatives, convinced a judge to let Sally's adoption of Betsy stand. Of course, we all know Jack would win the case. It's common knowledge that he'd do just *anything* for Sally."

Cotter let the pointed innuendo about Sally and Jack pass. He had seen Jack with his wife, Marianne, and with Sally, and there was no question in Cotter's mind about the nature of the relationships among the three of them. He was more interested in Sally's relationship with her daughter. "When did Sally adopt Betsy?"

"Sally took that baby in when she was only a few months old. She adopted her sometime later, when Renee got out of prison and didn't want her."

"So if she adopted her, then Betsy is her daughter."

"You can look at it that way, if you want. The facts are that Sally isn't *really* her mother."

Thinking of the way Sally had sung Betsy to sleep, of the way they laughed together, of the strong bond between them that was obvious to anyone who wasn't stupid and shortsighted, Cotter clenched his hands into fists at his side. "From what I've seen, Sally is everything a mother is supposed to be."

Jackie's smile was smug. "Oh, everyone knows how she loves Betsy. Why shouldn't she? She was in love with the girl's father."

Keeping up with the details had Cotter's head spinning. "Betsy's father and Sally were in love?"

"I don't know about him being in love with her, but Sally was crazy about Tommy Joe Brewster. Everyone in town saw them carrying on." There was a malicious, speculative gleam in Jackie's eyes now. She was obviously enjoying relating this tale to Cotter. "Only he was sleeping with her sister, too. Tommy Joe insisted Betsy wasn't his. But if he were alive today, he couldn't deny her. Aside from that black hair she inherited from her mother and Sally, she looks just like him."

The pure hatefulness emanating from his meek assistant shook Cotter. She sounded as if she'd had it in for Sally for a long time.

"Some folks say Sally didn't know about her sister and Tommy Joe," she continued. "But I just bet—"

Cotter slammed his fists down on the top of his desk. The lamp shade wobbled. His empty coffee mug bounced off the edge of the desk and crashed to the floor. And Jackie Bryant shut her mouth with a little squeak.

"Get out of here," Cotter thundered at her. "Shut up and get out of here."

"But—"

"But nothing." The blood was roaring in his ears. "Take your filthy gossiping mouth and your vicious rumors and get out of my office."

She had more spirit than he had yet to witness, for she continued to stand where she was, glaring at him. "I'm not a gossip. I'm only telling you the truth about that woman—"

"And I'm telling you that I don't want to hear it. Now get out of here. Get out of the hospital."

She blanched. "The hospital?"

"I've been wanting to get rid of you from the first day I walked in this office. This seems like a good time to do it. I'll have your desk cleared out by the end of the day."

"You can't fire me."

"I just did." Propelled by fury, he strode around the desk and to the door, which he opened. The two clerks who occupied one of the outer offices scurried away, like eavesdroppers caught listening at a keyhole.

Cotter ignored them and beckoned for Jackie. "If you don't feel up to leaving on your own, I can always ask one of the security guards to escort you to your car."

The look of outrage on her pinched little face would have been comical if Cotter had felt like laughing. As it was, he had to battle the impulse to slam the door behind her.

Then he went to his desk, called personnel and started making arrangements to hire a new assistant. He didn't waste much time in thought over all Jackie had told him about Sally. Most of it was probably malicious rumors. He had other thoughts to occupy his time, like steeling himself for the explosion he knew was coming from at least one member of the hospital board.

It was only an hour before Dr. LeBron Bryant blew into his office with the force only a pious, narrow-minded bag of wind could muster. Short and stocky, with a perpetually crimson face, Dr. Bryant was a prominent Oxford County physician, chairman of the hospital board and father-in-law to Jackie Bryant. He had questioned every change and innovation Cotter had tried to implement since taking charge. Cotter thought the man would probably still be applying leeches and dosing folks with laudanum if he could get away with it.

"I'm not going to tell you to hire Jackie back," Bryant sputtered, standing with hands on hips in front of Cotter's desk. "Frankly, she says she wouldn't come back if you begged her."

Cotter didn't move from his relaxed posture in his chair. "I'm glad Jackie sees this the way I do."

"She was only trying to do you a favor, you know."

"If that's what she wants to believe, fine."

The doctor's already prominent jaw squared even further. "The thing I don't believe you understand is that Willow Creek is a small town. Life is different here. This job is very different from the positions you held before coming here. Your salary is supported in part by tax dollars, so you should expect to be under a certain amount of scrutiny."

"All right. If I don't do my job, then I'll pay the price. As for my personal life—"

"It's your own," the doctor conceded. "But in a place as small as Willow Creek, professional and personal lives overlap."

"That isn't a situation endemic to Willow Creek. People socialize with business associates the world over, Dr. Bryant."

"Exactly my point. Whether we like it or not business is often conducted in social surroundings. And a social situation that makes people uncomfortable can sometimes have an adverse effect on business."

"Are you saying that my seeing Sally Haskins could make it difficult to do my job?"

Dr. Bryant chuckled, an unpleasant sound, lacking in humor. "I can't predict human behavior. But you are a young man with lots of new ideas, things you want to accomplish. I know you're smart enough to realize there are ways to go about winning approval. And ways that won't get you too far.''

It was easy enough for Cotter to read between the lines. Bryant was saying that if Cotter continued to see Sally, he might find it difficult to accomplish some of the goals he had set for the hospital. Cotter wanted to show Bryant the door in much the same way he had gotten rid of Jackie. That wasn't prudent. But Cotter had to do something. After Bryant left his office, he mulled the situation over for at least half a minute before reaching for the phone.

As he punched in a number, he muttered, "I'll be damned if I let a bunch of narrow-minded snobs tell me what to do.''

When Sally answered the phone, he invited her to lunch, at high noon, in the hospital cafeteria. When she accepted, he sat back, feeling pleased with himself and praying the cafeteria would be as packed as usual.

Friday night, Sally had told Cotter she was used to being stared at. That much was true. There were even times when she exploited the attention, enjoyed it. Part of accepting who she was had been learning to take others' perceptions of her in stride. Some days and situations were easier than others. And today, as she followed Cotter through the busy cafeteria, she felt distinctly uncomfortable with the looks they were getting. It hadn't been easy to get away from the restaurant at this time of day. She would just as soon not spend the next hour being studied like a freak in a carnival show.

Sally could well remember the first day she had felt as if she was on display. She had been twelve, and one of the chief joys in her life had been the middle school chorus.

When she was singing, it didn't seem to matter that her
clothes were shabby or her father was a drunk. Her voice
was as good or better than anyone else's. On this particular occasion, the weekly school assembly program in
early April, Sally was scheduled to join two other girls out
in front of the rest of the chorus for a special song.

She had prepared carefully, practicing hard and wash-
ing and ironing her best dress, a blue A-line with full,
puffy sleeves that Miss Louella had brought to their house
at Christmas, along with a bag of other clothes from a
rummage sale at the Baptist church. Sally had worn the
dress only once before, at the chorus's January presenta-
tion in front of the PTA. The dress had grown tight
through the bust and hips since January, but Sally had
studied herself in the mirror at home and decided she
looked okay. Her father was sleeping off a bender, her
mother hadn't been home in days and Renee was too
young to form any opinion on the dress. Sally knew she
couldn't wear any of her other, ordinary school clothes,
the cotton blouses and skirts, most of them too big, which
had come from other bags of hand-me-downs. The other
girls would be in their Sunday best. This dress was the best
she had. It was a cool April morning, so she donned a
sweater and went to school.

The sweater didn't come off until the chorus was lining
up behind the curtains on the stage at one end of the
school gymnasium. Sally liked to think her choral teacher,
who had always been kind, would have saved her if she
had noticed anything was amiss. But the teacher was busy,
and everything was fine until Sally and the other two girls
stepped forward to begin their song.

That's when an older boy in the front row called out
Sally's name and a crude remark about her breasts.

There was a commotion and laughter and more remarks, each of them lewder than the next, before the group of students was brought under control.

To this day, Sally could remember standing on that stage, her face scarlet, feeling as if the bosom she had been only vaguely aware of until that point was bared to the view of everyone in the room. Every instinct she had was to run away. Pride alone got her through the song.

But she did run home after assembly. She laid out of school for a week, only returning when her mother came home from wherever she had been and wanted her out of the way during the day. She dropped out of chorus. And she learned how to cope with the ogles and comments of boys and men.

The memory of that day in seventh grade came back to Sally with startling clarity as she placed her tray on the table Cotter had selected at one side of the cafeteria. She tried to shrug off the feeling that they were the subject of half the conversations in the room.

"I told you we would be front-page news," she told Cotter as he drew out a chair for her to sit in.

The glance he directed around the cafeteria was defiant. "I guess small minds can't help but get caught up in useless speculation."

It was his tone of voice, more than his expression, that made Sally think someone had been speculating about her to him. She unrolled her silverware from a paper napkin while he took his seat, then said, casually, "Have an interesting morning?"

"I fired my assistant."

Soupspoon halfway to her mouth, Sally stared at him in surprise. Cotter had already mentioned that his assistant was Jackie McGinnis Bryant and that he didn't like her. Sally didn't like her, either, but she hadn't felt it was her place to say anything. Having been the target of gossip for most of her life, she tried not to talk about people any more than necessary.

"Better eat that soup before it's cold," Cotter told her, laughing.

She set her spoon down. "You seem awfully cool about having fired the chairman of the board's precious little perfect daughter-in-law."

Cotter sprinkled pepper on his chicken potpie. "My, my, it sounds as if your feelings about Jackie Bryant are about as congenial as hers are for you."

"She said something about me?"

He speared a forkful of pastry and chicken with elaborate unconcern. "She said a lot of things before I fired her."

Sally put her hand on his arm, virtually forcing him to look at her. "Cotter, you shouldn't have done that."

"It was a good excuse to get rid of her."

"She can be pretty vindictive."

"What'd you do to her, anyway, Sally, steal her boyfriend in high school?"

"As a matter of fact . . ."

"I thought as much."

"It wasn't what Jackie thought it was," Sally said. "She and Mark, who's her husband now, broke up one summer. He's my age and, believe it or not, back then he hadn't let her and his dad get to him, and he was a pretty nice guy." As Sally remembered it, Mark had been shy to the point of muteness around her. She thought he had only asked her out to prove something to himself. He and Sally certainly hadn't been compatible, but she had been disappointed when he went back to namby-pamby Jackie a few weeks later. "We went out a few times. It was nothing serious." Her face darkened. "To hear Jackie tell it, however, I was the harlot who tempted her innocent sweetheart into sin."

Cotter's hearty laughter made heads turn their way.

"This isn't funny. Firing Jackie Bryant is like declaring war on that whole family."

"I don't give a s—" He cut himself off, remembering the attentive audience that surrounded them. He lowered his voice and continued. "I don't care about Jackie Bryant's family. She couldn't do her job the way I wanted it done. I didn't care for her attitude or for the way she tried to interfere in my personal life."

"She said you shouldn't be seeing me, didn't she?"

His gaze slipped away from hers. "Could we drop this? I'd like to enjoy my lunch, and thinking about that woman will give me indigestion."

"But, Cotter," Sally said, leaning toward him. "You didn't have to cause yourself so much trouble by defending me. It wasn't necessary."

"I was defending myself." He put his fork aside and took her hand. "The day I let people like LeBron and Jackie Bryant tell me how to run my life, is the day I lose all self-respect. I don't care for their sort of sanctimonious claptrap." He held up his hand when Sally started to protest. "And don't tell me anything about small-town ways."

Because that was exactly what she had been about to point out, Sally regarded him with despair.

"You know what?" he said, squeezing her fingers. "I really don't give a damn about what you might have done with Jackie Bryant's husband."

"I didn't do anything."

"Even if you danced naked with him around the Courthouse Square, I don't care," Cotter insisted. "I don't care about your sister and Betsy—"

"Betsy?" Sally cut in. "Jackie told you about Betsy?"

His hazel-eyed gaze didn't waver from hers. "She told me Betsy is your sister's biological child, but that you adopted her."

Quickly Sally began to explain. "I would have told you, Cotter, if I thought it was important—"

"It isn't important. I mean, it doesn't matter. It doesn't have anything to do with anyone except you and Betsy." He released her hand and picked up his fork once more.

Sally sat back in her seat. Of course he would say the facts about Betsy weren't important. Why should Betsy matter to him? Grimly Sally reminded herself of the ground rules about their relationship. Sex, as soon as they found some privacy. Friendship, in those times when privacy couldn't be found. Cotter wanted them to be friends who slept together. Nothing more. No getting tangled up in each other's lives. Cotter had had one marriage, one wife. He didn't want another. Sally might hope that the feelings would deepen between them. But for now, there was no reason for Cotter to concern himself with her daughter or her past.

But his next words took her by surprise. "From what I've seen, every kid should be as lucky as Betsy."

The compliment touched her. "Most of the time I forget that I didn't give birth to her."

"You're a better parent than I've ever been."

She remembered what he had said about not having time for Jamie in the past. "It's getting better with Jamie, isn't it?"

"I'm trying."

"That's all any parent can do."

"It doesn't sound as if your sister wanted to try at all."

Sally looked down at her cooling bowl of soup. Her sister, Renee, was only one painful subject that she didn't want to explore with Cotter. He said her past didn't matter. She wanted to believe him.

But, glancing up, she found an unreadable expression on his face. Speculation? Doubt? She wasn't sure what label to put to it. But it frightened her, made her realize just what was at stake with this man.

She covered her anxiety by changing the subject. He didn't resist. They finished their lunch, strolled to the front of the hospital, said a pleasantly lingering goodbye. He even brushed a light, sweet kiss across her lips, right in front of the information desk and the lobby gift shop. But Sally sat in her car for a long time out in the parking lot, shaking.

She had wanted many things in her life. But none more than she wanted to keep Cotter Graham's respect. Not love. Respect. In Sally's eyes, respect was a precursor for any other meaningful emotion.

Respect was the reason she had worked two and three jobs in order to buy the restaurant. Being in business for herself brought her a certain, albeit grudging, esteem in some people's eyes. Respect was the basis for her few friendships. Jack and Marianne respected her. As did her employees and some other people around town who had forgotten old scandals or didn't yearn for new ones. Respect was something Sally treasured. When it was given to her, she worked to keep it and responded in kind.

Friday night, Cotter had proven he had enough respect for her to wait before they entered a sexual relationship. She didn't want to lose that respect. She wanted it to grow. But he had to respect all of her, not some notion he had of her, not a half-truth, not just what she wanted him to see. He could say all he wanted about her past being no one's business, but Sally wanted it to be his business. She wanted Cotter to know all about her and still respect her.

For that reason, she knew she had to tell him everything. About Renee and Betsy and Tommy Joe and Jack and...well...maybe there were some secrets he shouldn't know. If she didn't tell him, someone like Jackie Bryant would. At least if he heard it from Sally, he would be hearing the truth.

Her mind made up, Sally drove back to the restaurant. She called Marianne and asked if Betsy could spend the night with Laura again. Then she called Cotter and invited him to dinner. When he accepted, she left the Dairy Bar in the hands of her part-time manager.

On the way home, after stopping at the grocery and the florist, she realized this was the first Monday afternoon in months that she and Lana hadn't sat in the restaurant, filling saltshakers and doing the books. Grinning, she thought she might as well do something more.

So she wheeled her car around and headed for the Town and Country Dress Shop on the Courthouse Square. A new dress and some lacy underwear would help her spirits, as well as give the ladies who ran the shop something to speculate about. Gossip already had her and Cotter in bed. She might as well toss out a few new tidbits for the sharks to feast on tonight.

Who knew? Perhaps after tonight, the gossip would be true.

Cotter hadn't known exactly what to make of Sally's invitation to dinner. She said Betsy would be gone, unusual on a school night. She also told him, almost as an afterthought, to bring an open mind instead of wine. He arrived at seven-thirty, intrigued.

Inside, she had set a seductive scene.

There were candles on the table. Long, white tapers in wooden candlesticks, their glow reflecting in the windows of the dining nook. There were flowers, too. Yellow chrysanthemums in a pottery vase, their color vivid against an ivory damask tablecloth. And, finally, there was Sally. Lush and vibrant in a dress of forest green, the shimmer of gold at her ears and throat.

Cotter paused in the arched doorway from the entrance foyer, admiring the table and her. "I'm impressed. And underdressed." He indicated his jeans and blue button-down shirt.

"Nonsense."

He caught her hand in his. "But this looks very special."

Her gaze met his and clung for a moment before skittering away. "We always seem to be surrounded by children. I thought it would be nice to act like grown-ups tonight."

"Jamie keeps telling me he's old enough to look after himself. So I guess I have the time to act very grown-up tonight, if you want." He drew her to his side, and with his lips scant inches from hers, murmured, "Although I think you usually like having all those children around to diffuse the situation."

"I told you Friday night that I'm not hiding any longer." But she stepped away before he could kiss her, the full skirt of her dress swirling around her shapely calves as she went to check the pot on the stove that was sending spicy aromas into the air.

It could have been his imagination, but he thought he detected a hint of nerves in her voice. Sally, nervous? Cotter was surprised. She was such a straightforward person and came across so warm and genuine that nerves weren't something he would associate with her.

Of course, she must know, as he did, that tonight they were going to be lovers. Lost in that thought, Cotter gave himself over to the pure joy of being here alone with her.

She moved, he thought, with innate grace. Pouring wine, serving a dinner of salad, pasta and chicken. It was a simple meal, made special by her presence, her laughter, by the ease of their conversation. But the ease disappeared with the ice cream and fruit she served for dessert. Their talk dwindled to nothing. Sally was silent, her elbows on the table and clasped hands resting under her chin, as if she was thinking very hard about what she wanted to say next.

Cotter let the silence spin out for a few moments, then asked, "There's something wrong, isn't there?"

She looked up at him, moving her hands to the edge of the table in front of her, where she pleated and unpleated the tablecloth. "I don't know how to begin this."

The guilty conscience that had been plaguing him all day made him ask, "Is it something about today?"

"Sort of."

"I'm sorry I dragged you into that cafeteria for lunch."

"What are you talking about?"

"Lunch with all those idiots looking on." He sat back, fingering the stem of his wineglass. "It was a selfish thing to do."

"Selfish?"

"I wanted to send a message—Cotter Graham can't be dictated to concerning his personal life or anything else." He gave a rueful sigh. "I used you to help me deliver that message."

"I've been used before."

The serious note in her voice made him look hard at her.

She cleared her throat and looked away. "What I wanted to do, Cotter, is talk about what Jackie Bryant told you about me. About Betsy. And my sister. And—"

"I told you—"

"I know," she cut in. "I know you told me that you don't care about what the gossips have to say. You gave me the impression that you didn't believe half of what Jackie said to you."

He shrugged. "I don't."

Her gaze met his straight on once again. "Maybe you should."

He wasn't certain of how to reply, so he opted for silence.

After a moment or two, Sally got up, arms crossed around her midriff as she rubbed her arms and shivered. "It feels chilly in here tonight. It's like the calendar moved to late October and the weather decided to cooperate."

"It's these damned brick floors," Cotter said, grinning. "I'd say the hell with historical significance, if it were me."

He was rewarded by a relaxing of Sally's shoulders and a slight but still perceptible smile. He got up and took her hands in his. "That's better." He touched her cheek. "Much better." Then he kissed her. Gently at first, with a growing power, until he pulled away and whispered against her mouth, "Much, much better."

She drew away, looking up at him. "I have some things I want to say, okay?"

"Then can I kiss you?" he teased, pulling her back toward him.

"Will you please listen?"

Because there was something akin to fear in her eyes, he stepped back. "All right, let's sit down and you can tell me what's on your mind." He took a seat at the table again, but Sally remained standing in front of him.

Chin tilted at a defiant angle, she asked, "What exactly did Jackie tell you about me?"

He sensed she wasn't in the mood for evasions, so he told her everything his ex-assistant had said, with as little emotion as possible.

"Well, that's a real surprise," Sally said when he was finished. "I wanted you to know the truth, and it sounds like that's what Jackie Bryant told you. Except maybe the part about Tommy Joe denying that Betsy was his. There was never any doubt that he was her father. There's also nothing to what Jackie hinted about me and Jack Dylan. I've always cared for Jack, but we're just friends."

"I never thought anything else."

"And what do you think about the rest?"

Again, Cotter wasn't sure what she expected from him. Censure? Sympathy? Neither of them seemed appropriate. "I'm not shocked, if that's what you're wondering. As life stories go, it's not the tamest. But it's not a tragedy, either. I mean, here you are. You've more than survived. You seem to be doing great. Betsy's a beautiful, lively and happy little girl. Your sister didn't take her away from you."

"And she never will."

The determination in her voice made him smile. "See that? That's why it's not a tragedy. Because you're a strong person."

"I wasn't always. I made mistakes."

Shrugging, he said, "All of us have made the wrong decision a time or two. Especially when we were young." He should know. He had made a few of his own. Marriage to the wrong person. A child who had taken second and third and fourth place in his priorities.

Sally managed a wry chuckle. "How does that old song go? 'Mistakes, I've made a few...' That's my theme song."

"It seems to me you had some help with a lot of those mistakes," Cotter said.

Again her expression hardened. "I don't make excuses for anything that's happened to me."

"But this guy, Betsy's father—"

"Tommy Joe Brewster."

"And your sister. Surely she's not blameless."

"Renee was always mixed up."

"Is that why she got involved with your boyfriend?"

"Maybe she did me a favor."

He raised an eyebrow.

"Tommy Joe Brewster was no prize."

"But you were in love with him?"

She lifted her hands in a helpless gesture. "Who knows if I was in love? Let's just say that he had a smooth line, and I was naive enough to fall for it. I was also naive enough not to realize how deeply he was into drugs." Her laugh was short and dry. "That's not exactly true, I guess. I knew drugs had been a part of his past. I was dumb enough to think I was helping him. He let me believe I had reformed him."

"Sounds as if you were caring instead of dumb."

She shook her head. "I was so naive that I didn't know anything about his dealing at all. I certainly didn't know about him and Renee."

Cotter was quiet for a moment, thinking her naiveté had spared her some horrors. He only wished she had been spared all of it. "Jackie said Tommy Joe is dead. Drugs?"

"You could say that." Sally's gaze shifted away from his. She shivered again, rubbing her arms as her mouth set in a grim line. "Right after Betsy was born, he took a bullet to the head in a sheriff's raid."

The controlled note of devastation in her voice brought an ache to Cotter's gut. Only by force of will did he resist the urge to get up and take her into his arms. She had been very young when all of this had happened. He wondered where she had found the strength to make it through intact.

"What about your sister?" he asked after a moment's pause. "Jackie said she was involved in drugs, too?"

"Oh, yeah. She was dealing, working with Tommy Joe. And sampling the merchandise, as well. I was so blind I couldn't see what was going on right in front of my face."

"I guess a person doesn't expect their sister to become involved with the man they love."

"By the time Renee was arrested, I didn't have time to think about that. I had Betsy to consider. I only thank God that nothing Renee did when she was pregnant had any effect on Betsy."

Cotter shook his head. "It never fails to amaze me how differently two people growing up in one family can turn out." He thought of his sister, Susannah, a teacher who was able to embrace life with an openness he had never attained. Yet they were raised in the same house with the same influences and the same values. "Here you are, so strong, and your sister was weak enough to fall into the worst traps life set for her."

But Sally defended her sister. "Renee and I weren't so different."

"That doesn't look to be true."

"She escaped into drugs, while I..." Sally hesitated, biting her lip. "I can't judge Renee too harshly. I don't want her in my life or in Betsy's, but I know where we came from. I understand her."

"That's generous of you."

"She's my sister."

"That doesn't mean she deserves your forgiveness."

Again she hesitated, then plunged ahead. "Renee and I had it hard at home. I told you before, Dad was an alcoholic. The only real time he ever spent with Renee and me was when he used to make us work with him. When he was sober, he was really not so bad. I guess that's why it hurt so much when he did drink. Renee was always trying to get his attention."

"What about your mother?"

Sally managed a tight smile. "Mother liked to travel."

"Travel?"

Again there was that lifting of her chin, that "I dare you to pity me" gesture. "There are always men blowing through town, even a little town like Willow Creek. Mother would pick one every month or so and take off. Then she'd come back. When she'd return, Dad would straighten up for a while. I think he really loved her. And sometimes she loved him—why else had she come back so often?"

"You think he drank because she hurt him?" Cotter asked.

"Who knows?" Sally murmured, a sadness too deep to mask settling over her features. "When I was sixteen, Mother didn't return from one of her trips. I haven't seen her since."

That slip of her carefully controlled expression told Cotter just how much her mother's casual coming and going had hurt her. This time, he didn't resist the urge to go to her.

Her hands were like ice in his, her eyes a troubled and translucent gray. But she forced a note of gaiety into her voice. "Maybe now you understand why everyone in this town likes to talk about me. My family's always been fertile ground for scandal. There have been dry spells when I don't know what the town would have done without us.''

He swore, a violent, direct oath that told her exactly what he would like to see happen to the good people of this town. "I know there must be some decent folks around here—''

"Of course there are.''

"Then where were they when you and your sister were dealing with a drunken father and an absent mother?''

"There were people who helped, who cared—''

"But not enough. Otherwise, you and she wouldn't have gone through what you did.''

"Back then people didn't think it was right to interfere in what happened within a family.''

"But they liked to talk, didn't they?'' He gripped her hands tightly. "They liked to gather in the diner and on the corners and talk. Instead of helping, they just observed. What a waste, what a—''

"You don't understand—''

"You're right,'' he muttered. "I don't understand. I don't even want to understand people who could turn away from a child in need.'' He drew one hand through her black, silky hair, gazing down into her face and clearly seeing the child she must have been. A proud, brave, strong child. The same sort of woman she had become. Circumstance shaped character as well as genes. Unlike her sister, Sally had taken the high road. She had his admiration for it.

"I don't know how you stomach some of these people,'' he said, anger thickening his voice. "These types like Miss Louella, Miss Clara—''

"You know what's funny about them?" Sally said. "They might have talked, but they were also the first people at the door on Christmas Eve with gifts and food."

"So they could feel damned superior, I guess. Spread a little holiday cheer and ease their conscience."

The look on Sally's face told him that's exactly what she thought, as well, but still she defended them. "I think they wanted to help, but didn't know how."

Rage tightened around him like a band of steel. "Jesus, Sally, how can you forgive all these people who have hurt you?"

Sally turned away. She couldn't tell him there were worse things than nosy matrons with good intentions. She couldn't tell him there were other moments, almost too horrible to remember, certainly too painful to recount, especially one moment and one person she couldn't and wouldn't forgive. Stacked against that memory, Miss Louella and Miss Clara and any other gossip in town were easy to forgive.

He came up behind her, his hands warm through the satiny material of her dress, his voice low against her ear. "They think you're such a sinner, don't they?"

"The scarlet woman of Willow Creek."

"But there's more saint than sinner to you." His voice had deepened, roughened, and now thrummed across her senses, as arousing as any touch. She allowed herself to lean back against him, savoring his strong, solid, male strength. "I think you're very special, Sally. A very special woman." Gently he pushed her hair aside and pressed a kiss, warm and lingering, on the side of her neck. "No one realizes how special you are."

His arms slipped around her, his thumbs just brushing the lower curves of her breasts. Sally felt her nipples harden in response. Her breathing quickened. Her heart tripped into a sharper rhythm. Then his lips parted. She felt the warm glide of his tongue against her skin, and something clenched inside of her, from her heart to her womb. An ache started deep in the secret folds of her femininity.

With a soft sound of entreaty, she turned in his arms, her lips lifted to his. But his mouth hovered, a breath away from her own.

"You should have had someone, Sally. Someone to slay your dragons."

"It was okay. I fought them on my own. It made me tough."

"And you don't need a fearless knight?"

"I need you," she whispered. "I want you."

"I think it's about time you got something you wanted."

Instead of taking the kiss he offered, Sally stepped back and took his hand. What she wanted was to take a risk on Cotter. Her final risk, she thought, but then nudged away that sad thought.

"Come to bed," she said. And because that felt so incredibly, perfectly right, she said it again. "Come to bed."

Chapter Six

Sally had never brought a man to bed in this house. The extent of her sexual experience, the stuff of legends in Willow Creek, was limited mainly to back seats and country roads. To grasping hands, mumbled apologies and awkward moments in the dark. Yet each time she had offered herself, she had imagined she was in love. Each time, she had ended up with a bruised heart and, at least once, a body bruised to match.

This time, she wanted it to be different.

Please make it different, she prayed. Then she wondered, as she always had, whether God really listened to people like her.

The room where she led Cotter with such a hopeful heart was simply furnished. A plain pine chest of drawers. An old skirted dressing table with an oval mirror. An iron bed she had rescued from rust and ruin. A trunk to one side of the bed held a white-shaded lamp and a bowl of rose petal potpourri. The fragrance, subtly sweet, pervaded each shadowy corner of the room.

"Even if I didn't know it, I could guess this was your room," Cotter said, drawing her tight against his side as they paused in the doorway. "It smells like you. Looks like you."

"Looks like me?"

"Welcoming."

She moved away from him, to the end of the bed, where she touched a hand to the painstakingly painted iron posts. "This was my bed when I was small," she told him. "Mine and Renee's. We used to lie in it and talk and giggle." Memories tightened her throat. "And sometimes we cried. Before Renee forgot how to cry, that is."

In the doorway, Cotter made a sound of protest, but he didn't try to stop Sally as she turned to the dressing table.

Light from the moon and from street lamps outside highlighted the flowered chintz skirt she had made herself. Briefly she smiled as she laid a finger on the bottle of perfume that had been a Mother's Day gift from Betsy. "This table was my mother's," she murmured, half to herself. "She used to sit here and put on her makeup and tease up her hair. And she told Renee and me that we had to stay out of her stuff." She paused, remembering. "So of course we didn't."

Still, Cotter waited in the doorway. The dim light from the hall outlined his broad-shouldered frame. His face was in shadow, but she could feel him watching her all the same.

Sally went toward the window, but paused by the bed once more, her hand trailing across the patchwork quilt she used as a bedspread. "Grandmother Haskins made this. She hid it in a trunk so that Dad wouldn't sell it for money to buy booze. She told me where it was hidden the day before she died. I was only nine, but I hid it again.''

She looked across the bed at Cotter, who hadn't moved one step farther into the room. "I guess this room really does look like me. It's all the pieces of who I am."

Then she turned her back to him as she unhooked the tiebacks and let the curtains fall across the broad, front window. They shut out the light and spread shadows across the room, across her past.

And in the shadows, Cotter found her.

He said nothing. He just kissed her. A heady, abandoned kiss. Openmouthed, devouring, beguiling. Sally slipped under the spell of his kiss with no hesitation. She would rather lose herself in this moment with Cotter than continue reliving a lifetime of sadness and disappointment.

They were intent on the passion of this kiss as shoes were kicked aside and clothes were shed. Kisses were punctuated by hurried movements and whispered encouragements. Her dress pooled on the floor. His jeans were peeled away and tossed aside, the buckle on his belt hitting the bed's iron foot rail with a loud clang. The sound startled them both, and they laughed, nervous laughter, ending in another head-spinning, heart-soaring kiss. Then, with fevered action, his briefs were stripped away, her panty hose and bra thrown toward the corner.

Cotter sank to the edge of the bed, legs spread, and pulled Sally toward him. His beard was scratchy against the skin of her stomach as he pressed a kiss just above her navel, well above the cream-and-black lace panties she had purchased just this afternoon.

"You're so soft," he whispered, running his hands down her thighs and then up to her hips again. "So soft, so curvy."

Sally felt suddenly shy. It was one thing to be comfortable with her body when she was clothed. It was another to be with this man this way, with nothing hidden. "It's those cheeseburgers, you know."

"I like the way you feel."

"I always wanted one of those boyish figures—slim hips, no breasts."

Cotter shook his head against her stomach, then drew away, his hands lifting to her breasts. "You look perfect. You feel perfect. Like a woman."

The stroking of his thumbs across her hardened nipples sent a liquid spiral of desire downward from her stomach. She swayed against him, her hands braced on his broad shoulders, her knees growing weak. As she bent toward him, his mouth replaced the actions of his thumb. Her breasts felt heavy, the nipples distended, aching, pouting for his attention. He complied with her unspoken invitation, his tongue licking, his lips tasting first one and then the other greedy peak. His hands now cupped her bottom, holding her still, and she was shivering from the force of the need he was fueling with his every touch.

"Please," she whispered, the word little more than a sigh. "Please, Cotter..."

With scant effort he drew the scrap of lace and silk down her legs. She kicked the panties aside. Cotter stood and caught her close, his erection pressing with hot urgency into her belly. She parted her legs instinctively as he kissed her. He bent to cup her bottom again, lifting her up against his body. The movement of his hair-roughened chest against the soft, sensitive flesh of her breasts and stomach created a satisfying friction. She could feel his throbbing heat; her body answered with a moist, spreading ache. She twisted against him, thighs parting still farther, seeking the intimacy they both craved.

He groaned her name against her lips and sank down on the bed again, carrying her with him. He fell backward, upper body braced by his elbows, feet still on the floor. She shifted to a kneeling position, straddling his hips, reaching for him. She was wet and trembling, more than ready for the hard shaft she guided inside her.

As she sank onto him, caught him in the slick folds of her woman's body, Cotter pushed himself up to face her. Her hips rotated downward to meet his welcoming up-ward thrusts. Her hands gripped his shoulders. She rode him with rocking, tantalizing motions, quickening here, slowing there. Harder, then softer. Her head was thrown back, hair loose and curling about her shoulders. The slender column of her throat was pale in the shadows. Below that, paler still, her lush, rounded breasts. Breasts made for a man's touch. When the temptation became too great, Cotter pressed his face to the perspiration-dampened valley between those full, swaying globes. Then he wrapped his arms around her, the heels of his feet dig-ging into the floor as he drove up and into her. Again and again. Arching toward a mutual goal.

And for the longest time, a stretch of heaven, they ground together, breath coming in harsh gasps, the tempo of their coupling a steady counterpoint to the drumming of his heart.

His climax tore through his body just as her name was torn from his lips.

"Sally," he murmured. "Sweet, beautiful Sally."

She turned to liquid in his arms, crashing around him like a wave rippling onto the shore. He held her tight un-til the last swell of trembling release had drained from them both. Then he eased them back on the bed, his body slipping reluctantly from hers.

They lay, side by side, on the quilt her grandmother had stitched by hand, their breathing the only sounds in the dim, silent room.

Then Sally let the laughter that was building inside of her escape.

She felt Cotter turn toward her. "What?"

"I was thinking about my panties."

He eased up on one elbow. "Your panties?"

"I bought them for tonight, down at the Town and Country Dress Shop. I took an hour picking them out and..." Her laughter choked the words.

"And what?"

"The good ladies down there would be so disappointed. You barely looked at those expensive panties."

He pushed himself up and off the bed.

She sat up. "What are you doing?"

"I'm going to find them."

"What for?"

He snapped on the lamp beside the bed. Sally blinked in the sudden light, then her breath caught in her throat at the sight of Cotter—tall and well-muscled, gloriously naked and proudly, distinctly male. Incredibly enough, given what they had just done, his body was stirring again. Incredibly she also wanted him again.

Hands on his hips, he grinned down at her. "I'm finding those panties," he repeated. "And you're going to put them on."

She smiled back. "Oh?"

"Yeah. You're putting them on." His grin broadened; a mischievous gleam grew in his gaze. "So I can take them off again."

She did.

And he did. Slowly.

With predictable results.

But this, Sally decided, was the sort of predictability she could live with.

Her head told her she had never been able to throw caution to the wind without disaster. That was one reason she had stopped taking risks. But this risk with Cotter felt like her last chance. So she ignored that nagging, negative whisper, and reached for the stars with him again.

The chiming of the clock on the Courthouse Square vibrated through the still night, shaking Cotter awake. Eyes opening wide, he stared up at the ceiling, counting each far-off, echoing strike. It was only midnight. Yet he thought he had lived a lifetime since entering Sally's house.

She slept beside him, evidently so used to the striking of the old clock that the sound didn't disturb her slumber. She was curled tight at his side, one hand on his chest, her full breasts pillowed against his arm, her bare legs tangled with his.

Tangled.

Cotter thought the word very appropriate. For what was he doing here? How had he ended up with his body curved so intimately around this woman's? And with his emotions in an equally tangled state?

It wasn't the sex that had him so confused. He had known before arriving at her house tonight that they were going to sleep together. Had known it, had enjoyed the anticipation. But with the sex had come the sort of complications and revelations he hadn't wanted. Since their confrontation on Friday night it had seemed damned appealing to become Sally's friend as well as her lover. He had ignored the warning his subconscious had tried to issue. He had imagined he could handle friendship. After all, he had set the ground rules out in plain English for her. She had agreed. They would be friendly lovers. Nothing more.

What a fool he was.

For he was the one who had forgotten the ground rules. He hadn't counted on the admiration she roused in him. He hadn't expected to ache for her. He hadn't known he would want to protect her, hold her, make the pain of her past go away. And he hadn't known that making love with her would be so powerful. Each touch, each sigh, every turn of her body, every pulse-pounding level of excitement, was burned in his brain.

God in heaven, how had he come to this?

He, Cotter Graham, had no business getting mixed up with a woman like Sally. A sweet, loving woman. Someone who, no matter what promises she had made, no matter what her articulated expectations, wanted a complete joining of souls. She needed far more than he could give. Underneath her strong front, Sally was a collection of vulnerabilities. She needed a hero, he thought. A dragon slayer, just as he had suggested before they had made love.

But he was no white knight.

Brenda had proven that to him. He knew no matter what he gave, in the end it would never be enough. Like Brenda, Sally, and perhaps every woman, required an emotional intimacy that he was incapable of supplying.

If he had what it took to sustain a lasting relationship, then why had an unbreachable gulf opened between him and his wife of sixteen years? He could remember looking across the breakfast table at Brenda and thinking he had no idea who she was. Even her illness hadn't opened any doors between them. He had been powerless to help her, to reach her on any significant level. And he had sworn, *never again*.

He had promised himself he wouldn't repeat past mistakes. Yet here he was. Lying in the dark with a needy stranger. He had allowed passion to rule his reason.

Beside him, Sally stirred, her skin soft, her delicate womanly scent wrapping around him like a fragrant, velvet cocoon.

All of a sudden, Cotter couldn't breathe.

He eased away, praying Sally wouldn't awaken. But of course she did, stretching like a sleepy child. "Cotter?"

"Go back to sleep," he whispered as he slipped from beneath the covers. "It's late."

"Where are you going?"

"Jamie's at home."

"I thought you said—"

"He says he can look after himself, but I should go home just the same. I should set a good example, you know." Cotter found his jeans hanging off the end of the bed's foot rail. His shirt was on the floor. But his briefs...

The lamp beside the bed clicked on. He glanced up, startled to see Sally propped against her lace-edged pillows, grinning at him. "I believe finding your clothes might be easier with the light on."

He turned away from her trusting smile, sickened by the knowledge that he had been trying to sneak away in the dark. He didn't want to face her now, with his thoughts jumbled, clouded by the memory of their passion. His back to her, he found his briefs and socks and shoes on the floor and proceeded to get dressed. Behind him, he could hear Sally getting out of bed, opening and closing the closet door.

She was wearing a red gown when he turned around, perhaps the same one he had glimpsed laying across this bed on the night he had first come to her house, the night this room had beckoned to him with its gentle light and soft colors. As he had known she would, she glowed like a jewel in that ruby hue. She stood in front of the dressing table, brushing her hair, her gaze meeting his in the mirror. The glow in her cheeks was more than the gown. He knew the look. That expectant look.

The kindest thing would be to say nothing about how he was feeling. He should just leave. They could talk another time.

And yet what was kind about leaving her full of hope? What was kind about putting off what was a certainty?

"This was a mistake," he stammered out, without giving full thought to what he wanted to say.

Slowly, with her smile dimming, she lowered her brush to the dressing table.

He cleared his throat. "I think I took advantage of you tonight."

She turned to face him. "What do you mean?"

"You were so emotional, talking about your sister and your parents. And this..." He gestured toward the rumpled bed. "This all happened so fast."

"Fast." The word was flat, devoid of feeling.

"Yeah, too fast." Cotter shoved a hand through his hair, nearly undone by the shuttered mask that had descended upon her features. Then a terrible thought hit him. He felt the blood drain from his face. "Good God, Sally, it was all so fast, so..." The word "spectacular" sprang to mind, but he didn't use it. "I forgot to...I forgot protection—"

"Don't worry about it," she bit out. "I assure you I don't have any diseases."

"That's not what I meant—"

"Don't give it another thought, okay?" The words were clipped, each one precisely spoken. She wheeled around, the red gown swirling as she headed for the door. "You should go."

"Sally—"

"You can leave a tip on the nightstand if that'll make it feel right to you."

That brought an oath to his lips and sent him across the room. He caught her arm, turned her toward him. "Sally, that's not fair."

Her face was stained with angry scarlet color as she snatched her arm from his grasp. "Look who's worried about being fair."

"Listen to me," he said urgently. "I just don't want to hurt you."

"Didn't we have this conversation Friday night?"

"Yes, we did. That's when I told you what I wanted. We discussed the boundaries."

"So?"

He gestured toward the bed again. "So we've stepped over them, all right? I can see what's happening with you. It's written all over your face. I see what you want."

She was silent for a moment, her gaze intent on his. "You want something more than sex, too. Don't say you don't."

He shook his head. "No, I don't."

"But tonight was more. It was special."

He drew in a deep breath, then released it. "Yeah," he admitted softly. "This was special. And you're special. And you deserve all the things that you want. But I'm not the one to give them to you."

She stepped forward, laying a hand on his chest. "Why do you say that?"

"Because I've done this before."

There was a pause. Then a quiet, "Your wife's gone, Cotter. You have to go on living."

"I know that."

"I'm sure she—"

"Sally, just stop it, okay? You don't understand." He cast about, searching for the right words. "Brenda was this great wife, you see. Perfect. The best. And I wasn't a very good husband."

"I'm sure that's not true."

"But it is," he insisted. "She did everything just right. The house, Jamie, the entertaining, supporting me in my career. She resented it at times, I know, but then I'd come home and she was always...always there. And then..." He swallowed around the sudden constriction in his throat. "Then she was sick. And she was gone so fast. And I was so...so...sorry."

Sally's hands were now holding fast to the unbuttoned sides of his shirt, her eyes wide and full of questions. "Of course you were sorry," she murmured. "Of course—"

"And guilty," Cotter said, still trying to find the exact phrase that would convey his meaning. "It was guilt...you know...this terrible guilt."

But Sally still stared up at him, clearly not comprehending.

He opened his mouth, then shut it again. Good God, no wonder his marriage had failed. It was nearly impossible for him to express how he felt. That lack simply proved how unwise it was to embark on a relationship that required any amount of real communication. He had a hard enough time trying to communicate with his son. He didn't need another burden. He didn't need Sally.

"I'm sorry," he said, stepping back. "I'm sorry, Sally. I should have known this wouldn't work."

"You haven't given it a chance."

He didn't pause to listen to her arguments. He simply turned on his heel and left.

In the stillness that followed the closing of the front door, Sally whispered, "So much for risks."

Throughout the sleepless night that followed, she told herself she wasn't surprised. She greeted the dawn with world-weary resignation. She went to see Betsy before school. She went to work. And she told herself she should have known better.

Oh, Cotter wasn't the jerk some of the other men in her life had been. He had been honest. He had treated her with more respect than anyone else she had known. She had been the one who invited him to bed. He had waited for that. But from the beginning, he had told her what he wanted. Her foolishness had lain in thinking she could change him. Her insanity had been in seeing something below the surface that simply didn't exist.

Over and over again, she replayed what he had said about his wife before he left. Perfect. The best. Just right. The adjectives told her that no one was ever going to measure up to this woman, this paragon. In his mind, Cotter Graham was still married to the most wonderful woman in the world, a woman for whom he thought he wasn't good enough. Who was Sally Jane Haskins to think she could measure up?

Mid-afternoon, when Sally was drooping with weariness and thinking of going home, the florist made a delivery at the Dairy Bar. Two dozen roses. Gloriously budding, fragrant coral-pink roses.

"Wow," Lana said when Sally opened the big, white florist's box. "I've never seen that many roses all together except over in the flower bed at City Park."

Trying not to betray her dread, Sally took a small white envelope out of the box. She stared at it for a long, long moment. She was very aware of Lana's interest and of the florist deliverywoman, who was lurking near the door, ostensibly chatting with Audrey Fisk, who was seated in a booth, enjoying a hot-fudge sundae, which her hips didn't need. Sally knew both women were waiting to see her reaction to these flowers.

"Well, open it," Lana urged. "Although I guess you know who they're from. God, Jamie's dad is so cool."

Cool. Yes, be cool, Sally told herself as she slipped a card from the envelope. The message wasn't typed. Cotter had been sensitive enough to the gossips in the town to write the message himself. It said, simply, "I'm really very sorry. Cotter."

If she had been alone, she might have cried, might have pressed her face into those pink, fragrant flowers and sobbed like she hadn't sobbed since the night Betsy was born and Renee told her Tommy Joe was the father. If she were alone, she might have smashed every glass in the place. Gone outside, shouted at the sky, screamed at God.

But she had an audience. And she was Sally Jane Haskins. So she did what was expected.

She smiled. It was a calculated smile. She knew it was mysterious. She knew it would make everyone wonder just what was written on that card. The deliverywoman would report it to the florist. Audrey Fisk would tell everyone at the real-estate office where she worked. And from there it would spread.

Grinning so hard that her cheeks ached, Sally put the card in her pocket and picked up the box of roses. "Lana, honey, could you take care of things here for a while. Craig'll be in in another hour or so, anyway."

There might have been a flicker of doubt in the redhead's eyes. After all, she was an accomplished actress herself. She might recognize the signs. But all she said was, "Sure, Sally. Where're you going?"

"Shopping."

The doubt washed away. "Another new dress, huh? For a big date?"

"Maybe."

Then Sally went home. She threw the roses in the trash, cramming them down to the bottom of the kitchen garbage can. The delicate petals crushed as easily as her heart. She stood there trembling, feeling like the worst fool in the world. Worse, she must look like a fool to Cotter. Her chin lifted, resolve stiffening. She would show him. She went in her room and took out her shortest skirt, a little black number that hugged her bottom and her thighs. She put on a red sweater, also snug, and big black earrings, on the gaudy side. She fluffed up her hair, reddened her lipstick. And then she went downtown.

On the sidewalk outside the post office, she flirted with the young reporter from Marianne's newspaper. She did the same with Old Man Conner at the furniture store. Then she strolled by Louella's Diner, pausing to wave at the customers who lined the tables in the front. Ned Turlow came all the way outside to whistle and tell her she was the prettiest thing in town.

At the Town and Country Dress Shop, she swept in the door, laughing. The owner, Lolly Kingston, looked up from behind a display case.

"Well, Lolly," Sally said, loud enough to attract the attention of the one other customer she could see in the store. "You were right yesterday. I should have taken that little black teddy you showed me."

"Oh?" Lolly, whose clientele came largely from Willow Creek's small affluent population, was a lady through and through. But she couldn't disguise the curiosity in her voice. Just as she hadn't been able to disguise it yesterday.

"I'll take it now" was all Sally told her. "I *definitely* have to have it now."

She knew that black lace teddy, along with Cotter's flowers, would have them all guessing for weeks. Cotter would be guessing, too, because the town gossips would report her afternoon walk to him. When the hubbub died down, no one, especially Cotter, would think her heart was broken. By then, she would have probably forgotten all of this herself.

With that accomplished, she went home again. And this time, she did cry. But not for long. For there was Betsy to pick up from after-school care. And dinner to make. And a life to live.

But no more risks to take.

Never, ever, again.

Though it was mid-November, the trees in the circle in front of the hospital still wore their vibrant autumn dress. Cotter noted the colors from the window of his office. He frowned because he couldn't remember when the leaves had changed. It had been six weeks since he noticed much of anything.

Six weeks since he had seen Sally.

He had worried about avoiding her in a town this size. It had been surprisingly, almost disappointingly easy. He had warned Jamie about orchestrating another scene like the one at the football game. His son had complied with his wishes, though he had labeled Cotter nuts for having let Sally slip away. Cotter told him no details, just that it was over. For good. There had been no argument. No angry scene. For that, at least, Cotter was grateful. He knew Jamie still went to the Dairy Bar, still hung out with that red-haired waitress. She had been in Cotter's home a time or two, and she was a little chilly in her manner toward him. But nothing was ever said about Sally.

He and his son continued to stumble along, not as estranged as before, but not really together, either. Cotter had redoubled his efforts with Jamie after the debacle with Sally. He was more determined than ever to be a good father. He thought more time with Jamie would put a dent in the loneliness that threatened to swallow him up these days.

But Jamie had made plenty of friends at school. He was even, wonder of wonders, talking about trying out for the track team in the spring. He seemed receptive to time spent with his father, but he had other things to occupy his free hours.

So Cotter was adrift.

He had been offered half a dozen dates, including Miss Louella's niece, the one with a laugh like a braying hound. He gave in to a fleeting grin, thinking how right Sally had been about that one. So far, he had avoided all arranged social engagements. And at the grocery store on Saturday, when he was browsing through the frozen foods, he had heard someone whisper that "that Sally Jane Haskins" had dumped him and broken his heart. He thought that story was as good as any.

He also thought he would forego any chance at romantic entanglements in the near future. He didn't know if he would enjoy living like a monk forever, but that was more attractive right now than the alternative. If he was physically frustrated, well . . . he would just have to run harder and longer. He figured by wintertime he would be in the best shape of his life.

The intercom on his desk buzzed, and he turned from his perusal of the fall foliage to pick up his phone. His new administrative assistant, a sharp and intelligent woman of fifty-two, told him he had a visitor.

Sally Jane.

And in a moment, she was walking into his office.

"Cotter," she said, pausing just inside the door.

He stared at her without speaking. She wore black. Trim knit slacks, stirrups he thought the women called them. And a loose black sweater over them. She was pale, her skin white against the ebony gloss of her hair, her eyes looking larger than he remembered, the fine bones of her face sharply defined.

Closing the door behind her, she approached his desk. "I know you're surprised."

He finally found his voice. "How are you?"

"Well..." She took a breath and let it out again. "That's why I'm here."

"You're not ill?"

"No." She paused, bit her lip.

"Sally?" he prompted, concerned by her deepening pallor. "Are you okay?"

"Actually, Cotter, I'm not."

"What's wrong?"

"I'm pregnant."

Chapter Seven

As Sally expected, Cotter took the news like a bullet. He actually staggered back a step.

"Maybe you should sit down," she suggested. "I know I'm going to." She was feeling none too steady on her feet, hadn't felt altogether composed since she had realized the truth of her predicament.

Cotter still didn't speak. He was staring at her with the stunned expression worn by hurricane disaster victims Sally had seen on the nightly news. His face mirrored her own turmoil. She wanted to turn around and walk away. But she had to get through the next few minutes.

She squared her shoulders and gestured toward the sofa and chair grouping in one corner of the office. "Can we sit over here?"

"Of course," Cotter said, looking like a statue come to life. "Please sit down. And I'll get us some...water, I think." His movements were stiff and jerky as he moved across the office. He disappeared into another room, from which Sally soon heard the sound of running water.

She sank down onto the taupe leather couch, laid her head back against the soft cushioned back and closed her eyes, glad to relax for a minute before she had to face him again. When she looked up, Cotter was standing beside the sofa, a glass of water in his hand. From the damp, spiky look of his eyebrows and lashes, and from the dark patches on this gray-and-red patterned tie and white shirt, she guessed he had splashed some water on his face.

"Take this," he said, offering her the glass. "You look like you need it."

"Thanks."

Instead of taking a seat in one of the adjoining chairs, he sat on the edge of the heavy wooden block coffee table. He braced his hands on his spread thighs, and regarded her with concern. "You sure you're okay?"

She managed a wan smile as she set the half-empty glass on the table beside the sofa. "How about you?"

Impatiently he ran his fingers through his hair. "I'm stunned, Sally. And sorry."

She looked down at her hands. "I am, too."

He surged to his feet, one fist punching the air like some unseen adversary. "Of all the stupid things I've done in my life, this is the worst. I'm almost forty years old. I know better. I knew better that night. I just...just lost my head like some...some—"

"You can't take all the blame."

He spun around to face her. "But I should have taken care of this."

"So should I," Sally shot back at him. "I was no innocent little virgin, remember? I had every intention of protecting us both. And then I...I just...I didn't think." The excuse was lame. She knew that. "That's a pretty sorry reason for an adult to allow something like this to happen." It was especially ironic for her, Sally Jane Haskins, a woman most folks would think had the sense and the experience to avoid an accident like this. An accident. God, that was some way to be talking about a precious little baby. Her baby.

Cotter hung his head, briefly, then straightened as if he knew what he had to face. "It doesn't matter who's fault this is."

"No, it doesn't," Sally said, squaring her shoulders, as well. She, too, knew what they had to face. "I didn't come to see you because I wanted to assess any blame. God knows, my whole life has been one disaster after another. I'm not going to start blaming other people for my mistakes now."

"Don't do that," Cotter ordered, sitting back down on the edge of the table. "Don't go forgiving me for this."

"There isn't anything to forgive."

His features hardened. "Yes, there is. I went over to your house knowing what was going to happen between us. And I didn't take care of you. In my book, that isn't how a man treats a woman. It's not what you deserved."

Those were fine words from a man who had walked out after one night of passion, a man she hadn't seen in six weeks. But that didn't matter now. What mattered was the life that was growing inside of her. The wounds Cotter had inflicted to her ego and her heart had faded under a growing suspicion that she was pregnant.

When her period was late in mid-October, she told herself it was stress. When it never came, when the date of a second period came and went three days ago, she had known she couldn't hide from the inevitable. She might have behaved irresponsibly the night this baby was conceived, but she knew she couldn't any longer. A home pregnancy test confirmed her fears. Yesterday, a doctor in Knoxville, the largest city close to Willow Creek, had proven the test results were right. Ever since, Sally had been thinking, planning what she would do.

That was the question Cotter put to her now. "What do you want?"

"I'm going to have the baby."

He sat immobile, saying nothing.

She put a hand to her stomach. "For me, the thing I want to do is have this child."

He was still silent, his hazel eyes narrowing.

Suddenly as nervous as she had been when she walked in the door, Sally looked away, lifting her chin and forcing herself to remain as outwardly calm as possible. "I'm not asking you for anything, Cotter."

"Let me ask you something."

She still couldn't look at him. "What?"

"Marry me."

Now it was her turn to stammer in shock.

He pushed himself up from the table, his face set in grim lines. "This child is mine, too. I don't think I could win any father-of-the-year awards. But I do know that I don't want a child of mine walking around without my name, without knowing me."

His child? His name? The possessive, outrageously autocratic male tone of his voice made Sally sputter. "You're out of your mind."

"Oh, come on, Sally," he snapped. "Are you really going to have a child out of wedlock in this town, with judgmental types like Jackie Bryant and Miss Clara always wagging their fingers and clucking in disapproval? You and I may be little more than strangers, but I do know that you are a warm and caring mother, and I don't think you want our child to suffer like that. I can't imagine you considering that."

She got to her feet, her cheeks growing warm. "Don't you think I've thought of all of this? After all, I know how Betsy has felt without a father."

"Exactly," he said in triumph. "As difficult as it has been to raise Betsy by yourself, why would you do it again?"

"It hasn't been so tough."

He made a dismissive gesture. "Don't pull that with me. I'm raising a son alone. He's almost grown, but I know damned well that it's not easy to face it all by yourself."

"But you're not—"

He cut her off with, "Don't say it's harder for me than it would be for a woman. Being a good parent of either sex is hard as hell and you know it."

Sally had to concede he was right. She had never meant to imply it was easier to be a mother than a father. She was rattled and showing it. She drew in a breath, trying to calm down. It had never occurred to her that she would be having this conversation with Cotter. Marriage had never once entered her mind.

"All right," she told him finally. "Being a single parent is never easy. And Betsy has suffered some. I can remember the first time she asked why she didn't have a father. I know that there are times when she feels abandoned and confused, and I'm sure that down the road she will have other questions, may have more problems—"

"Then how can you consider doing that to another child?"

"Because I also know there are worse things than being illegitimate. Remember? I grew up in a home with two people who shouldn't have married."

"But I'm not like your father. You're not like your mother."

"People change. They grow bitter and they hurt each other. And when there are kids, they suffer right along with the parents."

"I'm not saying this would be easy."

She forced out a choked laugh. "That's an understatement."

"But we have to try. The only important thing is what's best for our child. And I think a home with two parents is best."

She still couldn't believe what she was hearing. "How can you consider marrying me? Six weeks ago you couldn't even commit to sleeping with me again."

"That doesn't matter now."

"But it does matter," Sally retorted, jabbing a finger into her chest. "It matters to me. We can't consider a marriage that we don't really want. This isn't the 1950s. Every family doesn't have to be the *Leave It to Beaver* ideal in order to work."

Cotter just shook his head, refusing to listen to her. "What's ideal is putting this child first. We didn't put any thought into creating him...her. But now we've got to think and think carefully about what we do."

Biting back a curse, Sally spun around and snatched up her purse from the sofa. "I'm not wasting my time talking to you about this anymore. I only came up here to tell you because I thought you deserved to know—"

"Decent of you," he interjected with heavy sarcasm.

She wheeled to face him again. "Well, I didn't have to tell you at all."

"Like you would do that. Like I wouldn't have found out about it in this town. The first day you put on a ma-

ternity dress, there'd be half a dozen people up here ready
to tell me about it."

"I could have lied and said it wasn't yours. Nobody
would doubt it. Probably not even you."

He laughed at her, a sound owing more to anger than
mirth. "That's not true, Sally. I would know. And you're
too decent a person to tell a lie like that."

"That's not an opinion many people share."

"Oh, I'm aware of the way you allow people to think
of you. For some unknown reason, for all your life,
you've let half the town believe you're something quite
different from the woman you really are. You've only allowed a few people close enough to see the real you."

"Don't flatter yourself into thinking you're one of
those fortunate few. Like you said, we're strangers."

He caught her arm before she could open the door.
"You're wrong," he whispered. "I have seen the real
you."

She closed her eyes as he drew her back against him.
She did all she could to resist the intimacies his deep voice
made her remember. Not merely sexual. But what she had
told him of her life, the vulnerabilities she had revealed.
From the beginning she had opened up to him. What a
mistake. What a terrible mistake. It took all of her will,
but she broke free of those thoughts and of him and
reached for the doorknob once more.

"Just stop it, Cotter. Let it go. I'm not going to marry
you. That would just be another mistake."

But there was a fierce tenderness in his voice as he said,
"I don't want you to face this alone."

"I'm not afraid to be alone."

"Oh, really?" With gentle but insistent pressure, he
turned her toward him. With his hand under her chin, he
tipped her face upward so that his warm, hazel gaze

locked with hers. "I don't believe you, Sally. I think you're scared to death."

He saw too much, she thought, jerking away. Far, far too much. She had to get out of here.

Holding her head high, she opened the door. As she stepped into the outer office, she spoke over her shoulder in a falsely bright voice. "You think too much, Mr. Graham. It muddies the brain."

She left Cotter standing in the open doorway, enduring the interested regard of his office staff.

"Don't you have anything to do?" he thundered in his best Cotter the Barbarian voice. They scurried like deer fleeing the sound of a gun. And Cotter closed his door. Slowly, because he wanted to slam it. Slowly, because he didn't want any more talk than was already circulating about the woman who was carrying his child.

Inside the office, he felt the walls closing in. And so he left. In the middle of the afternoon, leaving no word of how he could be found, he just walked out. It was Friday. Jamie had taken a bus along with half of the high school student body to a football game in another county. So Cotter was alone at home.

He considered crawling inside a whiskey bottle and staying there for a couple of days. But that had never been his style. In the end, he sat alone in his darkened study, berating himself again and again.

A baby.

His and Sally's baby.

God in heaven, why hadn't he seen this coming? He had known that night that they had neglected to take the most rudimentary precautions. Swearing, he jammed his fists down on the arms of his easy chair. No protection. Not once, but twice. It was inexcusable, immature. He was ashamed of himself, and angry, too. He should have considered what might happen. He should have never been with Sally in the first place. If only he had listened to his head and ignored the dictates of his loins.

He was going to be a father again.

With a bitter sigh, Cotter considered all the people in the world who would give anything for a child. Yet here he was, already a less than exemplary father, and he would have yet another opportunity to get it right. If Sally gave him a chance, that was. If she even let him be a father.

Frustration squeezed his chest. Sally had to see this his way. When she gave it some thought, calmed down, she would realize there was only one thing to do. They had to get married. Soon.

It was strange, the way he had decided to suggest marriage. It had required little thought at all. Sally was pregnant. It was his baby. So he was going to do the right thing. The two situations simply equally the third.

Today, as he had sat there in his office, absorbing the reality of this dilemma, he had known right away that he wanted to marry her. There had been this blinding moment, foolish perhaps, a vision of Sally with his baby in her arms. Before he proposed, it had occurred to him, that maybe, for the first time in a long while, he would be doing something he knew to be totally, completely right.

Not that marriage didn't frighten him. He still had little confidence in his abilities in that regard. But that shouldn't matter now. There was a child on the way. A child who was as much his responsibility as was Jamie. Maybe with this child Cotter wouldn't screw it up. Maybe he had learned from his previous failures. Maybe if they tried hard enough, he and Sally, Jamie and Betsy and this baby could be a family.

This just might be his second chance. His redemption.

If only Sally would see it his way.

She had to see it his way.

That was the reassurance he repeated time and again over the next few days. Days in which he rarely slept and could barely eat. He couldn't even go for a decent run. He was out of his mind, wondering what to do next. He kept hoping Sally was going to make it easy for him, that she would show up or call, and tell him she had reconsidered. But she didn't.

Early Tuesday evening, Jamie came into the study where Cotter was sitting in the dark. He snapped on the desk lamp and regarded his father with a concerned expression.

"You all right, Dad?"

Cotter sighed. He wasn't all right. He was in here trying to get up enough courage to go beg Sally to marry him. But how did he explain that to a fifteen-year-old? How, indeed, did he explain the fact that dear old dad, the one who preached caution and thoughtful action and respect for women, had gone out and gotten someone pregnant? The scenario might have seemed funny if it were happening to someone other than him.

"Dad?" Jamie repeated. "What's wrong?"

There was no ducking this issue any longer. Cotter wasn't going to lie to his son or hide the truth from him, either. If Sally married him, it would impact Jamie, as well. Even if she didn't marry him, the baby was coming.

So Cotter took a deep breath. "Son," he said. "You're going to be a brother."

Sally and Lana were going through the Tuesday night closing routine, eager to get home, when Jack and Marianne came through the Dairy Bar's front door. Though Sally had called her friends last week and said she wanted to get together and talk, she hadn't expected to see them tonight. Two weeks ago, Marianne had given birth to a baby boy. The same week, Jack had won his bid for the state house of representatives. They had definitely been too busy to be bothered with Sally's problem.

From behind the cash register where she was counting cash, Sally challenged, "Don't tell me you've left Laura, Jessie and Sam home alone?"

Marianne laughed and called a greeting to Lana, who was mopping the floor behind the counter, before responding, "Yes, we've actually left those innocent children with someone else. And I must say it feels good to be out of the house."

"Delilah and Jeb are baby-sitting," Jack said, referring to Marianne's aunt and uncle. "They've been telling us to call them every night this week, so we finally took them up on their offer."

Leaning her arms on the counter, Marianne tried but failed to stifle a yawn. "I'm sure they're at home right now, wondering why they offered. Young Mr. Sam Dylan is already a demanding little hellion."

Sally grinned at Jack. "Sounds as if he does take after his father, as predicted."

"It's not so bad," Jack said. "Jessie is getting so big nowadays. She's not a baby at all. I'm sort of enjoying all of this."

"Yeah," Sally agreed. "Babies are pretty special." She wondered if she would feel the same way in seven and half months when this baby had her up half the night. Maybe Jack would come over and *enjoy* some time with her.

"Right now, I don't want to think about babies," Marianne said. "I want to forget about trying to lose all this weight I gained with Sam, as well. I want two scoops of raspberry sherbet."

Jack added, "Make mine two scoops of chocolate chip."

"Coming up," Sally said, turning from the counter. But as happened occasionally these days, a wave of nausea and dizziness assailed her. She put a hand to her forehead and swayed slightly as she groped for the edge of the counter behind her.

"Sally?" Lana said. The mop banged to the floor as she rushed forward to take Sally's arm. "Sally, you're white as a ghost."

Five minutes later, Lana and Jack had Sally sitting in a booth with a glass of water, while Marianne attended to the money Sally had left stacked on the counter beside the cash register.

Lana stood to one side, fussing. "She's been working way too much lately."

"Isn't this your usual night off?" Jack asked Sally.

"Craig has a test tomorrow," Lana put in. "Sally gave him the night off to study."

"Betsy's with a sitter," Sally put in.

Marianne slipped into the seat across from her, her face full of concern. "You do look awfully pale, you know."

"There's nothing wrong with me," Sally insisted, as she had been doing since the moment she had become dizzy. "Jack, why don't you go get that ice cream that you and Marianne want. And Lana, would you please..." She paused as she looked, really looked at the young waitress. Maybe she *had* been working too hard lately, for Lana didn't look like the same funky, slightly kooky girl who had been working for Sally for more than a year.

"You okay?" Lana said again, her expression concerned.

"I just realized you're wearing colors that match and a bow, an *actual* bow in your hair."

"It's my new image."

"New what?"

"Sally," Marianne cut in. "Don't try and change the subject. We were talking about you working too much and looking pale. And don't tell me there's nothing wrong. You're one of the healthiest people I know. What gives?"

Pointedly ignoring her, Sally glanced back at Lana. "You'd better get home, you know. Your mother will have a fit if you're late."

"But the floor—"

"I'll have Craig do it tomorrow."

Lana was gone in a matter of minutes. Jack finished dipping ice cream and came back to the table.

Marianne ate a spoonful of sherbet, her gaze never wavering from Sally's. "Now that Lana's gone, will you tell us what's wrong?"

Rolling the glass of ice water between her hands, Sally considered how to begin. It wasn't easy to reveal her secret. She had never been one for sharing her problems. Maybe it was because she'd had so few friends. As a youngster, she had been busy at home most of the time. The lion's share of responsibility for meals and laundry and caring for Renee had fallen on her shoulders. And later, the attention she received from boys had alienated her from many of the girls her age. Renee had naturally been her closest confidante. Until she changed. Until she betrayed her.

But Jack had always been a friend. And through him, Marianne. Sally trusted them both. And she knew she was going to need their friendship. She had told Cotter she wasn't frightened. But she was. The fear he had read in her was very real. All his arguments about bringing a child into the world without a father had struck home.

Jack must have seen the fear, too, for he reached out and stopped her nervous fiddling with the glass of water. "What's wrong, Sally? You haven't heard from Renee again, have you?"

"God, no. As far as I know, she and her husband have moved to California." Compared to that desperate time when Renee had sued for custody of Betsy, Sally realized this problem was small indeed.

So she told them. Everything. About the baby. And the father.

Jack was silent at first. But Marianne got up, scooted in on Sally's side of the booth and slipped an arm around her shoulders. "You can count on us to help you. You know that, don't you?"

"Of course."

"Absolutely," Jack said, reaching across the table to cover Sally's hand with his own. "You know we'll do everything we can to support you. But what's Graham going to do?"

"I don't want anything from him."

"It's his responsibility," Jack insisted.

"I don't care."

"Sally," Marianne protested gently. "Jack is right. This is Cotter's problem as well as yours. You don't have to do this alone."

Jack began, "If you want me to talk to him—"

"God, no," Sally said. "I don't need you strong-arming him. He already asked me to marry him."

"So are you?" The question came in unison from Jack and Marianne.

"Of course not."

"You won't even consider it?" Jack asked.

"No," Sally said. "We barely know each other. We have no business getting married. He doesn't care about me. He just wants to take responsibility for this baby."

Jack spread his hands wide. "What's so wrong with that?"

"I can't marry him on that basis," Sally told him. "It isn't enough for a marriage, I mean, he doesn't love me. I don't love him."

"Oh, really?" A knowing smile curved Marianne's mouth. "Don't you?"

Sally suddenly wished the people she had allowed to get close to her were a little less insightful. She was readying an emphatic denial of Marianne's suggestion when car lights swept across the windowed front of the Dairy Bar. And the subject of their discussion stepped out of his Bronco.

"Don't go," Sally told her friends. "I don't want to talk to him."

"You want me to tell him to leave?" Jack asked.

Sally wanted to handle it herself. She met Cotter at the door. Through the glass and under the neon lights that rimmed the outside of the restaurant, she could see he looked terrible, pale and bleary eyed, his jeans and shirt wrinkled, hair tousled.

But as she pushed open the door, she hardened her heart against his haggard appearance. "I'm closed," she said without preamble or greeting.

His lips tightened. "I didn't come for ice cream."

"I don't want to talk to you."

"Damn it, Sally, we've got to talk."

She felt rather than saw Jack come up behind her. "I think she said you should go, Graham," he said.

Cotter stared at him for a moment, his eyes narrowing to dangerous slits. "This is between me and Sally, okay?"

"But she wants you to go."

"And I want her to marry me," Cotter said, his voice rising, a wild, exasperated look on his face. "I'd like to know when it became a crime for a man to want to marry the woman who is having his baby!"

Sally felt Jack step forward, but she blocked his move. Marianne was behind him, pulling at his arm. In the confusion, Cotter made it in the door.

"I just want to talk to Sally," he said to Jack. "Just talk. That's all."

Marianne pulled her husband, whose jaw was still jutting forward in challenge, toward the door. "We're going." She caught Sally's eye and added, "For what my opinion's worth, I think you ought to listen to what Cotter has to say."

Some friends, Sally thought, as she faced Cotter in silence.

"I hope you listen to her advice," he said.

She stalked away and began clearing the booth they had vacated. "You're wasting your time," she said on the way to the counter with the empty glass and ice cream bowls. "I'm not marrying you."

"Even though it's the right thing to do?"

"I haven't bothered much with what's right in my life."

"Jamie wants us to get married."

She set the glass and bowls down with a little clatter, wheeling to face him. "You told Jamie?"

"I thought he had the right to know. He thinks our getting married would be cool. In fact, he's the one who gave me the courage to come down here and beg you. He says it's the honorable thing to do. The baby he's not too sure about. But I'm sure he'll come around."

"I can't believe you told him," Sally murmured, pressing her hands to her heated cheeks.

"Was he supposed to have a brother or sister he didn't know about? Was that your plan?"

Sally shook her head. "Of course not. I knew he would have to be told. He and Betsy. I knew, but..." She closed her eyes for a moment. "God, this is all so complicated. Don't you see that? There's more than me and you and the baby to think about. We've got two other lives to consider."

"That's just one more reason why we should get married."

She threw up her hands in disgust. "You're impossible to reason with."

"I'm impossible?" He laughed. "You're the one I can't figure out. Six weeks ago, you wanted a relationship. Now I offer you more than that, and you won't consider it."

"Six weeks ago I was temporarily insane. That's how this mess started."

There was a moment of silence. Then his soft, "Is it a mess, Sally?"

"Of course it's a mess."

"Having a baby is merely a mess?"

With a muffled exclamation, she swung away from him. Damn him, anyway. Damn him for being able to look so deeply into her heart and see the truth. For even though she was frightened, and the circumstances were less than ideal, this baby, *their* baby, didn't feel like a mess. It felt like a miracle. As sappy and goofy as that sounded, that's how she felt.

"It's the weirdest thing," Cotter said, still standing behind her. "But I keep thinking about this baby, and I want it."

She turned back to him, stunned by his admission. "How can you want this baby? That doesn't make any sense."

He shrugged. "Don't ask me to explain it, Sally. But I've done a lot of thinking over the past few days. It seems to me that you and I and this baby and Jamie and Betsy, we all need one another."

"You didn't think so six weeks ago."

He hung his head briefly, then looked straight into her eyes. "You're right. But everything is different now. I don't think either of us can look at things the way we did then."

She had to admit he had a point. The whole world seemed to have changed since she realized she was pregnant. Every priority in her life was shifting.

Cotter stepped forward. "I know you don't want to admit it, but you need me, Sally. Our baby needs me."

His earnest expression and sincere words began to get to her. She tried hard to resist. "This is insanity, Cotter."

"Not marrying me is insanity," he insisted. "Not trying to make it work is crazy."

She felt her resolve wavering and turned away. It was easier to fight him when she didn't have to look at him. "I'm not marrying you."

"You would really deny our child his father?"

She closed her eyes, trying not to be swayed by his argument. "We wouldn't have to be married for you to be a part of her life."

"I think that would be hard on you and him."

"Cotter—"

She hadn't heard his approach, but he stepped close behind her, his hands settling on her shoulders. "I want to be married, Sally. I want to do the right thing. I want to take care of you and our child."

"I can take—"

"—care of yourself," he finished for her. "I know that. I respect that. But it seems to me that all of us, all *five* of us, could do with a little help from one another." He paused to clear his throat. "The truth is, Jamie and I need you, Sally."

That made her turn and look at him, a surprised question on her lips.

"It's true. Our life together has been better ever since I came barreling into this restaurant. Just watching you with Betsy has taught me about reaching out, being a parent. The times when all of us have been together have been . . . special. Like a family. I've missed that since I walked out of your house six weeks ago. Since I screwed everything up."

He was pushing all the right buttons. Sally knew that. She had been manipulated by men before. She knew the technique. But somehow, this time, she wanted to believe. She wanted the picture Cotter painted. A family picture.

"Do you think Betsy would mind so much?" he asked.

She managed a trembling smile. "Betsy has been planning our wedding since the first day she met you."

"She's a smart girl. Let's plan it for tomorrow."

"Cotter, I can't—"

Suddenly, unexpectedly, he dropped to one knee in front of her.

"Cotter!"

His smile was sheepish, but he held his pose on his knee in front of her. "Damnation, Sally, I'm desperate, okay? Marry me."

"You're making this so hard—"

He caught both her hands in his. "Sally, I'm not promising you perfection. But if you marry me, I will be faithful to you. I will respect you, protect you. I won't lie, though. There are things I can't give you."

Like love, she thought sadly. The sort of love he had given his wife.

"But I do want you. You have to admit there's passion between us."

"Chemistry," she murmured. "Just sparks."

"We'll work on keeping the flame burning." His grin flashed. "Personally, I don't think that would be too unpleasant a task."

She flushed, her determination to oppose him tearing even further.

"I need you, Sally. We all need one another. Please marry me."

Need. It was an emotion she understood. For most of her life, Sally had been ministering to someone in need. Her flawed and beaten parents. Her troubled sister. The little girl she had made her own. Needs could forge strong bonds. But would need be enough to build the family Cotter was offering? Would need be enough to hold the two of them together?

She didn't know.

But she wanted to believe it could.

With a leap of faith she knew was foolhardy, she said yes.

And five days later, Sally Jane Haskins got married.

Outside the judge's office in the thin November sunlight, Cotter Graham imagined most of Willow Creek was whirling from the news. He didn't care. The people most affected by this news were in this room. These people were Cotter's responsibilities, both old and new. Jamie, serious and strangely grown-up in a dark suit and tie. Little Betsy, her brown eyes dancing with satisfaction, in a purple dress with a white satin sash. And Sally, with his baby in her womb, looking luminous in a cream satin suit.

Concentrating on these people and the vows he was taking, Cotter tried to ignore his doubts and his worries.

His success was minimal.

Chapter Eight

A purpling late autumn dusk had fallen on their wedding day by the time Cotter and Sally set their luggage on the porch of a cabin some forty miles from Willow Creek. In front of them, the ground sloped to the bank of a slow-moving river. Trees, still with a smattering of leaves in brilliant hues of orange and yellow, surrounded them. The air smelled of impending winter, of moist, rich earth. The only sound was the far-off chug of an unseen boat's engine. The cabin was secluded, private, a perfect hideaway.

Cotter felt his optimism rise as he looked around. He fished a key from his pocket and placed it in the lock. He grinned over his shoulder as the door squeaked open. "I suppose I should do the traditional thing and carry you over the threshold."

Sally laughed. "I wouldn't want you to strain something just for the sake of tradition."

He didn't pause to argue. He just swept her into his arms and pushed the door the rest of the way open with his foot. She was no lightweight, but he managed the move with suitable flourish, he thought. He wanted flourish. He wanted tonight to be special. Maybe then he could banish his lingering misgivings.

"My hero," Sally teased as he set her down on her feet inside the door.

With her pretty face upturned toward his, her gray eyes brightened with laughter, he couldn't resist pressing a gentle kiss to her lips. Today, when the judge pronounced them husband and wife, he had realized they hadn't kissed since the night she accepted his proposal. There had been no time for kisses or for romance, what with planning the wedding and preparing for a change in their living arrangements. Cotter had been so preoccupied with the logistics of everything that he hadn't even thought about a honeymoon until yesterday morning, when Marianne Dylan had stopped by his office for a talk.

Marianne had come to warn him, actually, about what would happen to him if he didn't treat Sally as she deserved. With a toddler on one hip and her new baby in a stroller, Marianne had stared him down with brilliant, flashing blue eyes. "Jack and I won't stand by and let you hurt Sally," she had said. "So don't think you can."

"Hurting her has never been my intention," Cotter replied, surprised by Marianne's animosity. After the advice she had given Sally Tuesday night, he thought Marianne was on his side. But perhaps he deserved this tongue-lashing. If he had truly wanted to do right by Sally, he wouldn't have made her pregnant and put her through the past few weeks of stress and worry.

"You had better treat her well, or you'll answer to us," Marianne shot back. "And believe me, you wouldn't want to face Jack when he's riled."

Thinking of the man who had almost taken a swing at him Tuesday night at the Dairy Bar, Cotter nodded. Jack would be a considerable adversary in word or action.

Apparently satisfied that her warning had been taken seriously, Marianne smiled. "Now what I want to know is if you've made reservations for a honeymoon."

He had stuttered and stammered, about plans to drive into Knoxville or the nearby Smokey Mountains and the resort town of Gatlinburg.

Marianne didn't buy that. "This is a football weekend at the University of Tennessee. You're not going to find a decent hotel room in Gatlinburg or Knoxville. But I have a solution." She offered her family's riverfront cabin. Furthermore, she said Jamie and Betsy could stay with her while Cotter and Sally were away.

Cotter didn't think Marianne would have taken no for an answer. And now, surveying the rustic charm of the cabin around them, he was grateful for her offer. The cabin's main room wasn't luxurious, with a well-worn couch and a couple of chairs arranged around a stone fireplace. A kitchenette was to the rear of the room. On one side, a door opened to the bedroom. No, not luxurious, but cozy enough. From the rug in front of the couch to the gleaming brass of an old lamp, it was scrupulously clean. Someone had obviously prepared for their arrival.

Smiling, Sally touched one of the roses in a flower arrangement near the door. "Marianne's been here. She or her Aunt Delilah."

"Looks like it," Cotter agreed. There were bouquets of flowers scattered throughout the room. Wood was laid in the fireplace. More logs were stacked on a rack to one side of the hearth. A note pinned to the lampshade announced there was champagne in the refrigerator. The setting was ripe for romance.

Romance. Suddenly, unaccountably nervous, Cotter glanced at Sally. No longer smiling, she was studying the flower arrangement with more concentration than he thought it deserved.

He gestured toward the door. "I guess I should go out and fetch the groceries we brought from home."

Still not looking up, Sally nodded.

Cotter set their two pieces of luggage inside the door and then clattered down the wooden porch steps outside.

Sally let out the breath she had been holding. She felt nervous enough to jump out of her skin. Until they walked in this door, she had been too busy to think about coming here with Cotter.

Today had been a whirlwind. The eleven o'clock wedding. A lunch at her house with the children, Jack and Marianne and Cotter's sister, Susannah, who had surprised them by driving up from Atlanta. It had been four o'clock by the time they left Willow Creek. On the drive up, they had talked about plans for Sally and Betsy's move to Cotter's house. Sally was none too happy about that, but she agreed with Cotter that it was the best solution for right now. They had so much to think about and plan for that she hadn't had time to become nervous about tonight.

"Nervous," she said aloud, disgusted with herself. There was no reason for nerves. It wasn't as if she and Cotter hadn't been together before.

But not as husband and wife.

The thought made her shiver. And as she twisted her broad, gold band around on her finger, she was reminded of a saying popular when she was a teen, about today being the beginning of the rest of your life. That directive was especially appropriate for wedding days. This was a beginning. And it had to work, she told herself. She had to make it work. Somehow they were going to be happy.

A voice inside whispered that happiness wasn't her right, that she deserved to suffer for getting in this situation, for being careless enough to conceive a child this way. She tried to will that voice away, but it didn't work.

No amount of positive self-talk could calm her. Neither could activity, her usual escape from troubling thoughts. She took their bags into the bedroom and changed from her wedding suit to jeans and a sweater. Cotter changed also, as she put the groceries away and started preparations for dinner. Then he started a fire. And throughout this flurry of work they said little to each other. Indeed, Cotter's gaze seemed to skitter away from hers in the same jumpy way she reacted to him.

They ate an uneasy meal in front of a cozy, romantic fire while night settled outside the cabin. Then they sat, one at each end of the broad, comfortable couch, with nothing to say.

Finally, when Sally thought her nerves must surely be screaming loud enough to be heard, she got to her feet. "I'm making some coffee."

Cotter seized upon the suggestion with an enthusiasm that would have been humorous if Sally had been capable of laughing. "We can have the rest of the wedding cake Marianne sent."

Fifteen minutes later, they were back on the couch, with big mugs of coffee on the tables at each end of the couch and huge slabs of thickly frosted cake on the plates in their hands. But still they said nothing. Sally couldn't relax. She perched on the edge of the couch, nibbling at her cake like she was attending some stiff and proper church social.

Feeling ridiculous, Cotter cleared his throat and offered a lame, "This is wonderful cake, isn't it?"

Sally actually jumped at the sound of his voice. "Cake?" she said blankly.

Cotter held up his plate, which held a piece too large for most mortals to consume. "It's great, isn't it?"

"Oh, sure." With a gusto she didn't feel, she lifted another forkful of the sweet stuff toward her mouth. But she was so nervous her hands were trembling, and she actually missed her lips and a left a streak of icing on her face before the rest of the bite toppled from the fork.

"Damn," she muttered, swiping at the cake that had landed in her lap. It fell to the floor, leaving a trail of crumbs. Flushing, she pursued the crumbs with a paper napkin. That upset the cake on her plate. It landed on the floor. As did Sally. She toppled off the edge of the couch, sprawling with something less than grace on the faded rag rug.

There was a moment of stunned silence. And because Sally was obviously mortified, Cotter tried not to laugh. Biting the sides of his mouth, he set his cake aside and bent to help her. Only she didn't anticipate his move and jabbed him in the eye with her elbow. Yelping in pain, he managed to slip off the couch, as well. In trying to break his fall, his hand slid into her overturned cake.

The situation was too ridiculous for Cotter to do anything but laugh, and that laughter finally broke the fine thread of tension that had been running between them.

While they were laughing at each other, Sally kissed him. He looked so funny, so unlike the cool, controlled man he was so much of the time, that she couldn't help herself.

"So seeing me fall on my face turns you on?" Cotter murmured, drawing away.

"Yeah," she replied. "And if one of us hadn't made a move, I think we would have spent the rest of the night at opposite ends of that sofa."

"I guess the next move is up to me," he said, kissing her before she could reply.

She tasted of cake, he thought. And of her own special sweetness. The combination was heady, almost overpowering. Groaning a little at the way she stirred him, he put his hand to her face, realizing much too late that his fingers were coated in cake and icing.

"Look at this," he muttered, dabbing inadequately at the cake and icing he had added to the original smear on her cheek.

"Don't worry about it." Sally captured his hand with hers. Then, slowly, her gaze locked with his, she licked the sweet, sticky icing off his thumb, then off the next finger, and the next. By the time she was finished, Cotter felt as if the zipper on his jeans would burst.

And there, on the floor beside the sofa, with laughter and cake, they consummated their marriage.

The cake had been delicious before, but Cotter discovered each bite was particularly luscious when he nibbled them from Sally's breasts. Or from her belly. Or from the dusky nest of curls at the juncture of her thighs. As for the way Sally consumed the delicate pink rosette she scooped from the top of the icing...well, Cotter didn't think the part of his anatomy she chose as a platter would ever be the same.

When the cake was gone, she welcomed him into her body with the same free and easy warmth he remembered. She wrapped her arms and legs around him, caught the rhythm of his strokes, and in that moment of pure, sparkling joy, Cotter lost every worry he had.

He wanted with all his heart to hold on to that feeling, to the hope for happiness which was what had drawn him to Sally in the first place.

That hope bloomed inside him at unpredictable moments during the next few days. When he watched Sally sleeping. When she turned from the stove to offer him a taste of her special spaghetti sauce. When she tucked her cold feet under his in the bed. When, naked, they sat wrapped in a blanket in the front of the fire and argued good-naturedly about names for their baby.

In all the time they spent alone at the cabin, there were a dozen times when Sally almost told him she loved him. But she always stopped herself just in time. For she didn't want to face how he felt. He didn't love her. Oh, yes, he needed her, and desired her. But neither of those emotions was love.

The knowledge took some of the joy out of these days with him. She couldn't help the pensive mood that settled over her on the last night of their stay. Because she didn't want Cotter to sense her sadness, she finally said she needed some fresh air and went out on the front porch.

The night was cold, much colder than usual for the Tuesday before Thanksgiving in Tennessee. Sally shivered a little, but not from the plunging temperature. She was thinking of tomorrow, of returning to the real world, to real problems, to the rest of their lives.

As usual, she lectured herself about positive thinking. But that had little effect since she knew Cotter had been trapped into marrying her. Even though the marriage had been his idea, he had been trapped into it by his own sense of honor and responsibility. She had always dreamed of marrying a man who possessed his sort of integrity. She only wished the circumstances of the marriage were different.

She wished he loved her.

In these three days they had carved out of the rest of their lives, she had glimpsed a small section of heaven. She wanted it all.

Behind her the door squeaked open. "You're going to freeze out here," Cotter said.

Sally didn't turn. "It feels kind of nice."

Without further comment, he settled his coat around her shoulders. She pulled it around her, enjoying the scratch of the wool against her chin. The coat smelled of him. Of the musky scent she now knew so well. That intimate knowledge made her sigh.

"You okay?" he whispered.

She nodded.

But Cotter stood beside her, studying the outline of her profile in the gentle glow of light from the cabin's front window, knowing she lied. He felt a familiar tug of frustration. He could remember moments like this with Brenda, when she was upset about something, and he didn't know what to do or say. Those moments had always confounded him, left him feeling that he should know, should be able to sense what was troubling her. If he loved her, she used to say, he would know. He thought he had loved her, but still she had remained a mystery. Love hadn't been enough.

Well, love wasn't part of the equation with Sally. So how could he ever hope to understand her?

She deserved love, he thought. She deserved a man who could see into her soul, would know that secret password of understanding that only true love was supposed to convey. She had so much joy and life to offer, she should have someone who could give her the same. All Cotter had done was compromise her. Even marrying her couldn't make up for the way he had already let her down. The night he proposed he had told her they needed each other, that need would pull them together. But if love hadn't been the right basis for his first marriage, how could he build this one only on need? Weren't they doomed to failure, no matter how hard they tried?

Doubts were slamming into him anew. He wondered how long it would be before Sally felt trapped by his limitations. How long before the silence that lay between them tonight became the norm? When the bloom was gone from their mutual passion, what then?

Fear sliced through him like a blunt-edged sword. Cotter didn't stop to analyze why he was so afraid of letting Sally down. He only accepted that he would. And there seemed only one way he could think of to stop the spread of his doubts.

He turned her toward him. His kiss was brutal, almost desperate. She didn't seem shocked. If anything, she met him with a desperation of her own. Her mouth opened beneath his. Her hands raced up his back, fingers clenching at his sweater. There was no protest when his coat fell from her shoulders or when he freed her breasts from the confines of her bra or when he forced her jeans down her hips. She clung to him, gasping as his fingers found her moist, velvety cleft. He stroked, seeking that most sensitive kernel of flesh.

When she exploded in release, he trapped her sounds of pleasure beneath his kiss, finding that communion intimate, unbearably arousing.

He took her then, in the cold, up against the rough outer wall of the cabin, with only the most necessary rearrangement and shedding of his clothes. Aside from the crudest, most essential words of encouragement or instruction, they said nothing.

It was a shattering, erotic coupling.

The glow of their shared climax spilled over into the rest of the evening.

Yet later, lying beside Sally in their honeymoon bed, Cotter could hear his heart pounding in fear.

Sally had known it wouldn't be easy to move from her house to Cotter's. Part of her heart, a large portion of her bank account and a whopping load of sweat and tears had gone into her home. Her house of dreams. But the finished areas simply weren't big enough for all of them. Cotter said he loved the house, too, but he suggested they get through the winter and her pregnancy before they sold his house and invested the profits in finishing hers. His plan made sense, and Sally preached patience to herself.

But on Thanksgiving night, she couldn't stop her tears as she carried a last armload of Betsy's clothes to the Bronco. She dashed them quickly away, before Cotter joined her.

But he wasn't fooled. "Sally, if this house is so important to you, we'll find a way to stay here."

She wiped an errant tear from her cheek. "How? There are only two bedrooms and one bath. The front rooms have no heat. The upstairs has major problems. It will cost a flat fortune to get it in shape. I know you make a lot of money, Cotter, but I really doubt that you and I together make enough to get this house ready for us to live in during the coldest months of the year."

He touched her cheek. "I don't want you to be miserable."

"I'm not." But that was a lie. For it wasn't easy to be happy in a haunted house.

Brenda Graham had never lived in the spacious two-story home that Cotter had bought upon moving to Willow Grove. But to Sally, Brenda inhabited every corner. She peeked around the corners of the formal French Provincial furniture in the living room. She stared up from the plush Oriental rug in Cotter's study. She whispered Sally's name from a set of ceramic canisters in the shape of strawberries on the kitchen counter.

Throughout the long Thanksgiving holiday and the weeks that followed, as Sally tried to settle into her new home, she kept turning around, expecting to confront the woman who had come before her.

There were only two rooms that didn't bear the imprint of Brenda's style. There was Betsy's room, which had been freshly painted the week before the wedding and now held her own furniture. And the master bedroom. While Sally and Cotter had been at the cabin, he had asked his assistant to supervise the removal of his old furniture and the placement of hers.

Sally thanked him for his thoughtfulness. She thought she would rather die than be asked to lay beside him in another woman's bed.

Oh, she fought back, of course. She was nothing if not a fighter. She did everything she could to make it *her* house. She set bowls of her favorite potpourri on tables throughout the house. Even when Jamie's dog kept turning them over, she insisted they stay. She served their family dinners on her own pottery plates. She replaced a painting in the family room with one from her house, and boxed up some of the knickknacks she didn't care for, always being careful to ask Jamie and Cotter if it was okay.

None of the changes elicited a protest. She didn't know why that bothered her. She thought she would rather

Cotter protested, so that she could challenge him about the woman who wasn't there.

She knew she was being unreasonable and emotional. But she couldn't forget the things Cotter had said about his first wife. About how perfect she had been. Brenda was gone, but he had loved her, and that left Sally feeling at a distinct disadvantage. Cotter's love for another woman, a love he didn't feel for Sally, was a barrier between them.

Despite these problems, there were rewards to those first few weeks of Sally's marriage. There were the nights in Cotter's arms. No one came between them when they were making love. And no matter what else she doubted, she couldn't question the strength of his desire for her, nor of hers for him.

There was also Sally's deepening relationship with Jamie. His easy acceptance of her had never faltered. He had even confessed to looking forward to the baby. From the start, he had treated Betsy with a combination of brotherly affection and sibling disdain.

Cotter was establishing quite a rapport with Betsy, as well. Even at ten, she was as football crazy as most of the kids in Willow Creek. She and Cotter watched football together most of the Thanksgiving weekend and were already planning their New Year's Day college bowl television festival. The gentleness and patience he displayed with her daughter warmed Sally's heart.

As Cotter had predicted, a family was being formed. Maybe this would work, if only Sally could shake the feeling that Brenda lived here, too.

In the early afternoon on the second Sunday in December, with Jamie out, with Betsy playing in her room and Cotter working in his study, Sally wandered throughout the rest of the house. She wound up in the upstairs hall outside the door to Jamie's room. She'd had little excuse to come in here. Not even to clean.

Cotter said their marriage was no reason to get rid of his housekeeper. He wanted Sally to slow down at the Dairy Bar as her pregnancy advanced, and he didn't think she needed a house and the practical concerns of two other people to worry about. Sally thought the slowing down part would remain to be seen, but she had no objections to someone else doing the cleaning, most of the laundry and some of the cooking. But without housework as an excuse, she had no reason to go into Jamie's room, no chance to study the framed photograph on his desk. A photograph of his mother.

Glancing over her shoulder at the empty, silent hall behind her, Sally told herself she shouldn't snoop. But as far as she knew, there were no other pictures of Brenda in the house. If there were photo albums somewhere, she hadn't found them.

With a last, furtive look around, she went into the room, stepped over the usual teenage debris of clothes and books and shoes and went straight to the desk.

The pleasant, pretty face that stared up at her had Jamie's hair and eyes and his gentle smile. Brenda wasn't beautiful. She looked nice. That's all. Yet Sally continued looking down at that face until something wet and cold pressed against the back of her calf. Swallowing a scream, she jerked around to find Jamie's dog, Jet, sniffing her leg. And standing in the doorway, there was Jamie, watching her.

She flushed, setting the photograph down quickly, not knowing what to say.

He moved first, stripping off his outer sweatshirt and tossing it in the corner of the room. "Something you want, Sally?"

She took a deep breath. "Jamie, I'm sorry. I just...well..." When in doubt, tell the truth, she told herself. "I just thought I would look at this."

"Yeah?" His gaze shifted to the photograph.

"I guess I was curious," Sally confessed.

"You can't tell much from a picture."

"No." Sally sighed, and after stooping to pet Jet's head, turned to go. "I'm sorry if I intruded in here. This is your room, and I'll respect your privacy from now on."

"You want to know something about her?"

She shook her head.

But Jamie was looking at the picture of his mother and didn't see her response. "She would have liked you," he murmured. Then he flushed and shrugged his shoulders in the way that boys had when they were uncomfortable.

Sally swallowed hard. She had to confess that the unflattering picture she had been painting in her head of Brenda Graham hadn't been of a woman who would have cared anything for the likes of her.

Jamie continued, half to himself. "Mom was neat, you know. She was easygoing about stuff. Not like Dad."

That surprised Sally. Brenda the perfectionist had sounded anything but easygoing. But the boy's assessment of Cotter intrigued her, as well. "You think your Dad's uptight?"

"Majorly."

Sally decided to take a chance and reveal a confidence. "He worries about not being able to talk to you."

Now Jamie looked surprised. "Dad worries about that?"

"Of course."

"Part of the time since Mom died..." Jamie stopped suddenly, as if he realized he was about to reveal something. "Never mind."

"No," Sally said. "What were you going to say?"

The boy took a deep breath. "I guess I kinda think Dad resents me."

She sank down on the edge of his bed. "Oh, Jamie. I can't speak for the time before I knew you guys, but I know that your father really loves you."

"I know he cares . . ."

"But what?"

Jamie sat down at his desk and fiddled with a pencil, not looking at Sally. "Before Mom got sick, Dad wasn't around all that much. He always had to work. He never had time for us. For me, especially."

Sally knew that was true, because Cotter had told her, had said he hadn't been a good husband or father. "He regrets that," Sally told Jamie. "He's tried to make it different here in Willow Creek, hasn't he? Haven't you guys spent a lot more time together?"

"I guess so."

An awful thought struck her. "Then I came along and screwed that up, didn't I?"

Jamie looked up, his denial quick. "I'm glad you guys got married. It kinda surprised me . . . you know . . . with the baby . . ." He flushed again. "It's not the kind of thing a guy expects his dad to do."

"I know," Sally said, flushing herself. God help them, she and Cotter should have been considering the children they already had on the night they created the one she was carrying. They deserved whatever embarrassment or unpleasantness that resulted. But Jamie didn't. "I'm sorry if we've embarrassed you."

"It's okay. I like your being here. You . . ." He wrinkled his nose and grinned. "And even Betsy."

She knew he did. Nothing he had done had made her think otherwise. But she wanted him to understand how much Cotter loved him. "Cut your Dad some slack, okay? He really does care. He's trying to be a little less uptight."

"I'll try," Jamie grumbled, though his good-natured grin remained.

Laughing, and relieved that her snooping had resulted in such a nice talk with him, Sally started to get up from the bed. But again Jamie stopped her.

"I was wondering," he said, slowly, not meeting her gaze. "Have you noticed how weird Lana's being?"

Quite honestly, Sally hadn't noticed much of anything that didn't have to do with herself or Cotter or the kids. Even the predictable stir her marriage had created around town had gone virtually over her head. "What's wrong with Lana?" she said, frowning.

"She's just being strange. It's that guy she likes."

"What guy?"

"Mr. Football."

Sally shook her head. "I don't know who you mean."

"Everybody in this town knows Tyler Franks."

Jamie was right. Tyler Franks was the star quarterback who had guided the Oxford County Hawks to one victory shy of the state championship. A handsome boy, son of the judge who had married Cotter and Sally, Tyler was being courted by a number of colleges. He certainly wasn't the sort of boy Sally would have thought Lana would be interested in. Not that he was out of her league . . . but, well, yes, he was out of her league. Too experienced. And certainly too superficial to appeal to a girl as sensitive and vulnerable as Lana.

"What's she doing?" Sally asked.

But Jamie didn't explain further, just said she was being weird. Sally made a mental note to talk to her.

From the hallway, Cotter spoke. "What's this? Are the two of you plotting something?"

Betsy ducked under his arm, came in and bounced on the bed beside Sally. "It's only two weeks till Christmas. Aren't we going to get a tree?"

"There's an artificial one stored out in the garage," Cotter said.

To Sally, that was heresy. "Artificial?"

Betsy folded her arms across her chest, her bottom lip jutting out. "We always have a real tree. I gave up my room and my house so you guys could get married. I'm not giving up my tree."

Over her head, Cotter's amused gaze met Sally's. "I guess that means we're going tree shopping."

In the end, they got two trees. One for the living room window. One for the family room. Sally did it so that they could mix together all their decorations.

And on the ride to the Christmas tree lot, she also got plenty of information about Brenda Graham. As if her interest in Brenda's photograph had opened a floodgate, Jamie talked freely about his mother. Mostly about holiday traditions Brenda had observed. A special set of crystal ornaments she had collected for the tree. The cookies she had baked. How she had allowed Jamie to open one gift at midnight on Christmas Eve. And the big holiday open house she always hosted for friends and family and Cotter's business associates on the Sunday before Christmas.

Cotter said nothing while Jamie was talking. But the square set of his jaw told Sally he wasn't pleased. Was it still so difficult to talk about Brenda? She didn't think that was healthy, and she was dismayed when, at the tree lot, Cotter pulled Jamie aside for a private word. She was sure he was telling the boy not to talk about his mother to her. It wasn't that she liked hearing what a paragon Brenda had been, but Sally knew Jamie needed to remember his mother, especially at this time of year when emotions were always heightened.

That night, in the privacy of their room, she told Cotter so. "Jamie's talking about Brenda doesn't bother me," she said, trying to sound offhand as she sat at her dressing table brushing her hair.

In the mirror, she could see that Cotter, who had been taking off his shirt, turned to look at her in surprise. "What brought that on?"

"I know you don't want him to talk about her. But he needs to. And I don't mind."

Cotter frowned. He was well aware that Jamie needed to remember his mother. He wanted him to. He just didn't think it was particularly thoughtful for the boy to do it so openly in front of Sally, especially since he had seen the stony expression that Jamie's memories had brought to Sally's face. No matter what she said, it bothered her. And it bothered him that Sally thought she had to sacrifice her own feelings for anyone else's. In his opinion, she had done enough sacrificing in her life.

He finished unbuttoning his shirt, put it in the clothes hamper and reached for the snap of his jeans, still frowning over the problem.

"Cotter?"

He looked up to find Sally still watching him. "What?"

"I understand that you and Jamie might need to talk about Brenda sometimes."

He turned away. "I don't need to talk about her."

The way he closed her out wounded Sally, but she wasn't going to push the issue. There was something else that Jamie's memories had made her think about. "Let's have a party," she told Cotter.

He had stripped off his briefs and was en route to their bathroom, but he turned to face her. "A party?" The teasing light in his eyes told her he was putting a private slant on her suggestion.

She returned his grin. "Is that all you think about?"

He crossed the room, pulled her up from the dressing table chair and into his arms and playfully nuzzled her neck. "Is there anything else?"

"Yes," she murmured, thoroughly enjoying the feel of his mouth moving up her throat. "It's the holidays. You probably should have some people over from the hospital."

He pulled back, his eyebrows drawing together in a frown. "It's not that necessary."

"But it would be appropriate, wouldn't it?"

"Well..."

She stepped away from him, certain she knew what he was thinking. "Listen, I know I don't know anything about this sort of stuff. I know I grew up on the wrong side of the creek—"

"Don't say that," Cotter interrupted.

"But it's true."

"I don't think it makes a difference where you grew up."

"Well, I know I'm not up on social etiquette."

"Sally—"

"But I do know that a party of some sort would be an appropriate thing for the hospital administrator to host. I'm your wife now, and I'm willing to do it."

He hesitated, then shook his head. "Sally, you've got enough to do."

So he didn't think she *could* do it. Probably not as well as Brenda had done it, anyway. Sally's determination strengthened. "Just tell me a date."

"Sally, really—"

But Cotter's protests were to no avail. Sally insisted on an open house to be held the next Sunday. Cotter did everything he could to talk her out of it, but as he had discovered, his wife could be stubborn.

That week, as the house became a hotbed of preparation for an event he didn't particularly want, Cotter couldn't help remembering the parties Brenda had planned and given. Perfectly staged affairs, they had aided him in his career. At the time, he thought them necessary. He didn't now. Just as he didn't care about an immaculate home or Sunday dinner at the country club. He had had all that with Brenda. And it had turned out to be cold, bitter and empty.

He knew that was his fault. He knew his ambition had forced Brenda into the role of a superwife. He knew he had been too demanding. Cotter the Barbarian had reigned at home, as well as at work. He didn't want to make the same mistake with Sally. Yet, here she was, racing around, trying to please him with this party, not believing him when he told her she didn't have to do this sort of thing.

All he wanted was her warmth. He wanted the passion they were able to generate in bed to spill over into the rest of their lives. The past few weeks had been pleasantly surprising. A sense of family had settled on this house. He wanted it to continue. And yet he didn't know how to communicate that to Sally. She became upset and defensive when he protested about the party, about the elaborate Christmas decorations, about the way she was exhausting herself, trying to make this the most memorable holiday any of them had ever seen.

He decided all of this nonsense was what she wanted.

Finally, he let her be, pitched in where he could and hoped for the best.

Chapter Nine

Stacked up against most of the disasters Sally had known in her life, the open house was a minor debacle. It loomed large only because her expectations were so high.

That Sunday morning started badly. It was pouring rain, one of those chilly December rains that encouraged people to stay indoors. The cold Sally had been fighting all week had turned into a sore throat and a fever. While she was arguing with Cotter about going down to the hospital to be checked out, two trays of her special sausage balls baked to hard little bricks in the oven. Later, instead of the welcoming blaze that she had envisioned in the fireplaces, Cotter's best efforts produced only black belches of smoke. And finally, the blue velvet dress Sally intended to wear couldn't even be zipped. It was the worst possible time for her pregnancy to become so apparent. She took half an hour she didn't have to dig up a red skirt and blouse that fit well enough to wear.

Despite those setbacks, they were ready at two o'clock when the festivities were set to begin. Jack and Marianne were already there, but they didn't count as guests. Lana was manning the kitchen, looking astoundingly put together in black slacks and a *matching* sequined sweater. Sally made another mental note to find out what was going on in the girl's life even as she went with Cotter to answer the doorbell.

Predictably, Miss Louella and Miss Clara were the first on the doorstep. But others soon followed. Colleagues of Cotter's for the most part, but some neighbors, too. Others whom Sally had known most of her life. The house was soon bulging.

Sally knew she was on display. She saw the glances that went around the comfortably furnished rooms. Those rooms weren't a real representation of Sally's own taste, but she knew they were attractive. She also knew she had spent far too much money on decorations. There wasn't a corner that wasn't decked with holly, bows or Christmas lights. She saw the sideways looks she got from some of the women. She thought she could hear what those glances said. *That Sally Jane Haskins made herself quite a catch.*

In response, upraised eyebrows asked, *Wonder how?*

Even with those undercurrents, things went well for about half an hour. Then Jet, who was supposed to be penned in the garage until the party was over, somehow got loose and bounded into the dining room before Jamie or Cotter could catch him. He paused to shake his wet fur right beside Miss Louella, who shrieked, startling the woman next to her, who, in turn, upset the nearby punch bowl.

That was minor compared to the pot holder that Lana caught on fire in the kitchen, setting off the fire alarm and causing a near stampede for the door.

Or the fact that Ned Turlow, whose advances Sally had been rebuffing for years, had a few too many bourbon balls and spent most of the afternoon ogling her in full sight of his wife.

Sally was able to laugh most of it off. She was able to avoid the grim I-told-you-so look on Cotter's face. She told herself that these mishaps were things that could happen to any hostess, perhaps even Brenda Graham.

But around four, when the crowd had peaked and was tapering off, the real catastrophe struck. For that's when Jackie Bryant, Cotter's ex-administrative assistant, appeared at the door with her in-laws. Sally braced herself for trouble, while praying it wouldn't come.

But it did.

In the crowded living room, as Sally was handing a cup of punch to an elderly neighbor, Jackie asked, in a bright, loud voice, "When's the baby due, Sally?"

Everything stopped. All movement. All conversation. As had happened so many times in the past, Sally found herself the focus of attention.

Smile frozen on her face, she straightened from her neighbor's side and turned to Jackie. This woman had been waiting since high school to have Sally in a position where she could hurt her. Sally had to admire her timing.

Pretending to be appalled, Jackie continued, "I'd hate to think I was just repeating gossip."

Sally managed a smile, a bright one, she hoped. "Why, Jackie, honey, you'd never gossip, would you?"

A nervous titter ran through the people in the room.

A splash of crimson darkened Jackie's cheeks. "It isn't gossip if it's the truth."

"I suppose you could look at it that way."

"So?"

Sally pretended not to understand. "So what?"

"Are you pregnant?" came the pointedly direct question.

"Why, yes," Sally answered, clinging to her smile for all she was worth. "Yes, I am, Jackie. It's nice of you to ask. Cotter and I are very excited."

"And you're due . . ." Jackie's gaze dropped to Sally's waistline, which suddenly felt as if it were bulging anew. "When did you say?"

"Summer."

"*Early* summer?"

Cotter broke free from the crowd that had clustered in the living room doorway. He had heard just enough of this conversation to know what Jackie was up to. Gaining Sally's side, he slipped an arm around her. "Yes, it's early summer," he said, his defiant gaze moving from Jackie to the rest of the interested bystanders. "Anything else you want to know that's none of your business?"

Sally touched the hand he had clasped to her waist. In warning, he thought, but he shook her off. "Well?" he prompted the sputtering woman who still stood in front of him.

Jackie turned on her heel and left. The room was silent until Marianne came to the rescue with some sort of nonsensical comment that broke the tension. Movement and conversations resumed. And with a furious glare at Cotter, Sally pulled away.

Perplexed by that glare, he started after her, but there were guests who were leaving and wanted to speak to him. People like James and Deanna Kincaid, friends and colleagues whom he didn't want to ignore. Not everyone in this town was cut from the same cloth as Jackie Bryant and her in-laws, who, thankfully, must have slipped out the front door.

Nodding at people who smiled and called her name, Sally made her way through the house. She held her head high, though what she really wanted was a few minutes alone. Incredibly enough the kitchen was empty. So she stood, staring down at the sodden mess in the sink where Lana had earlier thrown the burning pot holder. Sally's head was pounding, her throat was raw and she was angry with herself for thinking she could get through this day without something like this happening.

Of course everyone in town had been wondering how Sally Jane Haskins got Cotter Graham to marry her. Pregnancy would have been one of the possibilities being bandied about by people like Jackie Bryant. Certainly Jamie or Betsy might have told a classmate about the pregnancy, though Cotter and Sally had asked them to wait. The pregnancy wasn't something that was going to be a secret much longer, especially at the rate her stomach had begun to expand. But Jackie was one of the few busybodies Sally knew who had enough gall to come right out and ask when the baby was due. And then Cotter had to—

"Sally Jane?"

The sound of her name made her turn. She was surprised to see Miss Clara and Miss Louella come into the room. The two women had remained throughout all the crises and dramas of the afternoon, and from what Sally had been able to see, they had looked over every nook and cranny of the house. She wondered if she would find white gloves covered in dust tucked away in the neat purses that hung from their arms.

Miss Clara spoke first, her thin lips wrapping distinctly around each word. "We wanted to talk with you for a minute, Sally Jane."

"To congratulate you," Miss Louella added, with her characteristic girlish laugh.

"Congratulate me?" Sally repeated, wondering where this was going.

"On the party," Miss Clara said.

Miss Louella's third chin wobbled as she nodded her head. "This was just lovely."

"And you've got yourself quite a handsome husband," Miss Clara pronounced. "Successful, too, from the looks of things."

They should know, Sally thought, since she was sure they had done everything but find the bank account book and go through it. She managed a smile. "Thank you, ma'am."

"And you're having a baby, too," Miss Clara said.

Instantly Sally was on her guard, but she wasn't about to apologize or get angry as Cotter had. He didn't understand that the best defense was to pretend it didn't matter what people said or thought. "Yes, ma'am, we are having a baby," she said, with a broad smile. "Isn't it wonderful?"

"Yes," Miss Clara said. "I think it is."

"Yes, indeed," her sister agreed.

Their sincerity was impossible to doubt. Sally gaped at them in surprise.

Miss Clara drew herself up to her full height. "*Some* people in this town have ugly minds, Sally Jane."

She almost choked.

"They're malicious," Miss Louella put in. "And downright tacky, too. Of course, that Jackie Bryant has never known any better. Her folks moved here from up *north.*" The word was whispered, as if that place was too horrible to be contemplated. "Sally Jane, Jackie has been jealous of you since that summer you—"

"Sister," Miss Clara interrupted. "Does any of that really bear repeating?"

Amazingly Miss Louella flushed. "No, Sister, I guess it doesn't. The main thing is that our Sally Jane is doing very well for herself. Even though she has made the Dairy Bar so appealing that my diner lost some customers, I can't be mad."

"Not at all," Miss Clara said. "It's good to see a young woman making something of herself. We just hope your marriage doesn't mean that you're abandoning your efforts at restoring Clementine McAllister's house. It's much too important a structure to let sit empty for long, my dear."

Their Sally Jane stood in mute shock, barely able to say goodbye when they bustled out the door. She was still immobilized when Marianne found her.

"Are you okay?" the other woman asked.

"All I can say is that the minister over at the First Baptist Church must have delivered a doozie of a sermon this morning on the evils of gossip."

"Huh?"

Sally told Marianne about the comments of the "Misses."

"You're set for life now," Marianne pronounced, laughing. "They have conferred their official seal of approval. Just wait until Jackie Bryant finds out you're in and she's out."

"I don't care what Jackie Bryant says or does," Sally said. "Or whether I'm in, out or sideways." She pushed away from the kitchen counter and walked toward the door. If people were to believe she didn't care, she needed to stop hiding in the kitchen.

Marianne said, "Nobody would have blamed you if you had whacked Jackie across the mouth."

"Oh, yeah, that would have gone over big, wouldn't it?" With a last grin for her friend, Sally rejoined the party, where most of the guests were on the way out the door.

No one said a word about Jackie's confrontation or about the baby, but Sally could guess what would be a hot topic around the supper tables tonight. She studiously avoided meeting Cotter's gaze. He was playing the perfect host, but she knew him well enough by now to read the meaning behind the tight lines around his mouth.

When everyone was finally gone, she was exhausted. But there was still work to be done, so she started through the rooms, picking up discarded plates and cups.

In the dining room, Cotter took all of them out of her hands. "You're going to bed," he said firmly. "You've got a terrible cold, and you've worked yourself to death over this."

"The house is a wreck."

"I can get the worst of it now, and the housekeeper will be in tomorrow to finish things up."

"The kids are going to want dinner."

"I've already sent Jamie and Betsy off with Lana to get a pizza. You belong in bed."

Truthfully, the only place Sally wanted to be was in bed, but she was still irritated enough by his interference with Jackie to want to argue with him now. Stubbornly she went back to stacking plates. "Don't pull the barbarian routine with me. I'm not too sick to clean up *my* house." It seemed somehow imperative to assert her possession. She was daring Brenda Graham's ghost to show her gloating, satisfied presence after today's chaotic excuse for a party.

"All right," Cotter muttered, setting his stacked plates on the dining room table with a clatter. "Go ahead. Don't let me help you. Get mad. Just like you did when I tried to help you with Jackie Bryant."

"That wasn't necessary."

He planted both hands on his hips, demanding, "So I'm supposed to just stand there while she insults my wife?"

"I was handling it."

"Yeah, you were handling it," he retorted with heavy sarcasm.

Anger was pumping through her veins. "I should remind you that I have a lot more experience with this sort of thing than you do. People have always been interested in the gory details of my life."

"So you just stand there, smiling, and give in to her holier-than-thou nosiness?"

She spread her arms wide. "What was I supposed to do? Lie? Tell her I'm not pregnant?"

"You should have told her straight out to mind her own damn business."

Now it was Sally's turn for sarcasm. "Like that would have been the end of it."

"Who cares?"

"Obviously you do. Otherwise you wouldn't want me to hide the truth."

"For God's sake," Cotter muttered, adding another, more profane curse for good measure. "Sally, I don't want you to hide anything."

"Except my pregnancy. I'm not ashamed to be pregnant, Cotter. I'm not going to lie about this child."

"Fine," he bit out. "I just don't like seeing you hurt, that's all. That's why we shouldn't have even had this party."

"Because I screwed it up?"

"Of course not," he said, though she didn't believe him. Today had fallen so far short of perfection that he would have to be an idiot not to compare it to the elegant parties Jamie had told her Brenda used to arrange.

"You didn't screw anything up," Cotter continued. "We shouldn't have had the party because someone like Jackie Bryant was bound to say something that would hurt you. You don't owe any of these people anything, not an explanation, not an excuse."

"I know that," she protested.

"Then why did you feel compelled to answer that stupid woman's questions?"

"Denying my pregnancy wouldn't have ended the talk, Cotter, especially considering that I'm probably going to be big as a house before spring. Willow Creek might be a backwater, but even here, folks don't buy those stories about nine pound seven-month babies."

"None of that matters."

"People are going to believe what they want to believe. Why not just tell them the truth, especially when it's exactly what they expected, anyway?"

"That makes no sense at all."

"No one will be very surprised to hear that you married me because I was pregnant. It's what people expect from me. All I did today was end the speculation."

"Oh, is that the deal?" he asked, his voice sharp. "Do you always do the expected? Is that why you cultivate this image as the town's scarlet woman? Are you just satisfying some predetermined image?"

"I am always just myself, Cotter."

"But who you are, at least the you that I know, is not some local girl gone bad from the wrong part of town. That's not you."

"It's part of me."

"I don't see that part."

"Maybe you choose not to see what you don't like."

He caught her arm as she spun away. "What does that mean?"

"Just that I am where I came from, Cotter. I am that little girl, with a drunk for a father and a tramp for a mother. The girl who went to school in hand-me-downs picked off of church rummage-sale racks. I am the girl from high school who all the guys said would *do it* on a dare."

Cotter's face hardened. "They only said it. I know you weren't that way."

She managed a laugh as she pulled her arm from his grasp. "I wonder if you would have known that back then. Back when I was this child in a woman's body, a child who was desperate for somebody to think I was special, desperate for someone to love me."

Horror came to his face. "Sally..." he began.

He was afraid, she thought, afraid of what she might have been, what she might have done. "Oh, don't worry," she told him through the sob that built in her throat. "My search for love ended pretty fast, before I could do much more than lose my virginity. It isn't my fault that some immature males like to boast. It isn't my fault that other men lie when they haven't anything of truth to brag about. It's amazing what folks will believe about you when you grow up in a tin-roofed shack."

He stepped forward, his hands gripping her upper arms. "Sally, stop this. I don't—"

"You don't want to know?" she asked, tears burning in her eyes. "You don't want to understand why the woman you married gets herself talked about?"

Holding her tears at bay, she told him about the bullet holes in the wall at the Dairy Bar, put there by a misguided admirer who wanted to prove his manhood by waving a gun around. That incident brought the mothers and fathers of the kids who hung around her place out in droves to denounce her. If a few good people, like Jack, hadn't stood up for her, she would have gone under. Then there was the jealous wife who had slashed her tires last spring and threatened to do worse. All Sally had done to earn that was lend a sympathetic ear to a husband who was upset because he thought the wife was cheating on *him*.

Cotter stood there, his hands dropping away from her shoulders, his expression unreadable as he listened.

"You want more?" she asked finally, looking up at him. "I've got plenty of stories that don't need gossip to embellish them." Pretending to be deep in thought, she tapped her forehead. "Let's see, I would tell you about being hoodwinked by my sister and my lover. But, gee, you already know that one, don't you?"

His expression softened. "That's right, Sally, I know about that. I know how your sister and that creep hurt you. You can pretend to be tough about it, but I know the truth."

She managed a shrug. "I should have known it would happen. No one but me was surprised."

"You sound as if you think you deserved it."

"Everyone said I did."

"They're all idiots."

"Are they? Most of these people have known me for my whole life compared to the four months you've been around. Who would know me better?"

He stood there, saying nothing.

Her gray eyes held a sad, resigned look. "It gives you something to think about, doesn't it?"

Cotter opened his mouth to protest when the front door opened, admitting Jamie, Lana and Betsy.

"Hey," his son called from the entry foyer. "We got pizza here for anyone who wants it."

And with that, the opportunity to pursue this argument with Sally was lost. Finally giving in to a headache and sore throat, she went up to bed right after eating half a slice of pizza. She was asleep by the time Cotter had settled Betsy for the night and made a start on the mess from the party.

In the morning, there was this remoteness between them, the distance he had been dreading.

A dozen times over the next few days he wanted to reach out to her, to begin the discussion again, to explain some of the things he thought she had misunderstood. Especially the nonsense about hiding her pregnancy. He wasn't ashamed she was pregnant. He just didn't want the narrow-minded hypocrites of this town judging or ridiculing her. But somehow that had come out all wrong.

And then she had hurled all that stuff at him about her past. As if to shock him or drive him away. Surely she already knew he didn't care about her past. He deplored the way she had been hurt. He sensed there was even more pain in her past than she had admitted. He admired the way she had made something of herself, despite the expectations people had of her. But she seemed to anticipate him judging her in the same way this town did.

Only one point of what she had said had any merit. That was about his not really knowing her. For now, more than ever, he realized they were really only strangers, drawn together by passion and bound by a child they had created by accident. When you stripped their relationship down to its barest form, that's really all there was.

He had begun to realize that he wanted more.

Before the party, Cotter thought there might actually be more growing between them, much more happening in the family they had formed. But now Sally seemed angry and hurt, and even the passion they had shared was gone. And he didn't know what to do.

Tension settled over the entire household.

Sally spent the week of Christmas battling her lingering cold. That, as much as the scene with Cotter, left her feeling out of sorts.

She wasn't sure why she had gotten quite so angry with him. She felt like he was ashamed of her. Why else had he wanted her to avoid revealing the truth about the child she carried? And then there was the party itself, that horrible party. It didn't matter what Miss Clara and Miss Louella had told her or the admiring phone calls she had received about it from rather unexpected sources, like Dr. Kincaid's wife. In Sally's eyes, it had fallen far short of her expectations and her intentions.

Christmas felt just as awkward. The robe she had chosen for Cotter seemed trivial in comparison to the beautiful diamond and pearl earrings he gave her. She was sick and didn't feel like cooking, so he prepared most of their holiday meal. He got Betsy and Jamie involved, and they spent half the day in the kitchen, laughing and dirtying every pot. Cotter said he enjoyed it. But Sally felt inadequate. She wasn't the wife Cotter wanted. She wasn't the person he loved. If she weren't pregnant, he probably never would have spoken to her again.

The one bright spot during the holidays was another visit from Cotter's sister, Susannah. Tall and thin like Jamie, with a face that was a feminine version of her brother's, Susannah was refreshingly honest and blunt. She taught art in one of Atlanta's toughest school districts and loved the challenge. She was also very perceptive.

On New Year's Day, she and Sally sat in front of the living room fire, talking, while Cotter and the kids watched bowl games in the next room. Sally, who was feeling worse than ever, was wrapped in the quilt her grandmother had made, her inner self wrapped in self-pity.

"It's been a rough start for the two of you, hasn't it?" Susannah said when a lull fell in their conversation.

Sally could have pretended not to understand what Cotter's sister was talking about, but she supposed it would take someone without any command of their senses not to see that all was not right in this household. "No, it hasn't been easy," she admitted.

"Cotter can be a flat-out mystery, can't he?"

The criticism surprised Sally, but she agreed. "Most of the time I don't know what he's thinking. He doesn't share much."

"He's always been that way. I think Mom and I did it to him. The two of us always just poured our troubles out on his shoulders. He got used to listening to our problems and didn't share many of his own feelings."

Sally took a deep breath and asked what was most on her mind. "Was he the same way with Brenda?"

"Probably worse."

"You're kidding? I thought—"

"—that they had this perfect marriage?" Susannah laughed. "Not by a long shot. That's the thing about when people die young. The ones they leave behind tend to edit out all the flaws." She shook her head, turning to stare into the fire. "Don't get me wrong. Brenda was a good person. I liked her. But I don't think Cotter opened up any more to her than he's ever done with anyone else. I don't think they were so incredibly close or happy. That's just an opinion, of course. He would never discuss that with me."

Sally was shocked. "He seems to have loved her very much."

"Maybe he did," Susannah murmured. "In his own way."

They fell silent for a moment. Sally was turning the new information about Brenda in her mind. For the first time, she thought the two of them might have had something in common.

Finally Susannah spoke again. "There's one thing you have to remember about my brother, Sally. That's how seriously he takes his responsibilities. When we were kids, he was in charge of me most of the time, because Mom was always working. And he worked hard, and he had goals, and he never, ever, to my knowledge, ever failed at any of them. He never backed away from a challenge that I knew of. And he never shirked on his obligations."

Sally didn't think Cotter had changed much. The man his sister described didn't sound like someone who would turn his back on a woman carrying his child, no matter what the cost to his personal happiness. More than ever, she knew he had felt trapped into this marriage.

And she didn't want that. She didn't want him to remain married to her out of obligation. They had to talk.

She planned the conversation for hours on the day after New Year's. She was so sick that she could hardly hold her head up, but she forced herself into the Dairy Bar and plotted and planned that night's discussion with Cotter over and over.

But when she dragged herself into the house that night, she didn't have the energy for any big, emotional scene.

Cotter, who had been on her back for two weeks about going to the doctor, fussed and fumed around the kitchen while she forced down some of the soup the housekeeper had left on the stove.

"It's just a cold," she told him, just as she had been telling him all along.

"But you're pregnant."

"Exactly. Even if I go to the doctor, I can't take any medication. I have an appointment with my gynecologist next week. If I'm still feeling bad, he'll do something."

But Cotter didn't want to wait. Sally was in terrible shape, a horrendous rattle in her chest, her eyes red and streaming. Finally making up his mind, he stalked to the phone and punched in the number of the hospital emergency room. Someone was going to see her tonight. Before anyone answered on the other end, he turned to Sally. Just in time to see her slump over her bowl of soup.

Chapter Ten

Sally woke up disoriented. The last thing she remembered was driving home from the Dairy Bar, determined to have it out with Cotter. But here she was in a bedroom filled with the gray light of dawn. Not her bedroom at her house. Not the bedroom she shared with Cotter.

"Hey, you're awake."

Turning her head, she saw Cotter unfolding stiffly from a chair beside the bed. She opened her mouth to speak, but her mouth was too dry.

"They said you could have this," Cotter said, pouring some water from a plastic pitcher into a cup.

That's when Sally realized she was in the hospital. Blinking, she gazed up at the IV bottle hanging over the bed. And a cold dread swept through her.

"The baby," she croaked despite the cottony feel of her mouth. "What about our baby?"

"Our baby's fine," Cotter said, approaching the bed. Gently he helped her raise her head and take a sip of water.

"You're sure?" Sally said when she was through. "The baby's okay?"

He set the empty cup aside. "No problems. But you've got a severe case of bronchitis, complicated by exhaustion and dehydration. They're going to fix you up."

"I can't take anything to hurt the baby."

He stroked her cheek, tenderly, the way he used to touch her before that disastrous party. "I promise you nothing they're doing is going to hurt the baby."

She lay back, eyes closed against the tears that were gathering. They seeped out, anyway, running down her cheeks.

"Oh, Sally," Cotter murmured. "Don't cry. It's going to be okay. You're going to be okay."

"But I just screw everything up, don't I?"

"You've just been trying to do too much with the holidays and all. You got too run down."

Sniffing, she looked up at him again. "I'm so sorry."

"You've got nothing to be sorry about."

"I just feel so inadequate, you know. I want everything to be right. With us. And with the baby."

"It will be."

His face began to fade from focus. Sally's words felt as if they came from far, far away. "Don't let me lose our baby, Cotter. I don't want to lose you."

Struck by the significance of those words, Cotter watched Sally drift back to sleep. If she lost the baby, she thought she would lose him. Was that true?

He sank back into the chair again, staring at her white, still face. She looked so ill, so fragile.

Curling one hand into a fist, he slammed it against the other palm. *Damnation*, he should have made her go to the doctor. He shouldn't have let the strain that had sprung up between them get in the way of his responsibility to her and their child. But he had. And here she lay, so still and so sick.

Cotter supposed he had been frightened before in his life. Like the day he realized his father was never coming home. Again, when his mother died. The day the doctor had told him and Brenda that her cancer was fatal. But he had never felt terror as sharp and sudden as that which had hit him when Sally passed out over her bowl of soup at the kitchen table.

Since he already had the emergency room on the phone, he simply told them he was on the way. That seemed quicker than waiting for an ambulance. Sally had roused a little when he and Jamie carried her out to the Bronco. But she had slipped back into unconsciousness quickly. Cotter had put Jamie in the back seat, to hold Sally up, while Betsy rode up front with him. He didn't relish frightening either of them, but they were already scared. He thought having them with him was better than leaving them at home to wait for a phone call.

At the hospital, Sally was rushed inside. And then they all had sat, for what seemed an interminable age, but was really only an hour or so. Cotter tried to send the kids up to his office where they would be more comfortable, but they refused.

At one point, Betsy climbed onto his lap, her brown eyes, normally so merry, very wide and fearful. As always, she had been a good little trooper, disarmingly adult in some respects. "Don't worry," she told Cotter. "Mom's going to be okay."

Her brave attempt to cheer him was touching. "Sure she is," he whispered. "You're right." But he pressed his face to her hair, inhaling her sweet, little-girl scent and prayed he wasn't lying. Sally was all Betsy had.

And yet she wasn't, he realized with sudden, amazing clarity. For Betsy had him and Jamie, too. Just like her mother, she had become an important part of their lives.

He looked up to find Jamie regarding him with the same fear that Cotter had in his heart. Jamie was probably staring down some particularly frightening memories right now. His involvement with hospital waiting rooms hadn't been too uplifting.

Cotter forced himself to smile. "It's going to be okay, you guys. Sally'll be fine."

And she was. The doctor on duty had come out to them then, explaining her condition. Her gynecologist appeared shortly thereafter, to examine her and reassure Cotter that the baby was in no danger at this point.

Cotter had called and asked Jack Dylan to take the kids home. Perhaps he imagined it, but there seemed to be an accusatory light in the other man's eyes when he arrived. But he had said nothing. In truth, there weren't any words that could make Cotter feel worse than he did.

He had sat here all night, watching Sally sleep and praying she would be fine. That their child would be fine. And his other prayer was only a minor variation on the wish she had murmured to him.

Don't let her lose our baby. Because I don't want to lose her.

That was still the wish in his heart. He knew their baby was the only thing holding them together right now. Without the baby, she might well walk out of his life. He wanted them to build on the connection the baby had formed between them. What they might build, he didn't know. He didn't have a clue as to how to build on it. But he knew he wanted to try.

Sally didn't lose the baby. She came home from the hospital three days after her collapse, with strict instructions to rest for a couple of weeks. Her gynecologist was very specific in his directions. She hadn't endangered her child so far, but she would if she didn't take better care of herself. She had been perilously close to pneumonia. To ward it off, she needed some real rest. That meant no work. Very little stress.

Though the housekeeper was there if she needed anything, Cotter took the day off after bringing her home. She had slept most of the time she was in the hospital. The two of them hadn't exchanged much more than updates on her condition. But he was very solicitous now.

He had red roses waiting in a vase on her dressing table, and those were in addition to the ones he had sent to the hospital. He hovered around, plumping her pillow, seeming to understand that merely the ride home had worn her out. He was full of reassurances about the Dairy Bar. He had made arrangements with her young assistant manager, whose winter term at college didn't begin for another week, to cover most of the shifts that Sally normally worked herself. Several of her other employees said they didn't mind pulling some overtime.

Satisfied that Cotter had taken care of everything, Sally went to sleep. When she awoke, he was right at her side, offering juice and magazines. Then he stationed himself in an easy chair in the corner of their bedroom, his laptop computer on his knees, while she drifted off still again. Jet, who had rarely consented to more than a rub on the head from Sally before this, stretched across the foot of her bed. And when the kids came home, they stayed in the room with her, as well. Betsy snuggled in beside her to do her homework. Jamie sprawled on the floor, watching television while he worked algebra problems.

Sally realized that anyone who might happen by this scene would think them a picture postcard perfect blended family. A stranger might not see the frayed edges. But she felt them. And she wanted more than this polite and solicitous man for her husband. She wanted him to be kind to her for reasons much deeper than duty.

Nothing had really changed, she thought. She and Cotter still needed to confront the fact that a marriage based on obligation wasn't the sort of marriage that would last. Only Sally didn't have the energy it took to talk to him about it. She was so tired. For days she continued to spend most of her time sleeping. When she was awake, she read and watched television, two daytime luxuries she had never had time for in the past. She finally also had the time she needed to go through an old box of papers and books that had been found in one of the unfinished upstairs rooms at her house.

On Monday morning, the week after getting out of the hospital, she had just made a startling discovery among those books when Marianne poked her head around the edge of Sally's door. "Look at you," she said. "Still in bed. Man, that looks like the life to me. Being the mother of three and a newspaperwoman to boot, I don't know anything about such luxury."

Laughing, Sally stretched. "Contrary to popular myth around here, I have never spent this much time on my back, either."

"Sally!" Marianne exclaimed in mock horror as she sat down in the easy chair that was pulled close to the bed. "How you do talk."

"Speaking of popular myths," Sally said, holding up an old yellowing book. "You're never going to guess what I discovered about the illustrious Clementine McAllister."

"The woman who built your house?"

"The finest woman ever to walk the streets of Willow Creek, according to Miss Louella and Miss Clara." Sally giggled at her choice of words. "Well, she wasn't exactly a streetwalker, but she wasn't quite the angel she's been portrayed as, either."

"What do you mean?"

"This is one of her journals." Sally handed the book to Marianne. "It seems she had a flaming, thirty-year affair with one of the town's first mayors. He was, I might add, a deacon in the very church Miss Louella and Miss Clara attend today."

Marianne quickly scanned some of the pages of the book. Her blue eyes were dancing with mischief when she looked up. "Oh, my lord, Sally. Do you think this book is genuine?"

"I've got some deeds and other documents here that have Clementine's signature on them. From what I can tell, the handwriting matches."

"That would be easy enough to authenticate, I suppose."

Sally could see that wheels were turning in Marianne's mind. "What are you thinking about?"

"Just that this little bit of trivia might make a terrific feature for the paper."

"You think people really want to read about someone who has been dead this long?"

"Sally, dear girl," Marianne retorted, shaking her head. "You of all people should know that scandals, even old ones, are always of interest."

Sally had to agree. "The only thing I hate is that Miss Louella and Miss Clara are going to be so shocked."

"Serves them right."

"Now, now, they were here to see me just yesterday. They even brought a crock of chicken noodle soup."

"Big deal," Marianne pronounced. "Those two women don't deserve your being nice to them, Sally."

"They're just two old biddies."

"Two old biddies who have gossiped about everyone in this town. Why, when Jack and I were getting together, they nearly drove me insane."

"You had been off in Washington. You had forgotten the interest that small-town folks show in one another's affairs."

Marianne snorted, rather indelicately. "You need to stop making excuses for people who treat you badly."

"Now you sound like Cotter."

"Hah! He's a fine one to talk."

"What does that mean?" Sally asked.

But her friend just pursed her lips and returned to talking about the long-time citizens of Willow Creek. It was a subject guaranteed to get her dander up. "I've always hated the divisions in this town, the outmoded economic and class distinctions perpetuated by small-minded snobs."

"It's just the way it's always been."

"Stop it," Marianne ordered. "Stop excusing bad behavior. You always do that. And you deserve more than that."

"Marianne—"

"No, now listen to me." Marianne's expression was quite serious as she sat forward in the chair. "For years I've watched you let people walk all over you."

"But that's not true."

"You know it is. You've let people, like Jackie Bryant, look down their noses at you. When it should really be the other way around. With all you've done in your life for other people, you're twice the person she or anyone else is."

Sally was embarrassed. "Marianne, I haven't done anything."

"What about being a mother to Betsy?"

"She was part of my family. Loving her was easy."

"Considering what Renee did to you, few people would have faulted you if you decided you couldn't take her child in."

"That's not true. Anyone—"

"Just shut up and let me finish, okay? I've been wanting you to know how much I admire you for a long time now."

"Don't, please—"

"You've done so much for the kids who hang out at the Dairy Bar."

Sally's laugh was dry. "There are some people who like to think I've corrupted a few."

"Those people are stupid. I wonder how many kids you've kept on the right track, just by being there and being willing to listen to their problems. What about Craig? He wouldn't be in college if you hadn't given him a job, if you didn't work around his hours? And there's Lana, too—"

Her cheeks flaming, Sally protested, "Please stop painting me as some kind of saint."

"You're not a saint. That's the point," Marianne said earnestly. "You're just a person, a very nice person, who should be treated with the proper respect. It makes me angry when you act as if you don't deserve that respect."

For a moment, Sally just looked at her. She realized, of course, that Marianne was right. She had made excuses for others. Even played into their low expectations, as Cotter had told her. And she did deserve more than that. Much more. Oh, she might have been telling herself for years that it didn't matter what people thought, but that had been an ill-disguised lie. The truth was that she had been hurt badly by the lies and speculation about her. In her struggle for the self-respect that she valued so highly, it hadn't been easy to face the disdain of others. Maybe it was time, as Marianne suggested, that she stop letting people get away with hurting her.

The atmosphere in the room was so intense that it had to be diffused. So she grinned at her friend. "Golly, Marianne, if I'm ever running for public office, I'll have to appoint you my campaign manager."

Smiling also, Marianne left her chair and settled beside Sally against the pillows. She gave her a playful little dig in the side. "Anytime you need a cheerleader, I'll be here."

"Thanks."

"I just hope Cotter Graham appreciates you as much as the rest of us do."

"He's been very nice these past few days."

"And is that enough?"

Sally studied Marianne in surprise. "What do you mean?"

The other woman took a deep breath, then plunged ahead. "I mean, are you happy with him, Sally?"

There was no avoiding Marianne's sharp gaze. From the beginning, from that first day in the park when she caught Sally and Cotter together, she had seen how Sally reacted to him. It was Marianne who had asked, that night that

Cotter proposed, if Sally loved him. And she had looked as if she knew the answer.

Releasing a deeply held breath, Sally said, "He doesn't love me."

"Then he's a fool."

"But I'm not the sort of woman he was looking for."

"He told you that?"

"From what I've heard, I'm not much like his first wife."

"So?"

"So she was great, okay? I mean, his sister says they weren't all that happy, but I'm not sure. He used his wife as an excuse not to get involved with me at first. And then, of course, I got pregnant." Sally closed her eyes. "God, Marianne. He was trapped into marrying me."

"That's nonsense. In this day and age, a baby on the way isn't necessarily a prelude to marriage."

"For men like Cotter it is."

Marianne sat for a minute, then said, "I guess you're right. Jack is the same sort of dinosaur, the kind of man who believes in honor and doing the right thing. But would you or I love either Jack or Cotter if they weren't that sort of man?"

"Of course not," Sally admitted.

"And you and I are the sort of women who fight for what we want."

Sally closed her eyes. "I can't make him love me, Marianne."

"He's halfway there."

"You don't know that."

"Listen to me. I was at the hospital. I saw how upset he was."

"He feels responsible for me, for the baby—"

"Oh, hogwash," Marianne interjected. "Here you go again, making excuses, settling for half of what you deserve. You deserve all Cotter has to give, Sally. You should demand it all."

That was fine talk. But harder to put into practice.

That night when Cotter came home, Sally wanted to make the sort of demands Marianne said she deserved to make. She wanted his love. But for someone who had lived most of her life without that tender emotion, just asking for it was nearly impossible. At the same time, the need to show him her love was strong.

Cotter had been sleeping on the sofa in his study so that Sally could rest better, but he had fallen into the habit of watching television with her in the bedroom before turning in. Tonight, when he rose to leave, she stopped him.

"You don't have to sleep down there, you know."

He gave her a long, considering look. Until this week without her beside him, he hadn't realized how used he had become to the soft curves of her body in his arms at night. Oh, he knew mutual passion was the one sure thing in their relationship. But he couldn't help but believe it muddied the issue, as well, kept them from focusing on the other aspects. They had come together in a fever and married in haste. Maybe he should try not sleeping with Sally for a little longer. Maybe they should concentrate on getting to know each other.

"Cotter?" she said now, her smile deepening as she patted the bed beside her.

"You should rest," he told her.

The light went out of her eyes. Her cheeks flamed. "Okay."

"Sally," he murmured, sitting down on the edge of the bed. "Don't be hurt."

She was picking up the old book she had laid aside, pointedly not looking at him. "I said that's fine."

"Sally, please—"

The knock at the bedroom door cut him short. Cotter wondered, for not the first time, how couples with children ever found any privacy.

Sally looked relieved by the interruption as she called, "Come in."

Jamie stepped in the door, wearing a jacket that dripped water onto the rug. Obviously he had just come in out of the cold and rainy January night.

Looking at his watch, Cotter frowned. He had thought Jamie was in his room. "Kind of late for a school night, isn't it, son?"

"Dad, please—"

"Now, Jamie—"

"Dad," the boy cut in. "I've got a problem, okay?"

For the first time, Cotter noticed the frightened look in the boy's eyes. He stood. "What's wrong? You haven't been in an accident, have you?"

Jamie shook his head, opened his mouth to speak, but nothing came out.

Sally swung out of bed, too. "Jamie, what's the matter?"

"It's Lana," he said finally. "She's downstairs, and she..."

"She what?" Cotter prompted.

There was misery in the eyes Jamie focused on Sally. "Some guy raped her."

Chapter Eleven

Sally went with Cotter to take Lana to the hospital. He wanted her to stay at home in bed, but she wouldn't, couldn't. Lana needed her.

The boy who had attacked her had been her date, a football player she had gone out with in a vain attempt to attract the attention of Tyler Franks. Like Tyler, the boy came from a well-off Willow Creek family.

"I didn't even really like him," Lana told Sally in the examination room. The doctors and nurses had taken their samples of blood and semen and looked at the bruises on Lana's body. Now they were waiting for the police. Cotter had gone out to try and find Lana's mother.

Gripping the girl's hand, Sally said, "Why go out with him, then?"

Lana's red-rimmed eyes filled with tears. "He's a friend of Tyler's. And I just..." She shook her head, obviously not quite sure of the logic that had led to this night.

"You were trying to make Tyler jealous?"

The girl's laughter was an empty, hollow sound. "Jealous? God, Sally, I was just trying to make him notice me. He would never be jealous over someone like me."

"Don't talk that way about yourself."

"But it's true. Tonight, when I said no, when I tried to stop everything, Jason told me I was getting what I had been asking for. He said they'd all been taking bets on who would get me first."

Ugly memories rose with bile in Sally's throat. She knew, as perhaps few others could, exactly what Lana had endured tonight.

The police arrived for questioning at about the same time Cotter came in with the news that Lana's mother hadn't been home, and the other children didn't know where she was.

The officer in charge, a woman, and a juvenile authority, questioned Lana, allowing Sally to stay with her. They were kind, but pulled no punches in telling Lana that date rape wasn't easy to prove. Evidence that Lana had engaged in sexual intercourse was there, and there were bruises to support her claim that she had been forced. But it was still a close call. The boy would no doubt say she liked it rough.

Lana said she didn't care. "He forced me," she told the officer. "He hurt me, and I think he should pay for that."

Feeling proud of Lana's stance but knowing the worst was yet to come, Sally went to get Cotter so that they could take Lana home with them for the night.

It didn't take long for the news to spread through the community. The boy was eighteen, of legal age, and his arrest was noted on the local radio station that morning, along with the rest of the police docket. Rape wasn't an everyday fact of life in this town. At least not an out-in-the-open fact. That this boy was a stand-out athlete in a football-crazy town made it even bigger news. The identity of rape victims was supposed to be private, but in a town like Willow Creek, the information was soon bandied about. It didn't help matters that Lana lived north of the creek.

The phone lines were soon humming. Sally took several calls before she turned on the answering machine. Lana spent the day sitting on the end of the couch, worrying more about her brothers and sisters, who had spent the night alone after her mother didn't come home, than about what she was about to face. Sally knew that was only temporary.

Cotter had gone out early in the morning to try and locate Lana's mother again. By noon he called to say he was out of places to look and was going to the office.

Jamie came home from school with a black eye and the news that everyone was talking about what had happened. Sally didn't need to guess where his black eye had come from. She knew the town had taken sides, some believing Lana, most not. Of course, Jamie had stood up for his friend. Some of Cotter's ideas about honor and responsibility had rubbed off on his son.

When he arrived home from the office, Cotter surveyed that eye with something like satisfaction. "I hope whoever gave you that looks pretty bad, too."

They shared a moment of masculine understanding. "Count on it, Dad."

Lana wasn't so happy to learn there were some people who thought she was lying, who said she had been coming on to this boy and to Tyler Franks and others for months. The full impact of what she was doing was beginning to sink in. It was one thing to say she wanted the boy punished, to endure what it would take to make that happen was another matter entirely.

Lana's mother, Mitzi Sanders, didn't show up until that night, and she didn't help. Standing in the kitchen in a cheap cloth coat, her eyes world-weary and accusing, she told her daughter, "That boy and his rich parents and their fancy lawyers will chew you up and spit you out."

Sally couldn't sit still for this woman to browbeat Lana. "She wants to make him pay for what he did."

"I'm sure they will pay," Mitzi retorted. "I bet they'll pay a bundle to make this all go away."

"Yes, I'm sure they will," Sally said. "But settling for money won't really help Lana."

Mitzi laughed. "You may have forgotten what it's like not to have money, seeing as how you got yourself over here on this side of the creek with a nice house and a la-di-da husband. But things are still the same as they've always been on the other side of town, Sally Jane Haskins. I think it's about time you stopped filling Lana's head with your high notions."

Cotter, who until this moment had been standing silently by, stepped forward. "Mrs. Sanders, I don't think Sally has anything to do with this—"

"Don't she? Ain't she the one who's talked Lana into charging this boy with rape."

"That was Lana's decision," Sally replied hotly. "And you should be proud of her for wanting to stand up for herself."

"Proud? You've got to be kid—"

"Mother, just stop," Lana said, suddenly getting up from the table. "This isn't about Sally. She didn't convince me to do anything. She's never given me any notions that I didn't already have myself."

"Well, there's one notion you're going to drop," Mitzi said, wagging a finger in the girl's face for emphasis. "I'm going to see this boy's father, we're going to get some money out of this and you're going to shut your trap about it."

"Mother—"

"Now get your stuff and come home," Mitzi said so forcefully that Lana scrambled out of the room to comply.

But Sally didn't want that. She stepped in front of the woman, pleading, "Mitzi, please, let her stay with us."

"No way."

Sally took another tack. "I could go to the authorities, you know, report how you left all your kids alone for the past forty-eight hours."

Mitzi didn't back down. Eyes narrowed, posture threatening, she said, "You do that and we'll see what kind of trouble I can make for you."

Cotter took Sally's arm. "Let her go," he said.

"But, Cotter—"

"Let her go." He took Sally by the shoulders. "This isn't going to help Lana."

"But she'll talk her out of prosecuting that boy."

"No, she won't."

And in the end, Lana went home with her mother.

Sally was furious with Cotter for his interference. "Lana should have stayed with us."

"I think you've done all you can to help her."

Speechless, Sally stared at him, remembering the way he had cursed the people who hadn't stepped in to help her and Renee when they were children. Those were just words, she thought, merely words. "I can't believe you want me to leave Lana's fate up to her mother."

"I feel very sorry for her, but I'm more concerned for you."

"Me?"

"I don't want you having to fight that girl's battles. Until yesterday, you were still in bed, remember?"

"I'm feeling fine."

"Probably just about good enough to have a relapse."

Sally was feeling a little weak around the knees, but she didn't feel she could desert Lana. Cotter wasn't going to help her, obviously. But that was really no surprise. They were so out of tune, she thought, so different. He didn't want to dirty his hands with this situation. And marriage to her was always going to be one situation right after the other.

But she couldn't worry about Cotter. Not right now.

The next morning, after he had left for the office, she repeatedly called Lana's home. There was no answer. Around noon, she got in the car and drove over to her house.

The ramshackle dwelling wasn't too different from the place Sally had once called home. Peeling paint. A drooping roof. Cardboard in place of a few broken panes of glass. The house looked deserted, but the rattletrap car that Lana had bought with money saved from her job at the Dairy Bar was parked to one side of the driveway.

Calling the girl's name, Sally banged on the door. It was five minutes before Lana finally appeared and let her in the drab, sparsely furnished living room.

She was pale, blue-black shadows under her eyes. "I've been sitting here thinking," she told Sally. "Maybe Mother's right. Maybe I should drop the charges."

Sally sat down on a threadbare couch, a protest on her lips.

But Lana stopped her. "There isn't anything you can do, Sally. I'm just going to forget this happened. I know he didn't get me pregnant because I got my period this morning, so I don't have that to worry about."

"I didn't think that was your main worry. I thought you were determined to see that he paid for this."

"Mother's right. No one's going to believe I wasn't willing. I mean, look at her, she's been willing so many times, most people will think I'm pretty much like her."

"You're nothing like her," Sally insisted. "You're a brilliant girl, too smart to think you'll be able to just forget this."

Lana shook her head. "I just want it all to go away."

"You think the guys at school will let it go away?"

The girl's pallor actually deepened, but she lifted her chin. "I can handle it."

Sally knew she probably could. But at what price? Sally knew the costs of keeping quiet, knew them by heart, and she didn't want this brave, special girl to have to pay them. But even when Sally told her own story, the *whole* story of what happened to her when she was fifteen, Lana still resisted.

The most she would promise to do was wait a day or two before dropping the charges.

Sally drove home, trying to come up with something that would convince Lana to stand up for herself.

The solution came that afternoon, when Sally picked up a blue memo that had spilled out of a notebook Jamie placed on the kitchen table. The high school PTO was meeting the following evening. Sally thought she knew just how to ensure there would be a crowd. In the process, she might just help Lana.

She found the phone book, looked up a number and dialed the phone. Miss Louella answered. Sally spent a few minutes talking about the papers and books of Clementine McAllister's. Then she brought the subject around to Lana's situation.

Evidently the pastor's sermon on the evils of gossip had worn off, for Miss Louella was eager to hear what Sally had to say.

And when Sally ended by saying she was going to be at tomorrow's PTO meeting, and was going to make a few public remarks about the situation, she knew Miss Louella would spread the word.

For the first time in her life, Willow Creek was going to hear the unexpected from Sally Jane Haskins.

It was nearly 6:00 p.m. on Thursday evening when Cotter heard that Sally was going to be the featured speaker at that night's PTO meeting. He was in the lobby at the hospital, heading for his car and home, when the volunteer worker who manned the information booth told him.

He shook his head. "I don't know what you're talking about."

"Oh, dear," the older woman murmured, coloring slightly. "I guess your wife just hasn't told you."

"Sally isn't speaking anywhere," he insisted. "She's barely recovered from near-pneumonia."

"Well, my daughter-in-law told me—"

"She's wrong," Cotter cut in. But as he drove home, he had a bad feeling in his gut.

The distance between him and Sally had been worse then ever since he had interfered when she had been arguing with Lana's mother. He just hadn't wanted her to get tangled up in this mess. She still wasn't well. She should be thinking of their baby.

When he got home, she was in the kitchen, dressed to go out. She said Betsy was at the Dylans' house. And Jamie was with Lana. Watching Sally slip into her coat made the bad feeling in Cotter's gut crystallize into a certainty.

"What are you doing?" he demanded as she put on her gloves.

Head flung back, eyes glittering with defiance, she faced him. "I'm going to a PTO meeting."

"Where you're the featured speaker?"

She chuckled. "Oh, is that what they're saying?"

"Don't tell me it's not the truth."

"Well, I don't know about the featured part, but I am going to speak. I'm going to talk about date rape."

"Why?"

"Because somebody needs to help Lana."

"And what will you talking about rape at the PTO prove?"

For a moment she appeared to falter.

"Why do you have to do this?" Cotter pressed. "This isn't your concern, Sally."

"I think it is."

Glaring at her in frustration, he tunneled his fingers through his hair. "You're not well enough to be going out in this rain tonight."

"I'm going, anyway."

"Okay, then. Fine," he exploded, with a swinging gesture toward the door. "Go on, go out, risk your health and our child. Go to this damn meeting and talk about something you don't know a damn thing about, for the benefit of a girl whose own mother won't stand beside her. All you're going to accomplish is to get yourself talked about, you know. All these fuddy-duddies in this town will just have one more Sally Jane Haskins story to tell."

"I bet you're sick of those Sally Jane stories, aren't you?"

"I don't care what anyone says about you. I've told you that from the beginning. What I don't want is to see you hurt."

"Oh, yes," she retorted with sarcasm. "I know you're so concerned for me. You care so much for me, don't you, Cotter? I guess that's why the two of us tiptoe around this house like strangers, because you care so much."

He stepped toward her, hands balling into fists at his sides. "Sally, I'm trying to protect you. I want you to see that if you'll just stop putting yourself in these explosive situations, you'll stop being the talk of the town, and you'll stop being hurt by that talk. I do care. That's why I don't want you hurt."

Her chin lifted another notch. "What's the matter? Tired of being married to the town bad girl?"

"That has nothing to do with this."

"I think it does," she retorted. "I think you regret getting into this 'explosive situation' with me, getting me pregnant, marrying me because it's the responsible thing to do—"

"That's not true," he broke in. "I want our child. I'm doing what I can to make our marriage work."

She made a disgusted sound and started toward the door. "I don't have time for this now. The meeting starts at seven."

"Don't do this," Cotter said, pleading now. "Don't put yourself through it."

She stopped with her hand on the doorknob, her back to him. "I have to."

"Stay here, please. We need to talk. I want you to understand how much I care for you—"

Wheeling to face him, she sputtered, "Care for me? Why do you keep using that stupid, meaningless phrase? Caring has little to do with it. You're only obligated to me because of this baby. Oh, you convinced me to marry you with a lot of pretty talk that I wanted to believe. But I know I'm not the woman you want. I'm not like Brenda—"

"I don't want you to be."

Sally wasn't listening. She was visibly trembling, her eyes filling with tears. "I'm not a perfect hostess. I'm not smart. And I've got a bad reputation that owes something to fact. I'm not a person you might have ever dreamed of marrying. I'm just this small-town girl who has been in love with you since the first day you walked into my restaurant."

Shoulders held straight and rigid, she repeated, "I love you, Cotter Graham. I have from the beginning. That's why I slept with you, that's what got us into this mess. I don't just *care* for you. I love you."

Emotions, too raw to be named, flooded through Cotter. It was amazing what hearing those words did to him. *I love you,* she had said. Right out in the open. *Love.* She had put a name to what he wanted to build with her. That one word encompassed all he felt as well.

But he was so damned afraid of that word. He didn't trust it. He thought he had loved Brenda, but what they had between them had never been enough. Those feelings, however, were pale in comparison to what he felt with Sally. Pale compared to the passion, the admiration, the blinding, painful need to protect her from hurt. He did love her.

"Don't go," he whispered finally, when they had stood staring at each other in the charged aftermath of her declaration. "Please stay here with me."

She shook her head. "I've got to be at this meeting, Cotter. You see, this is one time when I want to be the center of attention, when I want to get the town talking. I've got to do this. I've got to try and make some of those people understand what happens when you don't stand up for the truth, when you hide, when you let the fear of gossip or criticism keep you silent."

"Hide? Hide what?" he murmured, puzzled. "What are you talking about?"

"I've got to tell them," she continued as if he hadn't spoken. "I've got to make them see what can happen when people make assumptions based on the way a person looks or where they live. I've been criticized my whole life for getting into uncomfortable situations. Most of the time, I just took that criticism. I guess I figured I deserved it."

He moved toward her. "That's what I've been trying to tell you, Sally, you've never deserved any of that."

"Tonight I'm going to set a few local legends straight."

"Sally, don't. Just let the legends die." He caught her gloved hands in his. "It doesn't matter what anyone else thinks."

Her eyes were suddenly very clear and very gray as she focused on him. "But it does matter, Cotter. I've got to stand up tonight and show Lana and maybe someone else like her and me that the truth does count. Everyone's truth."

"What truth, Sally?" He asked the question, though he had already guessed the answer.

"The truth about when I was fifteen. When I was raped."

Cotter let Sally go then. Out into the cold, Tennessee winter rain. Out to face down a town that had never cut her one iota of slack.

He had known for a long time that there were some secrets Sally hadn't shared with him. After they argued following their open house, when she flung all those details about her past at him, he should have known what her secret was. When this situation with Lana had affected her so, he should have known.

But there were a lot of things he should have done where Sally was concerned. He should have embraced the joy and the zest for living that she had offered him. He should have stopped hiding behind his past failures and stepped into their future with an open heart. From the beginning, she had given him hope for happiness. He had just been too dumb to realize that some hopes do pan out.

Sally Jane Haskins, bad girl and talk of the town, was his dream come true. He might have known that if he hadn't stopped dreaming.

That just went to show how stupid a smart man could be.

He had to make these past cold and lonely weeks up to her. He had to show her that he didn't just care for her, that he loved her. But he couldn't do that here. The best way to show Sally how much he loved her was to be at her side tonight.

The parking lot beside the high-school cafeteria was packed. Cotter finally had to park in a fire zone. Then he had to force his way through the crowd that had jammed the cafeteria as well as the hall beside it. He was only halfway up one side of the room when Sally stepped up to the microphone. He stopped to listen.

In plain, blunt terms she told her story. About a young girl searching for love she had never found at home. A young girl who made a mistake early on with a boy who bragged and boasted of his conquest. Wounded by gossip and innuendo, she turned to a young basketball coach who gave her special attention. Only the night his attentions turned sexual and she resisted, he raped her. And he told her that since everyone knew she was a tramp, she wouldn't be able to do anything to him. So she kept quiet. She endured the snickers and talk and the gossip that followed. Every decision in her life was affected because she didn't believe the truth could save her. Without naming Lana, she said she hoped her story would make a few people pause and think hard before they decided what was the truth and what was a lie.

Cotter had begun to hate Willow Creek. But this night, while Sally spoke, while some people squirmed in their seats and some people cried, his faith in the essential goodness of men and women was restored.

They applauded her, every one of them. And then Cotter had to fight through the crowd gathered around the podium. Once at Sally's side, however, he slipped an arm around her. He whispered, "I love you," for her ears only. But for everyone else within hearing range, he said, "I'm just awful damn proud to be Sally Jane Haskins Graham's husband."

Later, after hours that had seemed like a dream, Sally snuggled close to Cotter in bed. They had been talking nonstop, making plans to begin their marriage anew, without the specters of her past or his first marriage hanging over them. Cotter, who up until now had been so guarded with his feelings, couldn't stop telling her how much he loved her.

"You know you're setting yourself up for a lifetime of trouble, don't you?" she asked.

Threading his fingers through her hair, he smiled. "A lifetime of happiness."

"Trouble."

"Sally—"

"I can't help it, Cotter. Facts are facts. And trouble has always followed me around."

He leaned down, kissed the rounded mound of her stomach, then grinned up at her. "I can handle anything. Except maybe twins."

For a moment, they stared at each other in stunned surprise.

"It won't happen," Cotter finally said. "It wouldn't dare happen."

Sally said nothing, only smiled as he came back into her arms. She wasn't daring anything. Sally Jane Haskins had learned long ago that anything was possible.

Epilogue

The twins were screaming about something, Jamie's stereo was blasting down from upstairs, Jet was barking and Betsy was refusing Sally's orders to get off the phone and set the dinner table when Cotter opened the front door.

Dismayed, he looked down at the white florist's box in his hands. So much for a romantic second anniversary with his wife.

He found her in the kitchen by the sink, fussing about cold brick floors while she offered apple slices to the two eighteen-month-old toddlers who were clinging to each of her legs. Betsy was on the phone, no doubt well into a second hour of discussing boys with Laura. Lana, who had joined their household after her attacker was convicted of rape, was sprawled out on the family room floor, surrounded by the college applications she had started filling out last night.

No one noticed Cotter as he paused in the doorway to take in the chaotic scene. Anniversary or not, it was just another day in the life of the Grahams.

"I told you a million times," he said when Sally directed another curse at the floor. "Let's rip 'em up."

At the sound of his voice, she looked up and smiled. "Historic significance" came her standard reply.

Cotter laughed. Her beautiful face lit up the room and his heart. The twins jabbered up at him from her knees, demanding his attention, but Cotter had eyes only for Sally.

He tapped a framed newspaper article that hung at the end of one cabinet. It detailed the less than perfect exploits of Clementine McAllister. "Miss Louella and Miss Clara haven't been nearly as interested in our house since Marianne published excerpts from those diaries. Let's get rid of these floors."

Again her smile flashed. "But I don't want to tamper with Clementine's house. She and I are kindred souls, you know."

Nodding, Cotter presented the florist's box. "Happy anniversary, you Jezebel."

"You remembered."

"It's hard to forget when my second chance at life started."

"Oh, Cotter." Misty eyed, she set the flower box on the counter and started to step toward him. But the children holding on to each leg stopped her cold.

Cotter scooped up their daughter, Amy, while Sally got their son, Mason. They kissed over the kids' heads and smiled into each other's eyes. But for only a moment.

Because a pot was boiling over on the stove. The twins' diapers were ringing wet. Jamie was rocketing down the stairs, proclaiming starvation. Lana was asking about premed classes. And Betsy was finally, unbelievably, un-gluing the phone from her ear.

Their wild and wonderful life demanded Cotter's full attention. But he still took just one minute more, while hefting a twin on each hip. Just one more minute. To smile at his wife and thank God that Sally Jane Haskins got married to him.

* * * * *

A Note from the Author

I'm just plain crazy about the heroine of *Sally Jane Got Married*. Sally Jane Haskins is no saint. Like most of us, she has made her share of mistakes. But she's also caring, bright, feisty, funny and brave. She has fought hard to attain self-respect. Above all, she wants to be admired, loved and respected for who she is.

Respect is a precious commodity for everyone, but especially so for women today. We are fortunate to have so many choices—pursuing the career we want, getting married or staying single, having children or not. Whether we choose one or the other or any combination, we want our choices to be respected. We deserve to be valued for who we are and how we decide to live our lives. I think, as women, it is most important that we respect one another's choices, that we support and celebrate the differences among us.

Since I began writing, I've made friends with a wide variety of strong and intriguing heroines. But Sally Jane Haskins ranks right up there with my favorites. She finds a wonderful man, and she's able to look in the mirror and know *That Special Woman* is the woman looking back at her. I hope you like Sally as much as I do.

Happy reading!

Celeste Hamilton

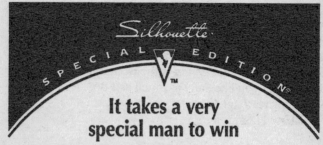

Silhouette

SPECIAL EDITION™®

It takes a very special man to win

That SPECIAL *Woman!*

ONE LAST FLING!
Elizabeth August

Investigative reporter Max Laird never knew what hit him when he teamed up with Bernadette Dowd. After learning a shocking truth, Bernadette was determined to put some adventure and excitement in her life. Falling in love made them both realize what they had been missing...and that this wouldn't be just another fling for either of them!

Thrill to Bernadette's adventure in Elizabeth August's ONE LAST FLING!, available in March.

She's friend, wife, mother—she's you! And beside each Special Woman stands a wonderfully *special* man. It's a celebration of our heroines—and the men who become part of their lives.

Don't miss **THAT SPECIAL WOMAN!** each month—from some of your special authors! Only from Silhouette Special Edition!

Relive the romance...
Harlequin and Silhouette
are proud to present

A program of collections of three complete novels by the most requested
authors with the most requested themes. Be sure to look for one volume each
month with three complete novels by top name authors.

In January: **WESTERN LOVING**   Susan Fox
                                             JoAnn Ross
                                             Barbara Kaye

Loving a cowboy is easy—taming him isn't!

In February: **LOVER, COME BACK!**   Diana Palmer
                                             Lisa Jackson
                                             Patricia Gardner Evans

It was over so long ago—yet now they're calling, "Lover, Come Back!"

In March: **TEMPERATURE RISING**   JoAnn Ross
                                             Tess Gerritsen
                                             Jacqueline Diamond

Falling in love—just what the doctor ordered!

Available at your favorite retail outlet.

REQ-G3

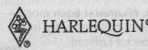

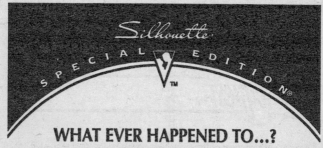

It's our 1000th
Silhouette Romance
and we're celebrating!

Join us for a special collection of love stories by the authors you've loved for years, and new favorites you've just discovered.

**It's a celebration just for you,
with wonderful books by
Diana Palmer, Suzanne Carey,
Tracy Sinclair, Marie Ferrarella,
Debbie Macomber, Laurie Paige,
Annette Broadrick, Elizabeth August
and MORE!**

Silhouette Romance...vibrant, fun and emotionally rich! Take another look at us!

As part of the celebration, readers can receive a FREE gift AND enter our exciting sweepstakes to win a grand prize of $1000! Look for more details in all March Silhouette series titles.

**You'll fall in love all over again
with Silhouette Romance!**

CEL1000T